ROGUE ENFORCER

ROGUE ENFORCER

John R. Monteith

Braveship
BOOKS
Aura Libertatis Spirat

Rogue Enforcer
Copyright © 2014 by John R. Monteith

Braveship Books

www.braveshipbooks.com

The tactics described in this book do not represent actual U.S. Navy or NATO tactics past or present. Also, many of the code words and some of the equipment have been altered to prevent unauthorized disclosure of classified material.

ISBN-13: 978-1-939398-25-3
Printed in the United States of America

To Aida

My Chaldean Queen

CHAPTER 1

Pierre Renard stifled the familiar adrenaline rush of another world-shaping deal. Through eyes that had reflected steel blue radiance during his last check in a mirror, he watched the Argentine president pass before his nation's blue and white standard and then stride across his office's hardwood floor. As he circled the polished meeting table that filled his office, his would-be client stopped behind the white leather-padded armchair at the room's opposite end and appeared to wrestle for his next thought.

Renard's hunting snout sensed that the president's bravado had yielded to edginess. Allowing his clever arguments in favor of bold military action to befuddle his victim, he salivated behind his vulpine fangs and perked his pointed fox ears to listen for an opportunity to pounce on his prey.

"I knew you would convince me this is the proper course of action," the president said in English. "It's what I want to do, and I knew it was the right path to follow ever since our first conversation about it. But now you must convince me it will work."

As he lowered his cognac tumbler to the cherrywood desk, Renard accepted that his victim required additional convincing. He twisted to project his French-accented voice across the office.

"You know my reputation," he said. "I have a distinguished track record of keeping regimes intact."

"Yes, I am aware," the president said, his words echoing off framed paintings of Argentine heroes past. "Your recent success in Taiwan is why you have my attention. But Taiwan has advanced naval and air forces while I have thirty-year-old destroyers and secondhand aircraft."

"I agree," Renard said as he turned and reached for his cognac. "But with Taiwan's modest numbers, I held off China's equally advanced and numerous forces. It's not about the raw firepower. It's about setting up the rules of engagement in one's favor and planning for victory with the available assets."

Renard heard the president's approaching footfall as he lowered his tumbler again.

"Your work in Taiwan was impressive," the president said as he moved into the Frenchman's field of view. "You showed cunning using seaborne hydrophone arrays and restricted nuclear warfare to defeat one of the world's largest submarine forces with a squadron of patrol craft."

"This is what I do, President Gomez. I advise leaders how to preserve their rule, I plan the campaigns that lead to success, and I broker the arms deals to assure that my clients are equipped for victory."

As Gomez returned to his chair, Renard noticed that the president stood at average height. It made sense, he realized, that a former A4 Skyhawk aviator would fit inside the cockpit of a small jet.

"Then I assume you have a plan already defined that will bring me success in the Malvinas?" Gomez asked.

"Of course," Renard said. "I not only urge you to take military action against the British Empire, but I've already taken the liberty of setting the plan in motion on your behalf."

"You haven't placed me at risk, have you?"

"Of course not. I am merely repositioning my submarine into the South Atlantic."

"You have a submarine of your own?"

"Indeed," Renard said. "After decades of building wealth, domain expertise, and trust with key allies, I was finally able to broker a deal for myself where I have my own vessel."

The president raised thick, dark eyebrows as Renard blew smoke into the air.

"Impressive, Mister Renard."

"I share this with you in strict confidence, of course," Renard said. "But I must also be candid about this asset that I intend to dedicate to your cause. It is a French-designed, Taiwanese-built *Scorpène* class submarine. State of the art electronics, weapons, and quieting supported by the MESMA air-independent-propulsion system. As the Taiwanese have built two additional submarines, they agreed to sell me mine with just one stipulation."

"Stipulation? Just one?"

"Training," Renard said. "I must train Taiwanese sailors. As part of the Cross-Straits ceasefire, the mainland Chinese have agreed to stop submerged operations within twelve miles of the Taiwanese coastline. The mainland fleet complies since it prefers to extend its operations and military influence hundreds of miles from its coast anyway, and it has no immediate intent to attack Taiwan."

The president nodded as he brushed the flame of a lighter under a cigarette.

"You claim responsibility for this victory?" he asked as small clouds rose in front of his face.

"Indeed. This is, of course, a tactical win for the Taiwanese, but it hinders their ability to train their submarine sailors for their primary duties. They are strained to their limits finding staff for the submarines they have. They, therefore, agreed to let me purchase my submarine from them at a modest discount in exchange for training more of their sailors. Since my crew had already used this very vessel against the mainland and was comfortable with it, I thought it an excellent opportunity."

The silent man seated next to Renard, the president's chief of staff, cleared his throat. The tall, lithe man had become an afterthought to the conversation, and the Frenchman hoped he would remain so, but that the shadows on the man's face revealed a potential adversary.

"Training new sailors from a foreign navy sounds like a liability," Gomez said.

"I must carry a dozen of their sailors aboard for training purposes," Renard said. "This, however, is a win for both parties. I don't have to pay for the extra hands, and I've already had great success thus far mixing my crew with Taiwanese professionals. They are a capable people."

"This worked for you in Taiwan, this hybrid crew?" Gomez asked. "In live combat against the Chinese?"

"Yes," Renard said. "Except for my commanding officer, my crew are veterans of the French Navy, and they have served together under my charge for years aboard *Scorpène* class vessels and their slightly larger predecessors, the *Agosta* class. My commanding officer is my greatest find–my protégé–a former American submarine officer who fell on difficult circumstances that I was able to exploit for recruitment."

Gomez reached across his desk and extended a pack of cigarettes.

"No, thank you," Renard said. "I have my own brand. But I would appreciate the light, please."

Chiding himself for his failure to give up smoking, Renard withdrew a pack of Marlboros from his sport coat. The president extended the flaming silver lighter, and the Frenchman enjoyed soothing puffs of nicotine.

"When you called on me," Gomez said, "I was somewhat hesitant about taking military action against the British Empire. But I now see that I must strike the Malvinas to divert the nation from the economic crisis, maintain my presidency, and prevent panic and chaos."

"Thirty-five years ago, the military junta that ruled your country arrived at the same conclusion," Renard said. "They failed to predict the British response, but they were correct that they needed to take military action. Such steps unify a nation."

"I agree. Plus, I also have the added motivation of the empire's discovery of the oil deposits."

Renard blew smoke into the president's chambers.

"Precisely. You have both nationalism and economic relief as your end goals—twice the motivation of your predecessors and, if you will allow me to serve as your advisor and arms supplier, ten times the preparation."

"To get to that oil and preserve my presidency," Gomez said, "I will require a far different outcome than the campaign of thirty-five years ago. Back then, Prime Minister Thatcher surprised the junta and sent her fleet across the ocean and retook the islands. How can you guarantee me a different outcome?"

"He cannot," the chief of staff said.

The voice carried authoritative neutrality, and the man's dark eyes held glints of brilliance. Renard recognized the chief as the sole remaining risk to his deal.

"In fact, I can," Renard said. "The president's predecessors were unprepared. I will see that he avoids repeating their mistakes."

"This is a grave risk," the chief said. "We are choosing hostility when we should be remedying our economic problems."

"Take drastic maneuvers, you mean?" Renard asked. "Austerity measures on the people? Requests for loans to world banks that see far too much risk to lend Argentina another Euro? Internal governmental spending restrictions? I think not."

"Our economic experts believe we can persevere," the chief said. "We must be patient and let our policies run their course."

"I've waited long enough," Gomez said. "So have the people. I do not blame them for their impatience, their rioting. They need a leader who takes action."

"Thirty-five years of diplomacy, sir," the chief said. "Thirty-five years of turning adversaries into economic allies. Thirty-five years recovering from an embarrassing loss fighting for islands populated by more sheep than humans."

"Watch yourself," Gomez said.

"Sir, we call the Malvinas by their correct name, but the rest of the world calls them the Falkland Islands because the British named them as such, pledged to defend them from us thirty-five years ago, and then did so soundly with a modest flotilla of negligible anti-submarine capability and with a single squadron of inferior, limping Sea Harrier jet fighters–to our shame."

"That is no concern," Gomez said. "There has never been shame in my regime, nor will there ever be any. When I take military action, it is for the sake of victory. Nothing less."

"You would be angering a lion, sir. True, their global force size has shrunk since nineteen eighty-two, but their presence in the Malvinas has grown. Not with our entire maritime forces could you do this. I urge you as your lead advisor, the man you've trusted your entire political career– disregard the counsel of this Frenchman."

Renard swallowed, letting his adversary's words linger in the air. He then bared his fangs and launched them at his rival's neck.

"You have a vivid memory," he said. "And accurate. However, you cite the actions of a junta that assumed foolishly that the British would yield the Falkland Islands without a fight. Now, if you wish to relegate the name 'Falkland Islands' to the footnotes of history, give them their proper name as the Malvinas, and extend your territorial waters outward to the fisheries and mineral deposits that you desperately need and deserve, you will acknowledge that your president is not the same fool of history who blundered in his vital assumptions of the military campaign."

"I never even hinted that my president is a fool. You have no right to place such words in my mouth."

"Then give your president the respect he deserves!"

The chief angled his jaw toward his boss.

"Sir, I urge you to follow a wiser course of action. The British are prepared to defend the islands. There will be a time to retake the Malvinas, but it is not now. Wait until you are in a position of strength."

The president's eyes turned black as his palm smacked his desktop.

"While I am president, Argentina will always be in a position of strength!"

Deducing that the president's infamous short-fused rage would preserve the chief's silence, the Frenchman nudged the conversation back to his preferred topics of planning.

"Your strength and resolve will be the keys to a clean and fast victory," Renard said.

The color fell from Gomez's face.

"Yes," he said. "Strength and resolve."

"There will be challenges and evaluation points where you may have to turn back," Renard said. "But the odds favor you greatly. I would not be here otherwise."

"I understand and appreciate your position," Gomez said. "Let's get back to the business of how this will work–if there are no more protests."

The chief shook his head and pursed his lips.

"So, you've told me all I need to know about your perspective of my situation and the world's position on it, and you have me convinced that I must take military against the British Empire in the South Atlantic Ocean."

"Indeed."

"You must tell me, who knows that you are repositioning a submarine across the globe toward my operational waters? This is a risk of attracting unwanted attention."

"As a rule and courtesy, I always inform the United States of my intent for any submerged operations. But in this case, since I am having my vessel towed from the Pacific Ocean to your waters, I merely told my contacts in the United States that I was shipping my vessel into the area and would inform them later if I decided to undergo submerged operations."

"You seem to enjoy a great deal of flexibility with the United States," Gomez said.

"I've earned it."

"I have difficulty believing they would allow you such flexibility based upon your past deeds," Gomez said. "They aren't ones to incur unnecessary risk based upon historical debts."

Trying to suppress a smile, Renard glanced at the black sheen on his Christian Louboutin leather shoes. He realized that a quiet wisdom simmered underneath the machismo, durability, and flair that had earned Gomez the presidency.

"I have an open, unwritten contract to provide services should the United States fall short of available submarines, or, more likely, should they need a submarine to take action for which even the slightest possibility of their involvement being discovered would be an intolerable risk."

"Action, such as challenging a British naval vessel?"

"Indeed," Renard said. "More precisely, taking on a British submarine."

Beside him, the chief of staff stirred and aimed his index finger at Renard's nose.

"I agreed to remain silent about my misgivings in taking military action against the empire," he said. "But ship for ship, they are arguably the world's premiere submarine operators. You cannot hope to defeat a British nuclear-powered submarine with your ragtag mercenary crew."

"Indeed I can," Renard said, "if the proper trap is set. Submarine warfare is my primary and original area of expertise. I understand the advantages and disadvantages of nuclear power, having commanded the French nuclear submarine, *Améthyste*. Unless you have comparable perspective, I recommend you remain silent until you seek the counsel of your top submarine experts."

"I—"

"But wait," Renard said. "I shall spare you the effort. You have no experts in operating nuclear-powered submarines, because you don't have any nuclear-powered submarines."

"Now listen—"

"No, you listen," Renard said. "We shall next discuss the capabilities of my *Scorpène* submarine. It has acoustic drones capable of loitering in wait for passing adversaries, extending the acoustic detection range to thrice that of its organic, hull-based hydrophones. And thanks to a recent customization my Taiwanese colleagues added at my request, my vessel also has super-cavitating weapons capable of speeds of two-hundred knots."

The chief's features softened.

"Two-hundred knots?" he asked.

"Yes, and I would invite you to again hold your tongue until you discuss these abilities with your domestic experts. I would then, again, spare you the wasted time—you have no such experts because you have no such capabilities."

Gomez frowned.

"Enough, Mister Renard. I admire a man of confidence, like myself. You have my ear, and although I will examine your plans with extreme scrutiny, I will give you the benefit of the doubt in your claims of capability. Continue."

"Thank you, President Gomez. I mentioned that my submarine is being towed by a ship. That ship is filled with sea mines, which will be your primary weapon. Of course, this is why I am using very long cables to tow my submarine and have staffed my submarine with a bored but well-paid emergency skeletal crew. I could ill afford losing my submarine in transit to an accidental mine detonation."

"Mines?"

"With timers," Renard said. "Each mine is set to become inert within six months. Mines, as treacherous as they are, historically make for excellent deterrents. But you must take care to use them wisely to allow diplomacy after achieving your military goals. You will surround the Malvinas with mines as part of your action to retake them, but you want to show restraint as well."

"If this takes more than six months?"

"Then we will lay more mines," Renard said. "They are relatively cheap."

The president shifted in his chair and lit a fresh cigarette, spurring Renard to withdraw a fresh Marlboro. After lighting up, he offered one to his defeated adversary. The chief rolled his eyes but accepted.

"Cheap, I agree," Gomez said. "But who will lay them? British air and sea power is modest at the Malvinas, but it is a vigilant force supported by a surveillance network of merchant and fishing vessels. I do, however, have just enough attack aircraft to soften their defenses. Such action, of course, is brute force. You don't appear to be a brute force sort of man."

"Correct," Renard said. "I am planning to avoid brute force, wanton destruction. You will take temporary control of the air and sea around the Malvinas, long enough to lay the mines."

"Really? How?"

"Through the most delicate and risky stage of the plan," Renard said. "You shall have temporary control of a British *Type 45* destroyer. Specifically, six weeks from now, the HMS *Dragon* will relieve the HMS *Dauntless* of patrol duties in the Malvinas operational areas. Since I have already recruited a key member of the *Dragon* to lead a small team of mutineers, you shall have access to that vessel for at least three days where you shall control the skies over the Malvinas to lay mines–and to also soften the air defenses on the islands."

The president tightened his lips, and his eyes narrowed.

"Impossible."

"I would agree with you, President Gomez, except that recruiting traitors is also one of my key skills."

"You claim to be a man of many skills," Gomez said. "Give me an example."

"The commanding officer of my submarine," Renard said. "Ten years ago, I turned him against the United States. He's since earned his clemency with a select few government leaders by taking part in the operations that have also earned me favor with the Americans, but I turned him nonetheless. And he wasn't the first, nor will he be the last."

"Even if I grant you that a British mutiny is possible, you cannot possibly base your entire plan for my success upon making a Brit turn on his countrymen."

Renard exhaled smoke.

"No," he said. "But should this mutiny aboard the *Dragon* fall short, we may have to resort to the artless brute force that you correctly surmised I detest."

"Such is warfare, Mister Renard. I trust you know how to deal with the unplanned."

The Frenchman's thoughts drifted to images of a crippled Trident missile submarine, its bow crumpled by a wall of ice, its missile compartment charred by fire, and its conning tower peppered by aircraft gunfire. Ever since he accomplished his intent with that doomed vessel, bringing its nuclear warheads to Taiwan, he knew he could adapt to all circumstances.

"I'm sure you know that I have," he said. "Like you said, President Gomez, such is warfare. Plans don't always survive contact with the enemy, and I've had my share of occasions to adapt. But, of course, I prefer to develop plans that beget victory."

"I have just one last question, and then I will take your plan to my military leaders for review."

"Excellent," Renard said. "I am more than happy to answer."

"Why, Mister Renard?"

"Excuse me? I don't understand."

"Why me? Why Argentina? The fees you request for your services would alter the life of the average man, but you are no average man. You're not doing this for the money. Why are you doing this?"

Renard's tail bristled with the thrill of a successful hunt completed.

"I enjoy empowering my clients to achieve what they can only otherwise imagine without my intervention."

"I believe you, Mister Renard. I truly do. But there must be more to it. Ego, perhaps?"

"You see much, President Gomez. If I had to put it in words, I would be challenged."

"Humor me. What does this mean to you, personally?"

Renard inhaled, pondered, and then exhaled smoke.

"I get to play God again," he said. "At least one more time."

CHAPTER 2

Jake Slate gulped fire. It strung his throat, and sweet vapor burned as the aftertaste.

"Bacardi dark," a man said over pounding house music.

When sober, Jake hated loud music and crowds, but alcohol's haze had drowned sobriety a dozen drinks ago. His head bobbed with the throbbing bass beat.

His new drinking companion and his younger, quiet sidekick had tipped their Detroit Tiger ball caps in response to Jake's request to share a table. Their broad shoulders filling flannel shirts, the duo introduced themselves as union welders. Consistent with his witness protection-like cover, Jake mentioned that he managed retail liquor distribution.

Nick, Jake's older but smaller brother, mentioned his unemployed state, a believable story a decade after the Great Recession's nuclear blast had devastated the city. Jake had warned Nick to avoid mentioning his career in deciphering psychic premonitions and helping people with his supposed healing energies.

Jake surveyed the room and admired its ethnic mix. To him, economic troubles, musical history, and automotive roots united Detroiters more than race divided them. What both irked him and enticed him was the smog of testosterone. Body odor and cologne hung in the air, daring the first bravado-fueled drunkard to throw a punch.

Against his failing wisdom, he wanted to be that first drunkard.

He scanned the bar for worthy prey. Something within his pseudo-fake life had snapped and turned him into an isolated, angry lion, and his inner animal tensed for rage.

He remembered a wild rage ten years earlier that a French arms dealer named Pierre Renard had exploited. With the promise of fortune and revenge, Renard had convinced him to hijack his Trident missile submarine. But stealing the submarine provided a short-lived distraction for Jake's deep and perpetual anger. A bar fight, he rationalized, was an acceptable way to vent.

"Chaser!" the welder said.

Jake swallowed a draft beer, and the coolness soothed his throat. His brother leaned in and whispered.

"I don't like it here, Jake." Nick said.

"You don't like it anywhere."

Jake noted that Nick had refused shots and nursed a diet coke, claiming designated driver rights.

"That's not the point," Nick said. "There are tons of bars closer to home, but you dragged me here looking for trouble."

"So what? You're not pulling your psychic shit on me are you? You know how that crap bothers me. You think you can foretell the future. Are you getting a bad omen here?"

"No," Nick said. "This has nothing to do with omens. Well, for the record, yeah, I have a bad sense. But that's not why I spoke up. I mean that I thought you outgrew your angry phase, and now it looks like you're getting ready to pick a fight."

Snapshots of Jake's life flashed through his clouded mind–photographs of a father he never knew, a mother's alcohol-related car accident, a submarine's commanding officer who purposely gave him HIV, a fugitive existence followed by service as a puppet and pawn, dashed hopes with a wife's false pregnancy.

His nine-figure net worth, earned by a decade of supporting Pierre Renard's plans, accentuated his void of purpose and his disdain for a god he couldn't force himself to accept.

"It's still in there," he said. "The anger. Just let me keep drinking so I can douse the flames."

Jake gulped the liquid, lifted his empty beer glass, and shouted across the table.

"Fill it up, boys. And get a new pitcher and shots. I'm buying the next round."

He reflected that he could buy the bar and everyone in it, but the sense of belonging in the crowd escaped his reach. Except for the mastery of submarine tactics that made him an asset, he belonged nowhere and to no one. He knew his wife loved him, but her attempts to bond clanked off his heart like ice picks on steel.

The welder leaned forward, pointed, and yelled. Jake followed his finger behind his shoulder and noticed two young ladies.

"See that beauty behind you?"

"Yeah," Jake said. "Sure."

"Can you get her attention? I know her," the welder said.

"Which one?"

Jake turned and aimed his palm at the lady behind him.

"This one?" Jake asked.

He shifted to the next, accidentally brushing the back of her sweater.

"Or this one?" he asked again.

Jake's antics caught the intended girl's attention. She saw the welder, rolled her eyes, and looked away.

"That's her," the welder said.

"I don't think she knows you that well," Jake said. "Or maybe, too well."

"We used to date. Sort of."

Jake felt a rough tap on his shoulder. He turned and saw a man with cropped hair and hollow, dark eyes staring through him.

"You like touching women?" hollow eyes asked.

"What are you talking about?" Jake asked.

"Don't play stupid with me. I saw what you did."

"I think you saw it wrong."

"I saw what I saw."

"Are you accusing me of something? I didn't do anything."

"So you're a pervert and a liar," hollow eyes said.

"I'm not going to argue with you. Let's cut to the chase. What the fuck are you going to do about it?"

Shadows and lines cut across hollow eyes' face.

"I'll take you outside and teach you some manners."

Jake measured the man's build. He stood a few inches taller than himself, and his tee-shirt outlined bulky muscle. But he guessed that he had a twenty pound advantage, meaning that hollow eyes either knew how to fight bigger men, he had help, or both.

Jake leaned into Nick.

"Stay out of this. No matter what. I mean it."

Careful to avoid exposure to a cheap shot, Jake sprang upward, moved beyond arm's reach, and faced his adversary.

"I'll be outside if you want to talk," he said.

He worked through the crowd and pushed open the bar's back door, feeling the encroaching winter's chill. Stopping besides a dumpster, he bounced, twisted, and whipped his arms in circles to warm himself.

As minutes passed, Jake wondered if his bluff would die uncalled. But then three men, led by hollow eyes, walked out the door and stopped several paces away.

"Three against one," Jake said.

"You asked for it," hollow eyes said.

"Yeah," Jake said. "I guess I'm just in the mood to kick someone's ass, and you're the dumb shit who volunteered. Am I going to pound your buddies here, too, or are they just gonna watch you bleed?"

"They're gonna watch me tear your eyes out."

As tactics to inflict pain and render hollow eyes unconscious flickered through Jake's mind, a crack hammered through his head, his drunken field of vision tilted sideways, and his world turned black.

When his vision returned, he felt men holding his arms to their chests, exposing his torso to hollow eyes' punches. With two men cheering their leader, Jake counted five total adversaries, and the ache in his jaw told him that he had let someone sneak up behind him for a sucker-punch.

"Punk!" hollow eyes said as he embedded his fist into Jake's ribs.

Caught unprepared, Jake forewent the advanced technique of softening his midsection to diffuse the blow and instead tensed his muscles as armor. He screamed to tighten his body at impact.

His ribs felt bruised as he conceded that hollow eyes punched with power. Fearing that another blow might break bones, he tested his restraints.

The man on his right held a skillful thumb lock and leveraged respectable pressure against Jake's elbow. His other arm enjoyed more freedom, its captor using unskilled strength and weight to hold him.

Jake dropped himself, forcing his restrainers to lurch forward. He then jumped up, lifted his left foot, and jabbed his heel into a captor's foot.

He yanked his left arm free and pivoted to his right. His skilled captor made the mistake of remaining committed to his joint lock, and Jake punished him by ramming the butt of his free hand into his jaw. The man dropped to a knee.

The wounded-foot man staggered and telegraphed a right hook. Jake slipped aside the blow, parried it, and launched his leg under the extended arm. As he planted his knee into the man's stomach, he felt the man's body convulse and drop.

With two attackers down and two men appearing content to observe, Jake squared his shoulders toward hollow eyes.

Hollow eyes withdrew a knife from his jacket, and its blade reflected the parking lot's overhead lights.

He led with a stab that Jake dodged, but he left no immediate opening for a counterattack. Taking the offensive, Jake channeled his anger into a series of brute force kicks into the man's side. He then sneaked a snap kick between forearms and caught hollow eyes in the mouth. His assailant stunned, Jake stepped forward to achieve his evening's goal.

Unleashing his inner lion, he swiped his elbow across the man's temple, and hollow eyes went down. As the blade clanked against pavement, Jake straddled his victim, grabbed his jacket lapel, and roared.

"Fuck!"

Jake thought about his broken childhood, and he drove his fist into the man's face.

"Fuck!"

He remembered the anger, fear, and betrayal that had ended his naval career, and he drove his fist into the man's face.

"Fuck!"

He felt hopeless and void of purpose, and he drove his fist into the man's face.

His vision blackened, and he repeated the blows in endless rhythm with his angry heart until one of his recovered victims stood over him and yelled.

"Dude, that's enough!"

Jake looked at the man who stood rubbing his jaw.

"You want to go another round with me, jackass?"

"No, dude. It's over. Just stop."

Red rage subsided, and Jake lowered his fist. As he rose to his feet, he realized that hollow eyes lay motionless, his lungs unmoving.

"Oh, shit," Jake said. "Call nine-one-one."

"What?"

"Just do it!"

As the man stepped back and lifted a phone to his ear, Jake trotted into the bar. He grabbed his brother and commanded him to drive him home.

He climbed into the passenger seat, and in silence, Nick drove into the night. Once on the interstate, Jake picked up his phone.

"Who are you calling?" Nick asked.

"My babysitter."

"Your wife is home with your step kids. You don't have a babysitter tonight."

"I mean the guy who babysits me."

Few men committed treason and returned home, but after stealing a Trident missile submarine, Jake had worked enough pro-American submarine missions with Pierre Renard to earn his way back to a policed life in the United States.

For the first time since the CIA had handed him off to the FBI to monitor his life of parole mixed with witness protection, Jake appreciated having a federal agent at his disposal.

His latest FBI-parole officer had started his assignment three months ago and sounded groggy as he answered the phone.

"It's late, Jake," the FBI agent said. "What's wrong?"

"I screwed up."

"How bad?"

"I got into a bar fight," Jake said. "I hurt someone bad. I may have killed him."

"You know that's stupid, but I'll spare you the lecture on drinking and fighting."

"That sounded like a lecture," Jake said.

"Focus. What bar was it?"

Jake gave him the name and the city.

"I'll monitor police and first responder traffic. Do you know who you hurt?"

"He drew a fucking knife on me!"

"That's not what I asked."

"I have no idea who he was. Damn it, I'm a stupid shit. I went out looking for this."

"Calm down. How many witnesses saw you?"

"Shit, half the bar plus the guy's posse. A good two dozen people at least."

"Do you think anyone saw your car?"

"I don't know," Jake said. "How the hell should I know? Maybe not. We were parked far away."

"I'll get my hands on the police report. You might get lucky. It depends who saw what, who your victim is, and how bad you hurt him. It also helps if someone will confirm that he drew the knife."

"Maybe," Jake said. "But what if this blows up?"

"There's a contingency plan for you getting into legal trouble. The FBI would claim you as our subject of interest for some multi-state crime spree, take over the case, and haul you across the country to start your life over. But you're getting ahead of yourself. You sound drunk. You need to sleep it off."

"Can I just go home?" Jake asked.

"Yeah. Go ahead. But keep your phone on. I'll call you if local authorities happen to connect the dots to you tonight."

"Thanks."

Jake hung up and sank into his seat, but his brief relief evaporated as a sick guilt rose within him.

After Nick drove him to his home in suburban Detroit, Jake collapsed onto the couch in his office. Inebriation dragged him into a shallow and fitful sleep, and he awoke in the middle of the night. His heart raced, pumping alcohol's toxins and self-loathing through his veins.

Anxious curiosity compelled him to roust his computer to life and log in to his secure communication page. As he hoped and feared, his FBI babysitter had left him a message.

The news hit hard. He had spent a decade sending countless men to their graves in naval exchanges and even with small arms, but he had never beaten a man to death–until now.

Dead on arrival due to closed head trauma.

The report mentioned that his victim was a mid-ranking member of a gang under surveillance for drug trafficking and that his death would likely be ruled a hit by a rival gang.

Jake believed he would escape legal persecution, but bile rose within him. He closed the message but noticed another unread note.

He opened it and saw the request from Pierre Renard to join him on a new assignment.

Jake had attempted to refuse Renard on prior assignments. He had even left assignments in mid-execution. But after letting his rage push him across a line, he wanted to run away.

He digested the note's brief contents, and he ruminated over the concept of commanding Renard's submarine in support of Argentina's strategic interests. His tired, shaken, and poisoned mind struggled to imagine the purpose and the details, and he stopped trying.

He would be patient and call Renard later in the morning to unravel the mystery. He expected to learn of a mission, a client, and a strategy to establish national boundaries. Danger would come with the territory, but his present state of mind left him uncaring.

Flying to the bottom of the world to command a submarine for any reason, either imaginable or beyond speculation, offered him the escape he needed.

CHAPTER 3

Breaking a European sex slave trafficking operation had earned Olivia McDonald her street credibility in the CIA, but it had also caused her a lifetime of antiretroviral drugs to combat HIV and countless psychological therapy sessions recovering from her near-death raping.

She wanted more than street credibility.

Given her chance to rise higher, she had seduced Jake Slate while he tried to hide in France, and she had accomplished her ultimate mission of using him to gather intelligence on Pierre Renard. After meeting the adventurous duo, Olivia's life had become a multi-year roller coaster of missions protecting her country.

As a trained psychologist entering her mid-thirties, she enjoyed recent quiet years of analyst work–free of interference from Jake and Renard. The momentum of her high-profile field work, combined with favor earned by a high-ranking mentor, had placed her on a fast track to the organization's upper echelons. Rumors spread that she would someday become the Director of National Intelligence–as long as she found the right assignments to stay relevant.

When Pierre Renard called her, memories of danger had caused trepidation, but ambition had compelled her to answer. After quick pleasantries, she had agreed to meet him. Background jet noise during the conversation had revealed that he was en route to Virginia, as if he knew she couldn't refuse him.

Having indulged in an extra bottle of wine the prior evening, Olivia cursed the overhead lighting and the toxins in her body. The blood running through her temples throbbed against the rims of her sunglasses.

She picked Legal Sea Foods in McLean's Tysons Corner II mall for its crowd and background noise. Two tables away, a pair of CIA agents masqueraded as husband and wife and watched for suspicious eavesdroppers. Olivia sat close to Renard, huddled like a lover, to further conceal their discussion from would-be listeners.

"Sunglasses indoors?" he asked.

"Rough night," she said. "Forget about it. Let's get down to business."

"After we order," Renard said. "Come now, let's at least enjoy the meal and share news. I haven't seen you in years."

Olivia appreciated the Frenchman's natural charisma and ability to place her at ease.

"I guess you're right," she said. "How's Marie and the kids?"

"Angry with me, as usual," he said. "She expects me to retire, but I cannot help but run around the globe trying to reshape it. Jacques and Sylvie are well, but I must admit that I see too little of them. Perhaps I will retire after this next endeavor so that I can watch my children grow."

"I'll go out on a limb and guess that you said that before your last job in Taiwan."

"I'm sure I did, but I cannot confirm that. I probably suffer from selective memory."

A waitress brought bread and took Renard's order for shrimp cocktail appetizers.

"How about you?" Renard asked. "I'm sorry that I don't see a wedding ring. You had met a man during our operation with the hijacked Israeli submarine. Did that relationship fall short of meeting your needs?"

"I put my career first. I just didn't have time for love and let him get away."

"You are still young, talented, and beautiful. I'm sure you will find a partner when you are ready."

"I think it's best that I get my career established first."

"If you'll excuse my advice for its hypocrisy," Renard said, "please try to enjoy your life. I fear that ambition will smother you, as it has me."

Olivia ignored the warning and looked to the CIA couple for confirmation that nobody spied on her. She then scanned the room to verify her privacy.

"That's good advice but tough to follow," she said.

"I understand. In fact, I'm here to help advance your career."

"I'm all ears," she said.

"Very well, then. I've been retained by a powerful client in Argentina, and I would greatly benefit from an exchange of assets with you."

She knew Renard's shrewdness and her awareness heightened in defense. The waitress arrived and startled her as she lowered the shrimp cocktail. Renard ordered a fillet mignon, and Olivia ordered lobster tail.

"Okay," she said. "An asset exchange. What do you need from me?"

"Ordnance," he said. "Aging but usable missiles and bombs to arm Argentine attack aircraft."

"I don't know if I can make that happen, but I know the right people to ask. I imagine you know better than I do if the inventory is available."

"I have a good idea that it is, and it's likely that you have what I need. I am asking for old weapons that have been in the American arsenal for decades. I could make use of your oldest inventory. I'm offering a good use for them before they must be retired and destroyed for age."

"Do you have a shopping list?"

"Yes. It's the usual armaments you would expect– Sidewinder missiles for air-to-air defense, HARM high-speed anti-radiation missiles to suppress ground-based air defenses, and bombs for under-wing hard points."

"No naval weapons?"

"No, the Argentine fleet uses French weapons. I, of course, have access to those."

"Sure. So what are you offering in return?"

"The intelligence you need to give the United States advanced warning pertaining to a conflict that is about to take place between Argentina and Great Britain."

The news caught her off guard. Her latest reading of global status reports had shown economic crises in South America but no impending hostility between the two nations.

"They've been healing wounds from the Falkland Island conflict for decades," she said. "What makes you think there's something about to happen?"

"I am advising President Gomez to take the action."

"That's extreme, though maybe not for you. Why are you doing it?"

"It's bound to happen. The two countries can pretend to be civil about the islands, but the sea-based resources surrounding them and the symbolism of their ownership are too divisive. The islands will eventually end up in Argentina's possession. Whether it takes weeks, months, or decades, it will happen. I have devised a plan to make it happen now, with minimal bloodshed, and with optimal diplomatic oversight by the United States."

"That's a lot to swallow, but you have a point."

"Of course, I won't give you enough advanced warning to yield tactical value to Great Britain, since I cannot control if you share the information with them or not. But you will know each step of the Argentine plan with enough warning for your administration to prepare a diplomatic response."

The opportunity felt like a gift. It seemed like an easy agreement to get her name attached to another high-profile success.

"What guarantee do I have that you keep the information flowing after you get your weapons?"

"You mean other than my ironclad word?"

"Yes."

"You've known me for years, and I have never lied to you."

"Not that I remember. But there's always a first time."

"Half the world's second-tier nations want my hide," he said. "And I imagine that Great Britain will soon join the ranks of those who would like to stuff my pelt with straw and place me on their mantles. Since I would like to retire someday, I would like to do so without fear of the CIA handing me over to the highest bidder. I believe you hold the ultimate trump card and need not worry."

"You know how to disappear," she said. "There's no guarantee with this."

"There are no guarantees in life, but this is an opportunity with great potential for you and little risk."

She knew he was right, but she needed to know more.

"Gomez is committed?" she asked.

"Of course. I met with him three days ago. He recognizes that he needs to take this action to preserve his presidency."

Olivia brushed back her long strands of red hair as the waitress brought their lunches. She swallowed a bite of sweet, buttery lobster tail and shifted into her default analyst mode.

"After you called me," she said, "I studied Gomez's dossier. He's a bull in a china shop. He's ridden his military heroism from the original Falkland Islands campaign to the top, but he's not a statesman."

"He found himself a good chief of staff early in his political career, allowing his rise to power," Renard said. "But I fear his economic advisors have failed him. The situation is beyond repair by fiscal policy alone."

"I could argue that the situation is beyond repair–period. So why do you think attacking the Falklands will help anything? What's your plan, Pierre?"

She watched him swallow a mouthful of steak before answering.

"Since they are dispersed and distant, I will ignore the South Georgian Islands and every other remote island chain in that part of the world that is under historical dispute. The focus is just the Falklands."

"Focus is good, I imagine, versus spreading out their forces. But I'm no naval strategist."

"Correct. I'm not letting Gomez attack anything except the Falkland Islands, and I am organizing a plan of limited action and minimal damage to yield an optimal position in the subsequent negotiations for peace."

"Makes sense," she said.

"The Brits have over a thousand soldiers on the eastern island alone. I will instead advise him to blockade Port Stanley and sprinkle mines around the main islands to prevent sea-based commerce or military landings. It's a classic starvation by isolation approach, similar to the Chinese mainland tactics against Taiwan."

"Then why do you need weapons for aircraft?"

"Primarily to lay the mines. One needs control of the air to maneuver ships and aircraft into place to do so. The Brits know this, and they have four Typhoon aircraft on the island protected in hardened and guarded hangars. They also keep a warship assigned to the island for added, mobile air power. This is on top of their numerous land-based Rapier surface-to-air missile batteries. I need to eliminate these defenses to allow the laying of mines."

"That's sounds like a lot of firepower for an island with a smaller indigenous population than my high school."

"It is," he said. "And it highlights how seriously the Brits value holding it. They added these defenses immediately after Argentina tried to take the islands in nineteen eighty two."

As she swallowed a bite of baked potato, Olivia weighed the Falkland Island scenario against Pierre Renard the man. She knew him as a contradiction who sold arms and advised people in small-scale wars but who also loathed violence. Sending Argentine aircraft headfirst in an assault against a strong defense seemed vulgar and inelegant for him.

"You're leaving something out," she said. "There's a factor in this that you haven't shared yet, or refuse to share."

"Two factors," he said. "And since you must know, I will tell you. The first is that I will use my own submarine as part of a plan to keep the British submarines at bay."

"Jake?" she asked.

"Yes. Who else?"

"I just realized that he's involved."

"You still care for him?"

"Not like that."

"Not like what?"

"He's married. He's moved on. I mean I care for him because I still consider him a friend."

"And you have no time for romance anyway."

Unsure if he meant his comment to be a jab, she ignored it.

"That sounds risky," she said. "Aren't the British good with their submarines?"

"Some would say they are the best, even better than the Americans. But fear not, I have a plan to keep my team safe and protect my investments."

"You always do. Just try not to let Jake get killed."

"He is charmed, as I have always said."

She washed down another bite of potato with a dry Merlot, the wine helping to mollify her hangover.

"What's the other factor?" she asked.

"You remember how I originally met Jake, do you not?"

"You used him like a puppet. You have a gift for identifying distressed people and using their weakness against them."

"Provided that I can find someone facing an appropriately difficult circumstance who has access to an asset I need," he said.

"Who'd you find this time?"

"The executive officer of the HMS *Dragon.*"

"That's a British… what? Frigate? Destroyer?"

"It's the destroyer that will be assigned to protect the Falkland Islands next month."

"This whole plan sounds like a bunch of high-risk actions with tight dependencies. The slightest failure could make it fall apart."

"All my plans appear that way at first, but each one has succeeded, although I may need to make minor adjustments from time to time."

"When will I know that Jake and your executive officer of the *Dragon* have succeeded?"

"I will tell you immediately, of course, as these are crucial steps in the process. But if you mean to withhold the weapons from me until these steps are complete, I'm afraid that won't work. I'll need the aircraft armed and ready to attack while Jake does his part and while my recruited agent takes over the destroyer."

"That doesn't give me much protection against committing the weapons to you for a losing cause."

The waitress returned, cleared plates, and asked about desert. Olivia gulped her wine and asked for a refill.

"The risk is near zero," Renard said. "The Argentines are already armed. The problem is that many of the weapons have decayed with age and neglect to the point of being unusable. But how many weapons remain unusable is a secret. We only need to explain away the weapons that find their targets and detonate, and the illusion will be that they found enough usable weapons from their own inventory."

"I can live with that. But you mentioned that you're not attacking the islands. What's your criteria for victory?"

"The credible threat of invasion. Once the islands are isolated by mines, submarines, and naval vessels, Argentina will have the air power and maritime forces to land ground troops."

"A landing would be a lot of bloodshed. Boots on the ground, so to speak. That's always ugly."

"Indeed," he said. "That's when the negotiations will take place, and a settlement will be reached that will reflect what I feel to be proper ownership of the islands and their surrounding resources."

She reflected upon the possibility.

"I'm here because I trust you," she said. "But you're only human. We need to consider that something could go wrong. Then what?"

"Since you trust me, will you allow that I have a contingency plan for all foreseeable events?"

"It's a test of my trust, but yes. I've seen what you can do, and this is normal for you. I can't think of a flaw in your plan, either."

"I appreciate your confidence in me. Do we have an agreement then?"

She nodded and glanced at him. His silver hair and sharp features kept him attractive as he passed his mid-fifties. Before she could let a lewd thought enter her mind, he leaned in and kissed her cheek.

"Thank you, Olivia. I hate to be discourteous, but I must be going now."

He dropped a hundred-dollar bill on the table and crept away.

CHAPTER 4

The reddish brick edifice of Saint Thomas Chaldean Catholic Church rose above Maple Road with power and grace. Jake wondered why he had always ignored the building's subdued elegance, having raced by it to someplace more important, or having cast angry glances at the stoplight that detained him as it funneled West Bloomfield's Iraqi-descended faithful to its ceremonies.

Married to an Iraqi Christian, he had learned to appreciate the story of Christ, and he had begun a personal research project to know the truth. After several sessions, he had learned to trust his wife's priest's counsel.

He drove around the church and parked at the rectory. As he walked through the door, a bearded man in a robe greeted him with soft brown eyes and a peaceful smile. God's ordained servant, Francis Kalabat, stood at average height and build.

"How are you, my brother?" Kalabat asked.

His voice carried caring and intelligence.

"I'm okay," Jake said.

He extended his hand, but Kalabat spread his arms and offered an irresistible hug. After the embrace, the clergyman led him into his office.

A small mess filled the room with books, pamphlets, and trinkets strewn about shelves, chairs, and Kalabat's desk. Jake crossed his legs as he sat across the table.

"What brings you here, my friend?" Kalabat asked.

Wondering if the luck that had spared him from countless brushes with death would wane during the upcoming assignment in Argentina, he acknowledged his mortality.

"I need advice."

"That's what I'm here for."

Kalabat leaned back in his chair and cradled a wooden cross that gravitated toward his heart. He radiated an earnest enthusiasm to dig Jake's soul from its tomb, and wisdom governed his energy. The holy man radiated a divine charisma.

"I've done some bad things," Jake said.

"There's nothing you can do that is unforgivable."

"I mean," Jake said. "I mean, I've had to make a lot of life and death calls, and I'm not sure I've gotten them all right."

"It's stressful playing God. If you try it long enough, you'll eventually get it wrong."

"Then why do I keep trying?"

"The last time you were here, you told me you were forced to grow up too fast. It's possible that you don't know anything else. People who have to fulfill roles greater than their ability can end up feeling like they need to be God."

The advisor's insight made sense, but Jake found it useless.

"I get the point. I'm a classic overachiever by accident. But I don't know what to do about it. I'm just pissed off all the time."

"Anger is natural, and so is expressing it. Jesus overturned the tables of merchants because they were desecrating a place of worship. Anger provides strength to fight back against wrongdoing."

"When I get mad," Jake said, "I sometimes go overboard."

"How overboard?"

"Things I'd rather not say, especially recently."

"That's okay. You don't have to tell me. But you can talk to God, even just to test the waters and see if He's there for you. He understands that you're not ready to come to Him yet, but you can explore the concept of his existence for yourself."

"I may be willing to try talking to God, even praying."

The words surprised Jake as he heard them echo in his head.

"That's great! Go for it!"

"I'm not sure how."

"Would you be willing to recite any of these prayers and just see how it feels?"

Kalabat withdrew a pocket-sized paperback from his desk drawer and extended it. Jake accepted it and flipped through its pages. The submission, praise, and gratitude to an unseen, unprovable entity bothered him, and he lowered the book to the priest's desk.

"I don't think so," he said.

"That's fine. Try talking to God, out loud or silently. He'll hear what you say."

"Just like a conversation?"

"Sure."

"Can I say anything I want?"

"Sure. Biblical heroes did. The best example is Job. God worked him over hard, and Job told God everything he felt about it. God understood and kept Job in his grace. Don't hold back."

"I can do that," Jake said.

"I can't always predict how God will react, but in general, you'll find answers slow to come. Be patient."

"That's not my strong suit, although I'm getting better with age. At least I think I am."

"Age brings wisdom and patience."

Jake felt no less lost than when he entered Kalabat's office, but he sensed a dead end for the day's progress.

"That's it then, right? I've got my homework assignment. Talk to God?"

"That's it. I trust God to give you just enough feedback to encourage you along in seeking Him. That's how it works."

"I'll give it a shot."

"Is there anything else I can do for you?"

"I don't think so."

"I'll be here if you need me, whenever you're ready to come back. And if you look for Him, God will be with you all the time."

The holy man stood, and Jake found himself caught in a goodbye hug, wondering if he was wasting his time seeking a faith.

As he marched by the rectory's receptionist, the elderly lady turned from her musty desk, and her eyes offered a peaceful sparkle.

"How was your meeting with the bishop?" she asked.

He thought about disregarding her inaccurate question, but within his heart, decorum triumphed.

"You must be thinking of someone else, ma'am," he said. "I was talking to Father Frank."

She smiled and tilted her head, excusing his ignorance.

"Nobody's called Bishop Francis that name for almost three years," she said. "He doesn't mind if old friends call him Father Frank in private, though. He must consider you dear to him, if he didn't correct you."

The revelation flustered Jake. He thanked the woman for straightening him out, and he drove home to talk to his wife.

Knowing that she hated his pending departure, Jake tried to downplay the dangers.

He had told Linda that it was a routine training exercise and that he'd be back within two weeks. In truth, he hoped to be home in ten days, but he hesitated to bank on victory over a British *Astute* class submarine, no matter how elegant the trap. He knew she sensed his doubts about his survival. Worse, he knew she sensed his indifference.

She had professed love to him in a way nobody had before–she needed him, and his death would ruin her. He couldn't process the responsibility, nor could he believe it. His role since the cradle had been the expendable survivor.

As part of his glorified witness protection plan, he drove a two-year old blue Ford Fusion. Despite being a mid-grade high-volume car, the vehicle felt like luxury to him since he preferred simple surroundings.

As he cranked the engine to drive to Detroit Metropolitan Airport, Linda threw herself onto the hood and extended her limbs across it.

Whereas weaker women might crumble under fear of her husband's safety, Linda had worked through her suffering with prayer. She would send her husband off with a show of strength. Her smile radiated enough joy in being his wife that it drowned out her fear and sadness.

"Don't go!" she said.

The windshield absorbed her words, but he recognized them. He smiled, tapped the horn, and revved the engine.

"Get off the car, silly."

"Don't go!" she said.

He rolled down the window.

"Give me a kiss," he said.

She rolled off the hood and moved in front of him. Her face resembled a heart with wide, ruddy cheeks that highlighted her swarthy Iraqi tan. Dark soulful eyes conveyed a deep love while trying to hold back a tide of sorrow.

He kissed her and started down the driveway before she had time to breakdown.

Through his rear view mirror, he thought he saw sunlight glinting off tears on her cheeks, but he hoped the parting vision of his wife was an illusion of suffering.

As he turned onto his street, he realized that he had the perfect wife. But he also digested his incapacity to appreciate her. The greatest gift that fate, divine providence, or even God had bestowed upon him had fallen on his iron heart.

He cursed himself for being unappreciative, but then he remembered a line from C.S. Lewis claiming that the inability of humanity to have all its desires satisfied in this world served as proof of an afterlife. The thought would linger in his mind as he traveled.

Jake arrived in the Argentine beach resort town of Mar del Plata two days ahead of his scheduled deployment on Renard's submarine.

On the chartered flight from Detroit, he had studied everything public about the British *Astute* class nuclear-powered submarine, and he also had private insight into its capabilities based upon Renard's intelligence network. But he conceded that he knew too little about this frontline adversary to overcome it in a clean battle.

So he would fight dirty.

Although Renard's vessel awaited him, Jake drank away his first day in solitude on the beach. He told himself he would have plenty of clean and sober time cramped with other men on Renard's submarine, and he needed to blow off steam.

As countless South American vixens pranced by in skimpy beach ware, Jake appreciated that many of them returned his lustful stare. Of course, he constantly reminded himself of his commitment to his wife and later relieved himself of his frustrations in the privacy of his luxury hotel room.

The next day, he met Renard for lunch at an outdoor bar with a view of the harbor, cursing himself for poisoning himself with alcohol's toxins the prior day. The Frenchman appeared vibrant, mocking Jake's hangover.

He smelled his friend's light and fresh cologne as they exchanged cheek-to-cheek air kisses.

"You smell like used rum, my friend," Renard said.

"With body odor and bad breath, I imagine," Jake said. "I'm still recovering."

"I trust you'll follow your American naval tradition of keeping alcohol off the submarine."

"Don't worry," Jake said. "I'm not stupid enough to drink and drive, much less drink and go up against the target you've picked for me."

"We're not in a safe place to talk. I appreciate you sticking to generalities. You've read the mission brief, did you not?"

A curvaceous waitress in a shoulderless sundress brought water and took their lunch orders. Jake copied Renard and requested a medium rare hamburger with fries, plus bread to settle his stomach. He gulped water to rehydrate himself.

"Yeah, I read your mission brief. It's dangerous."

"Everything I've ever asked you to do is dangerous," Renard said. "This mission is no more risky than the others."

"That's debatable, given the target."

"Your target is the most predictable you've ever faced. The ruse will work, and you will enjoy the element of surprise and have complete control of the scenario."

A pang of nausea reminded him of his frailty, and the thought of a British torpedo vaporizing him flashed through his mind. The concept of a quick and painless passing seemed enticing to him, and he coughed to clear his head of such thoughts.

"Are you okay?" Renard asked.

"I'm fine."

He gulped more water, and the waitress brought Renard a coffee. The Frenchman sniffed it, reminding Jake of a predator evaluating the worthiness of its prey.

"Do I have my usual crew?" he asked.

"Yes, and then some," Renard said. "There is new eager talent from our old friends who sold me the vessel."

"Have they forgiven me?"

"Excuse me?"

"Have they forgiven me? I walked out on them in Taiwan."

"There is nothing to forgive. They understood, even before you came back to lead them to victory. They are quite aware that your gift for naval tactics comes with your demons. They accept the demons because your charm brings them home alive."

"I trust them, too," Jake said. "We've been through enough together."

"Indeed. Setting aside that half the people aboard are my personal friends, I also wouldn't risk my life's investment on a dysfunctional crew. The trust among the key players is sound."

"Fine," Jake said. "Do I need to worry about the commanders of the other vessels?"

"Hardly. Not that I know or trust them, but their roles in this engagement are simple and well within their capabilities. There is a briefing after lunch at the submarine squadron headquarters where you will have a chance to meet them."

The waitress brought bread, and Jake broke off a section. He popped a piece in his mouth, chewed, and swallowed. The grains absorbed stomach acids and settled his stomach.

"Our trials with the new weapon went well," Renard said.

Jake pondered the ability of a super-cavitating torpedo, capable of two-hundred knots of speed. Navies had been experimenting with the technology for decades, and the weapon had reached its time.

"Cool."

"Excellent performance. Acoustics, electronics, propulsion–all as promised and hoped," Renard said. "We fired at a surfaced target, but it will operate equally well for a submerged target."

"Good to know."

"Henri can walk you through the operation, but you will have to use your judgment and–dare I say, your artistry–to know when to use the weapon or when to stick with a conventional torpedo. A conventional weapon still has much better acoustic detection, wire guidance control, and steering capability."

"And stealth," Jake said. "Your target won't hear a conventional torpedo coming until it's too late, but they'll hear the new one."

"Indeed."

Jake devoured a piece of bread, washing it down with water.

"Any changes to the ship's operational parameters?"

"None," Renard said. "It behaves the same as when you last commanded it. I had the hull cleaned of barnacles prior to shipment, just to keep it streamlined for that precious extra half knot of speed."

"Good call."

"It has a new name, too, now that it's mine."

"Do tell."

"*Le* Spectre."

"The *Specter*? Like a ghost. Cool."

"I thought about naming after my children, or even myself, but that's too egotistical, even for me. I went with something more creative and inspirational."

The waitress brought the burgers, and Jake devoured half of his meal before saying another word.

"You seem to have lost interest in talking," Renard said.

"Yeah. Sorry, Pierre. I'm just not running at full speed today. I need to give my mind a break before we go to the brief."

"Very well, my friend. I shall not say another word."

Jake downed his food and slipped into a minor food coma while waiting for the Frenchman to finish.

Jake found the windowless briefing room austere, appropriate for a military environment. Air ducts that looked older than himself pumped cool air through concrete walls, and metal chairs covered a faded aqua carpet.

As a liquid crystal display showed an overhead view of shapes that represented submarines moving around the waters east of Argentina, Jake sniffed the air. He smelled body odor, musk, and cologne.

Beyond the unnecessary effort to effuse a masculine odor–or the lack of concern to avoid it–the Argentine submarine commander seated in front of him bothered him. The upward and cocked head angle hinted at arrogance, and when he had met the man prior to the brief, his body carriage suggested haughtiness.

Jake questioned if the man rejected his presence, despite the undeniable need for the *Specter*'s world-class abilities, or if the man habitually expected those he met to feel belittled.

He wiped negative thoughts from his mind and did his best to understand the Spanish words describing his upcoming mission. Fluent in French, Jake had been learning Spanish rapidly, but he digested less than half the words. As the Argentine general standing by the screen stopped speaking, the junior officer beside him repeated the meaning in English.

"The purpose of this mission is to instill fear and caution in the minds of the British submarine commanders," he said. "Once we have demonstrated the ability to engage British submarines, they will by necessity alter their patrol tactics. This will be to our favor, as it will lessen their attention upon harassing and engaging our surface vessels, which will enjoy more freedom to lay mines and control the skies around the Malvinas."

Jake knew everything about the mission and he expected that the briefing would serve as a confirmation that the Argentines saw it the same way. The Argentine admiral spoke again, followed by his translator.

"The Argentine *Type Seventeen Hundred* class submarine *Santa Cruz* will deploy to the northern operations area," he said. "Likewise, the *San Juan* will deploy to the southern operations area. The mercenary submarine *Specter* will deploy to the east, in the Malvinas operations area. The assumption is that one British *Astute* class submarine will be on patrol and will detect either the *Santa Cruz* or the *San Juan*."

Jake recalled the intelligence reports from Renard. The assumption made sense, given that the British kept one submarine on patrol around the Falkland Islands.

The translator conveyed the admiral's next lines.

"It is critical that the *Specter* deploys undetected. The *Specter* must remain concealed from British discovery until weapons are released."

Jake leaned to his right and glanced at the man beside him. Short with a wide head and thick nose, Antoine Remy, his ace sonar operator, reminded him of a toad. He whispered in French.

"You've run self-listening diagnostics on the ship?" he asked.

"Yes," Remy said. "We are quiet as a mouse. Even slightly quieter than we were in Taiwan in the broadband noise spectrum, thanks to Pierre getting our hull cleaned."

The musky commanding officer in front of him stirred and shot a condemning glance over his shoulder. Jake suppressed the urge to apologize for whispering in a foreign language and instead let his rudeness linger as an insult.

The translator again echoed the admiral's words.

"Each Argentine submarine will spend two days conducting simulated attacks on passing merchant vessels as training exercises. This will attract the interest of the British submarine. Then, six hours apart, each Argentine submarine will transit toward the Malvinas operation areas. We won't know if a British submarine is trailing either of our submarines, but we will assume that one is."

Jake shifted to his left and saw a handsome man wearing his mercenary crew's slacks and dress shirt uniform. He considered the white-haired, sharp-featured Henri Lanier as a reserved version of Renard with an uptick in dignity and impeccable penchant for dress. Jake whispered in French.

"How many drones do we have?"

"Four," Henri said. "We should need only one, at most two. The spares are for contingencies."

"Good thinking."

The translator spoke again.

"The *Specter* will be waiting in a classic delouse trap. Since the *Specter* will have the advantage of waiting in ambush, it will deploy drones for detecting the British submarine. If the *Specter*'s drones transmit active, it will be at frequencies similar to that of the system aboard the Argentine submarines, to create a deception."

Wrestling with a bout of nausea from his hangover, Jake tuned out the briefing and glanced at Renard, who puffed a cigarette in the corner of the room.

His mentor, his friend, his ally, his boss, and–a decade ago when they had first met–his savior. The Frenchman oozed confidence and brilliance, and Jake had once considered him immortal.

But the crow's feet grew more pronounced every year, the skin sagging, and the handsome features less sharp. If the tempting of fate failed to destroy Renard with each movement of his pieces across his global chessboard, time would stake its claim on him. Jake realized that Renard would someday reach the grave.

The Frenchman approached the screen, and the overhead view expanded to include the shores of South America and Africa. Renard pointed at a red line that formed to connect the continents.

"Based upon the latest intelligence, the British submarine on patrol will be the *Ambush*," Renard said. "Ironic, given that it is we who will be ambushing it. After the encounter with the *Ambush*, the *Santa Cruz* and *San Juan* will evade to the north and loiter south of this boundary, highlighted in red."

Renard exhaled a cloud of smoke, awaited the Spanish translation, and then continued.

"As the *Santa Cruz* and the *San Juan* reach the boundary, they will stand in front of the expected incoming British task force, threatening their transit toward the Malvinas Islands. This threat will strengthen your president's position in negotiating the return of the islands to their proper ownership. Meanwhile, the *Specter* will remain on station to protect the *Dragon*, which will be in our possession by that time."

As the translator opened his mouth to relay Renard's meaning in Spanish, the commanding officer in front of Jake raised his nose and interrupted him in English.

"And if you fail in taking the *Dragon*?"

"It is a fair question, Commander Gutierrez," Renard said. "The taking of the *Dragon* is a delicate operation. Should the *Dragon* remain under command of the Royal Navy, then you will receive orders from your admiralty to sink her, as will Commander Martinez of the *Santa Cruz*. I will also order Mister Slate of the *Specter* to do the same."

The news surprised Jake. He hadn't considered sinking the destroyer and sending another two hundred sailors to their deaths.

"Three submarines is overkill," Gutierrez said. "I can sink a British destroyer myself."

"Perhaps," Renard said, "But the *Dragon* has far too much firepower to be allowed to work against us. Alone, it can control the air around the Malvinas. If its crew is alerted to an attack, it will employ speed and evasive maneuvers, making chase by a single diesel-powered submarine a low-probability endeavor."

Revealing no concern in countering Renard's argument, Gutierrez lifted his arm toward the screen.

"Proceed," he said.

"Thank you, Commander Gutierrez," Renard said.

The Frenchman showed poise and respect that impressed Jake, who took a cue from his French friend and stifled his urge to stand up and punch Gutierrez in the mouth.

He remembered the results of his last fit of violence, calmed himself, and listen to Renard explain details about the operation that he had already memorized.

Glaring at the screen, he shut out Renard's words and saw an *Astute* class submarine materialize in his future.

Over one billion British pounds invested into seven thousand, four hundred tons of stealthy killing power. Two Rolls Royce pressurized water nuclear reactors giving a sustained eight-knot speed advantage over his *Specter*'s fastest hour-long sprint. Infinite endurance. A torpedo room filled with almost forty weapons. Sound-absorbent equipment mounting that, at slow-speed operations, could make its nuclear reactor as quiet as his battery-driven system. Acoustic detection and data processing on par with his world-class French-designed *Scorpène* class submarine's ability. A commanding officer of world-class ability, trained by arguably the best submarine pipeline on the planet.

As he caught himself talking within his mind, Jake realized that his thoughts formed a good first question to test for the existence of a god.

Okay, God, here comes the test, he thought. *If you're really out there, can you keep me alive long enough to get it right?*

CHAPTER 5

Inhaling the sickly sweet stench of atmosphere-cleansing chemicals and the staleness of shined metal, Jake passed through a hatch into the *Specter*'s operations room. Henri moved to his side.

"You will remember all the French crew from our deployment in Taiwan," Henri said. "Pierre wanted to keep the French contingent consistent to minimize disruption. All the Taiwanese sailors, however, are new."

"What happened to the ones who deployed with us?"

"They took take their knowledge back to Taiwan," Henri said. "Now we train their new blood."

"Circle of life," Jake said. "At least there's a familiar face."

Six dual-stacked French-designed Subtics system tactical monitors spanned the compartment's left side. Before one panel sat the toad-like figure of his sonar systems expert, Antoine Remy.

"Am I the best sonar expert you know?" Remy asked.

"Of course you're the best. Why would you ask?"

"Because we're facing the best submarine we have ever faced. I need to know that you have confidence in me."

"Confidence comes from within," Jake said.

"For you, perhaps," Remy said. "For the rest of us, it comes partially from within ourselves, but partially from the extra you have to spare."

Jake chuckled.

"It's good to see you, my old friend," Jake said. "I'd bet my life on you at least once again."

Jake noticed young Taiwanese sailors offering hopeful and uncertain stares. Henri made introductions and assurances of the competence of the trainees. Jake found their English respectable and saw a healthy mix of bravado and fear in their eyes.

Their uniforms, or lack thereof, surprised him. They wore the beige slacks and white dress shirt uniform of Renard's mercenary crew. He pointed at a random man.

"In case we get captured?"

"Yes," Henri said. "Plausible deniability on the part of the Taiwanese government."

"If we get captured, it won't take a genius to connect this ship and its extra crew to its origins."

"Nonetheless, the civilian clothing is Renard's wish, whether we are captured or not."

"Let's not find out," Jake said. "Who else is aboard? Do I have an officer with any tactical training?"

"Not this time," Henri said. "Renard's agreement with the Taiwanese Navy was to train their people how to operate the shipboard systems. Their officers can learn tactics in a simulator."

"Makes sense. A newbie would probably distract me with too many questions anyway."

"Agreed."

"Who is the best drone operator?"

"You just met him."

Jake glanced at the pimple-faced Taiwanese sailor seated beside Remy. He looked twelve years old, and that suited Jake, who considered drone operations more like a video game than warfare.

"Pimple face?"

"Yes, Jake. Otherwise known as Petty Officer Kang. He is the best in the Taiwanese fleet at drone operations."

"The best available they could spare, you mean?"

"No, Jake. Drone operators are the one area they are developing ample talent. He is the best–period–based upon simulators, of course. But the simulators are dreadfully accurate."

"So his backup is good, too, just in case we need him?"

"Of course."

"Good. I assume you have verified all systems?" he asked.

"I rechecked all of them twice."

"You know I'm still going to walk the ship."

"I would expect nothing less," Henri said. "And I expect that you will be impressed, as usual."

Jake passed through the aft battery compartment and rear auxiliary machinery room, reaching the hull section where his memory expected to see the air-independent ethanol and liquid oxygen MESMA plant. He looked upward at a high-pressure tank of compressed explosive gas. His fingers tapped cool, dormant piping as he moved by.

He ducked through another watertight door and underneath the wide air ducts leading to the quad diesels. He saw the main motor further aft, hidden intermittently by a man pointing to gauges on a control panel. Four sailors–all wearing dungarees of the engineering crew–stood behind their instructor, who nodded at Jake.

Jake respected Claude LaFontaine, a former engineer officer on the French nuclear-powered *Rubis* submarine who had become an expert on diesel power plants after deployments aboard *Agosta* and *Scorpène* class boats.

"Claude," Jake said. "You look as edgy and wiry as ever."

"Some things never change, even with age."

"We're all getting older," Jake said. "And hopefully wiser."

"Wiser," LaFontaine said. "And better for our experiences. I trust that your wisdom is growing? You're approaching the age of a standard navy's submarine commander."

"True," he said.

"We're taking on the greatest adversary we've ever faced," LaFontaine said. "Everyone needs to be in top condition, especially you."

"I'm fine, Claude."

"Good, Jake. I'm ready for this, as is the crew. Make sure you are ready to stick this out from start to finish."

"You can be angry, but you're either going to have to get over it or fight through it. Take your pick."

"I will do my duty, Jake. As always."

"I know. I'd kick you off this ship if I didn't believe you. Introduce me to the new men on the engineering team."

Jake studied LaFontaine for signs of doubt. Nothing. He concluded that the Frenchman showed teeth and spine to express his anger but that he still trusted him.

"Yes, Jake. Like last time, they are the best from Taiwan."

Jake shook hands with Taiwanese mechanics. One had a thick accent, but Jake judged the English skills sufficient.

"How is the propulsion system?" Jake asked.

"It still runs like clockwork," LaFontaine said. "Predictable. Reliable. Not a hint of protest at depth, speed, or maneuvers."

"The MESMA system?"

"I gave it a second shakedown and pushed its endurance as we were towed across the Pacific. I knew that we could refuel oxygen here in Argentina."

"You made a good decision," Jake said. "After we spring our trap, we may not get a chance to snorkel and run the diesels. This may be our first time where we need to put the MESMA system through its paces for submerged endurance."

"It should give us four to five knots plus electronics and life support for three weeks."

"Good. The battery will need to be strong, too. Have you exercised it recently from full charge to full discharge?"

"Yes, Jake. It holds ninety-nine point seven percent of its full charge when this ship was brand new."

"The engineering spaces are ready," Jake said. "Now I've got one last item to check."

Ten minutes later, Jake stood at the frontal compartment of the submarine. Two sailors operated hydraulic valves, and a torpedo glided on rails through the breach door of its tube. Spare electric-propelled Black Shark heavyweight torpedoes filled the room, along with Exocet anti-ship missiles, a pair of super-cavitating torpedoes, and mines stretching under the shadows to the hull's insulation.

Henri stood by his side.

"The load out is a balanced mix of torpedoes, Exocets, and mines," the Frenchman said.

"Why the mines and Exocets?" Jake asked. "I don't intend to mine any harbors, and I sure as shit don't plan on attacking any British surface combatants."

"Pierre wanted us ready for all missions."

"Let's focus on the weapons I care about."

"Yes, Jake. The Argentine torpedoes we had modified in Taiwan."

"Right. Those are the only ones I give a damn about at the moment."

"I triple-inspected the weapon load out. The proper weapons are aboard."

"You know I trust you one hundred percent on this, right?"

Henri nodded.

"You also know why one hundred percent trust isn't good enough and that I need to see this for myself?"

"Of course," Henri said. "I had this team study the tube backhauling procedure, knowing that you would want to inspect them."

As the propeller and stabilizers of the cylindrical weapon slid by, Jake read the words imprinted on its plastic green shell. They were in Spanish, and they told him the right Argentine torpedo had been loaded.

Henri gave the order, and a sailor applied a battery-powered tool to screws that secured a plastic cover. With the cover removed, Jake aimed a flashlight into the torpedo's warhead compartment and studied its contents. He approved what he saw.

"How was this tested?" he asked.

"During an exercise scenario against a Taiwanese submarine," Henri said.

"A Taiwanese *Scorpène* class submarine?"

"Yes, Jake. It was a very simple training scenario. The Taiwanese submarine raced by us at a high bearing rate, we shot the training torpedo at them, and it performed perfectly."

"How fast was the target submarine going?"

"Flank speed."

"Twenty-five knots for a *Scorpène* submarine on its best day," Jake said. "A British nuke will hit thirty-three knots easy, maybe more."

"The weapons are smartly modified, and each one will work, Jake. You trust Taiwanese design and quality, do you not? They even sealed them with Argentine markings so that they appear Argentine if they were to land in the wrong hands."

"Good points. Close it up."

The team reloaded the tube and repeated the backhaul process on the other modified weapons. After Jake inspected all weapons to his satisfaction, he led Henri up a ladder to the control room.

He leaned over the central table and slid a stylus across a chart showing water to the north of the Falkland Islands.

"We've got some ground to cover."

"Agreed."

"But we're going to start slow."

"How slow, Jake?"

"Very. We're going submerge pier side."

"I was afraid you would say that," Henri said. "You wish to submerge while under the canopy so that we are unseen from the beginning."

"From the beginning."

"The water will be deep enough, but it will take careful maneuvering to keep us from hitting bottom."

"When we leave Mar Del Plata, we will head due south for seven hundred and fifty nautical miles. We'll cover one hundred and ninety miles per day. That's averaging almost eight knots, and the MESMA system won't be able to keep up. We'll have to stop and snorkel twice to recharge the battery, but once we're on station, the MESMA system will keep us at full battery charge and submerged."

"Agreed."

"Once we're on station, we'll deploy a drone and use it to delouse ourselves and make sure we weren't followed. That's critical. Then we wait for the Argentine submarines. The first will arrive two days later. Then the fun begins."

"I would hardly describe it as fun," Henri said. "It's a sort of morbid thrill to which we've all become addicted."

Jake wondered if Henri and the others enjoyed cheating death, if they subconsciously sought death, or if they cared as little as he did about the distinction.

"Take a fifteen-minute break," he said. "Then gather the ship-handling team here for a review of drills. I want to make sure everyone knows what to do in crisis situations."

"I have trained them, Jake. You will be impressed."

"I'm sure."

As Henri departed, slid around a polished railing, and stepped up to the elevated conning platform, Jake reached toward the bulkhead and flipped down a foldout seat.

He dialed Renard's number and placed his cell phone to his ear. He heard nothing, extended the phone, and glared at it. Recognizing that the phone's wireless signal failed to penetrate the *Specter*'s steel hull, he felt stupid and cursed under his breath.

Stuffing the phone into his pocket, he stood, walked forward, and then climbed a ladder into the ship's conning tower. Fluorescent lighting cast shadows within the tower's damp, echoing metallic confines, and Jake twisted to reach the exterior door.

He creaked open a latch and shoved his shoulder into the metal separating him from the wharf's briny air. Stepping, establishing his balance on the textured non-skid surface, and closing the door behind him left him leaning against the tower's outer wall of steel.

As he lifted the phone to his ear, he looked upward and saw the electric brightness bathing the covered pier in an artificial glow. The overhead crane network and the thin metal skin of the wharf's canopy protected the submarine from unwanted visual observation, but his phone's wireless signals escaped from openings at either end.

The phone rang and he awaited Renard's voice.

"Hello, my friend," Renard said. "I trust you find the *Specter* to your liking."

"It's in top shape, Pierre."

"Then why do you sound so despondent?"

"Was it that obvious? I was trying to sound cheery."

"I suspect it's due to the proper level of fear within you."

"I don't know, Pierre. I think you're wrong about this one. I should be afraid. I should be terrified. But I'm not. It's like I just don't care what happens, but I just know that I need to be here."

"This must feel bizarre to you, facing a British adversary. But trust me as you always have. I promise you, my friend, I've always had your best interests in mind. You are charmed, and you will succeed unscathed."

"I'm having trouble believing you now."

"The worst demons are in your mind, Jake. They are not aboard a British submarine. If you arrive at the ambush site with control of your own mind, you will have already succeeded."

Jake studied the length of the submarine and noted its minimal connection to the concrete pier. Four synthetic nylon lines maintained cleat-to-cleat links between the ship and land, and a lone grouping of twisted, shielded electric lines fed power from a wheeled diesel generator to sockets above the vessel's propulsion spaces.

"Jake, are you listening?"

"Yeah, Pierre. I'm fine."

"Focus, man," Renard said.

"Any changes to our mission parameters?"

"None, my friend. Everything is unfolding per my plan."

"Then I'm ready. I'm getting underway."

"Excellent. I wish you a safe and productive journey."

As Jake slid the phone into his pocket, he thought about calling his wife. But he knew that hearing his voice would only distress her, and he sought refuge from his philosophical problems within the bowels of the *Specter*.

Inside the control room, Jake saw Henri and a handful of Taiwanese and French sailors awaiting his command to simulate emergency procedures. He looked away, waved his hand, and found his way to the foldout captain's chair.

"We've got a ton of time to practice drills on the way down there," Jake said. "Let's just get this ship underway."

"Nightfall isn't for another thirty minutes, Jake," Henri said.

"That's fine. We'll take our time and make sure we do this right. No scratches, bumps, bruises, or any unwanted marks on our freshly cleaned hull. Do you have communications topside?"

"Yes, Jake."

"Very well, Henry. Divorce us from shore power and make ready to get underway on the battery."

Jake watched and listened as his crew prepared the ship for operation. Their speed and efficiency impressed him, although he expected nothing less with Henri in charge.

When his key Frenchman appeared to have a moment, Jake gestured for Henri to join him.

"Is our police escort ready?"

"Yes, Jake. Two shore authority vessels will keep unwanted sea traffic out of our way in the channel until we are in open water."

"As long as they know where we are, you mean. They won't be able to see us any better than anyone else."

"But they know where we plan to be, exactly. And you know my skill with inertial navigation systems and ship handling."

"Yeah, I do. That's why I have no doubt we'll reach open water just fine without so much as having to raise a periscope or a mast."

"But you will be tracking contacts in the system, will you not? Just to be sure?"

"Yes, Henri. And I'm willing to raise the periscope if things get hairy. Let's just hope they don't."

Several minutes passed as Jake watched Henri collect the final reports and glance at dials and gauges. The knowing look on the Frenchman's face told Jake the story he needed.

Battery voltage and current draw were nominal, the MESMA system showed safe temperatures and pressures, the rudder, stern plane, and bow planes were working under hydraulic power, the trim and drain system was moving water to the appropriate tanks to keep the ship level when submerged, and lubrication oil temperatures at the propulsion motor showed that an adequate warm up had taken place.

"We are ready to get underway," Henri said.

"Cast off all lines," Jake said.

Henri grabbed a sound-powered phone connected to circuit that conveyed his voice through the steel hull to the men who remained topside. Minutes later, three sailors descended into the control room and confirmed that the nylon mooring lines had been thrown to the pier, the cleats turned upside down and fared flush with the hull, and that the ship was sealed watertight.

Jake looked at a fathometer showing eight meters of water below the keel. From reviewing the nautical charts of the egress channel, he expected little margin in his effort to keep his ship's conning tower concealed just below the water's surface, until he reached open water.

He had ordered Henri to trim the ship light, keeping its internal tanks filled with minimal seawater so that its submergence would be gradual.

"Henri," he said. "Submerge the ship."

Seated in front of a control station on the starboard side, Henri flipped switches that opened the vents atop the main ballast tanks at both ends of the vessel. As water displaced air within the tanks, Jake watched the depth gauge tick downward. The increasing numbers on the depth gauge and the decreasing numbers on the fathometer told him that the *Specter* slipped below the still, brackish water beside its pier.

When the numbers settled, Jake realized the ship had reached the silted bottom.

"A little heavy, Henri?"

"Not bad, I should think, given how gently I submerged us and given that this class of submarine is designed for resting on the bottom. Nothing extending below the keel to be damaged."

"Fair enough. Make us lighter and get us off the bottom."

Minutes passed as Henri energized the drain pump to push water out of the ship. With a meter and a half of water underneath his ship, Jake was ready.

"All ahead one-third," he said. "Make turns for three knots."

Imperceptibly, the *Specter* crept forward, carrying Jake and his mercenary crew toward a destiny carved from nightmares.

CHAPTER 6

Commander Gutierrez leaned back in his chair and waved his hand in dismissal.

"Make sure to get rest, Commander Martinez," he said in Spanish. "I need you to be ready to perform better than your abilities. You must outdo yourself."

The younger submarine commander stopped at the door and appeared to stifle a retort.

"Good night, gentlemen."

Martinez closed the wardroom's door, leaving Gutierrez with the president of his nation.

"You are harsh with him," President Gomez said.

"That he is our second best commanding officer is telling of the mediocrity of our submarine fleet."

Gomez lowered his thick, dark eyebrows and blew smoke that rose into the overhead ventilation system.

"After you accomplish this mission, submarines will be seen as the sword of the fleet. The brightest men will seek to join your ranks."

"We already are the sword of the fleet, even armed with only relics. That tells you how badly our navy is in decay."

"I grant you that this submarine smells of stale dirt and oil embedded in its very atoms. But they are capable enough. You will win this campaign with the equipment at your disposal."

"Only with the help of a mercenary ship. Even just one modern vessel would have allowed me to handle this without having to reach out to strangers for help."

"Patience. After the recently discovered oil reserves around the Malvinas are under my control, I will have a combination of cash flows and borrowing powers to purchase a new navy."

Anticipating the latest rendition of Gomez's personalization of a promised rewards, Gutierrez inhaled the soothing taste of his cigarette.

"Before you return home," Gomez said, "you will be promoted to the rank of captain and placed in charge of our submarine fleet, which I personally guarantee will involve no less than four new, state-of-the art submarines. Perhaps six new submarines, depending on the price negotiations."

Visions of controlling a navy with dominance rolled throughout Gutierrez's head.

"What type of submarine?" he asked. "Which builder?"

"German, of course. *Type Two-Fourteen.* I will give you the keys to the kingdom, so to speak, and it will be to you to shape the fleet per your liking, with a very generous budget."

"Will I have the pick of the nation's finest to recruit to my submarine navy?"

"Of course. And after I force the admirals who opposed this campaign to retire, you will have flag rank within a year."

Gutierrez had speculated that his role in the campaign against Britain would earn his way into the admiralty, but Gomez's first overt promise raised his heart rate. He craved the power and drew from his cigarette to calm himself.

"I will do my part," he said. "But I am concerned about those outside of my direct control. The Frenchman, his American puppet submarine commander, his treasonous tool on the British destroyer. Each man must prove himself dedicated and capable, and I have no reason for confidence in any of them."

"The Frenchman has an impressive history of success. Those in his charge perform admirably."

"Those in his charge are pampered with the best equipment, and he coddles them with choreographed scenarios. Halfwits could succeed under those circumstances. But will his men show creativity and judgment to my level of satisfaction when faced with adversity? I think not."

"We've agreed upon a plan that will catch our adversaries by surprise and render them helpless. You have no reason to complain."

"We'll see if the Frenchman can deliver," Gutierrez said.

A steward entered from the galley, served coffee in porcelain cups, and departed. He watched the president sip and lower his beverage to the table.

"What assurance do you give me that you will offer me these promotions and strengthen a fleet for me?"

"You think nothing of challenging me overtly. It's fortunate that you are a better naval officer than politician."

"I have little respect for politicians."

The president stood, slid into his suit jacket, and opened the door. Gutierrez pushed back from his seat in a half-hearted attempt to see Gomez to the exit hatch.

"Don't bother seeing me out, commander. My trust in you is based upon your ambition, not on your adherence to protocols of pleasantries. But since you asked, you needn't worry about me favoring you as my preferred naval commander."

"Why is that?"

"Because yours is the only ship, submarine or otherwise, that I'm visiting prior to the campaign. As you may not understand the subtleties of political positioning, this means I would appear contradictory if I were to promote anyone higher or faster than you. My visit about the *San Juan* this evening means that your future is secured."

The president left Gutierrez alone with his thoughts, which his aspirations ruled. Promotions to captain and then the admiral ranks, and then leading the strongest submarine fleet in the nation's history felt like an interim step. He believed that he deserved control of the entire fleet, including the nation's air, surface, and maritime naval forces.

When he drained his cigarette to the butt, he dabbed it into an ashtray and reached for the temporary land line phone on the counter beside him. He had bid his wife and children farewell earlier in the day, stating he was restricting himself and his crew to the ship for the night to be ready for an early morning deployment. So he dialed the number for his mistress.

Her young, seductive voice aroused him.

"I'm lonely and waiting for my brilliant naval officer."

He thought it masculine to keep her in check.

"I will be there when I am ready," he said. "Show me patience, or I will find a mistress with better self-control."

Uncaring if she intended to voice a response, he returned the receiver to its cradle.

He departed the *San Juan* and drove to the hotel where his mistress awaited. When he had finished having his way with her, he returned to his ship, slept half the night, and awoke to get underway in a standard egress maneuvering operation.

The next evening, he recalled the touch and scent of his lover, and he wanted more. After his pending mission, he looked forward to exercising his right of enjoying as many mistresses as his appetite would allow.

He stood on the elevated conning platform and looked down upon his underlings. Under reddish nighttime lighting, they moved in a choreographed saga of rehearsed actions, each bending to his will to manage and filter data into the ship's tactical system.

His monochrome cathode ray tube monitor showed an overhead view of symbols representing the *San Juan* and freighters transiting through a nearby shipping lane. The arrangement displeased him, and he yelled to his executive officer.

"Lieutenant Commander Fernandez," he said.

"Sir!"

"Come!"

Fernandez emerged from a pack of sailors. His soft features appeared downcast, the way Gutierrez preferred it. Obedience by fear instilled his brand of discipline.

"Yes sir."

"Why don't you have a course and speed set for target number six?"

"It's bearing is constant, and its signal strength is weak. It's far enough away to be ignored while we focus on the closer vessels. I have firing solutions on the other five, one solution each entered into five of our torpedoes."

He recognized that Fernandez's argument carried merits, but he refused to hear them. Thwarting a mindset of counterarguments–veiled excuses– would preserve order.

"We have a sixth torpedo tube, do we not?"

"Yes, sir."

"If we are fortunate enough to engage a British task force, their ships will emit one-tenth the noise and move twice as fast. I want an accursed solution for every ship out there."

Two minutes later, the course and speed to the sixth merchant ship transiting by the *San Juan* appeared on Gutierrez's screen. He let ten more minutes elapse to verify that the solutions to each vessel correlated to the updates from the sonar systems.

"Stop!"

The din in his submarine's control room ebbed.

"I said stop!"

Silence.

"You've all barely managed to track half a dozen merchants. They move in straight lines and at slow speed. They are noisy. You got lucky that these ships are moving at predictable and constant speeds and directions in the shipping lanes. What will you do when faced with destroyers and frigates? They move swiftly. They are quiet. They turn at random intervals to throw off our tracking solutions and our torpedoes."

Silence ensued, and Gutierrez continued.

"I will tell you what you will do. You will wish that you can use a periscope for targeting. But you cannot. British detection systems can see our periscope. I will not risk it. Learn to track vessels with sonar alone. Maybe, if you get lucky, you'll be able to track a submarine."

He stepped to the periscope.

"Diving officer, make your depth forty meters."

His diving officer acknowledged, and the deck tipped upward as the submarine ascended. He twisted a ring that ported hydraulic fluid underneath the huge cylinder of metal, lifting it. With his eye to the optics, he snapped open and torqued two handles to swivel the periscope clockwise.

Keeping his face pressed against rubber, he barked his next order.

"Diving officer, make your depth thirteen meters."

The deck tilted as a surface swell extended its reach to the submarine. As the periscope broached, stars backlit darkness. Settling his field of view in the direction of the closest freighter, he saw a green running light.

"Raise the radio mast and get me a communications download."

A crewman acknowledged his order, and he heard the clunk of a hydraulic gate valve above him. The crewman announced that the radio mast had reached the surface and had linked with shore-based communications.

"Line up to snorkel," he said.

He knew that the ventilation system had been lined up to run the diesel engines, but he wanted his staff's formal verification. A minute later, the snorkel mast joined the periscope and radio mast above the water's surface.

"Cycle the head valve," he said.

The diesel air intake's covering clanked open and shut, sending echoes into the *San Juan's* steel frame. Assured that he could close the huge intake hole leading into his vessel if the submarine lost depth, Gutierrez was ready to charge his battery.

"Commence snorkeling," he said.

The quad diesels rumbled to life with baritone tones vibrating throughout the cylindrical hull. Cool, moist air filled the compartment, refurbishing the atmosphere as it fed the engines.

"The radio download is complete, sir," Fernandez said.

"Very well," Gutierrez said. "Lower the radio mast. I will stay shallow to continue snorkeling."

He grew weary watching shipping traffic, but he refused to trust anyone else. A single missed sighting could allow a catastrophic collision. He remained diligent.

"The battery is fully charged," Fernandez said.

"Very well," Gutierrez said. "Secure snorkeling."

The rumbling subsided, and he lowered the periscope. As his eye adjusted to the red light, his executive officer handed him a clipboard with a printout of the radio traffic download.

An intelligence update on the activity of the *Ambush* excited him. According to several sources, the British submarine was transiting in his direction.

"They're taking the bait," he said. "They are coming. Less than a day away."

"This is excellent," Fernandez said. "We must make noise so we are heard. I will have the crew begin the maintenance and repair exercises we have scheduled."

"No," Gutierrez said.

"I don't understand. These are our orders."

"Let Commander Martinez and the *Santa Cruz* make noise. Let him be the bait. Why waste my skills when I'm superior to that halfwit in every respect?"

"Do you mean to disobey orders, sir?"

"A mere slight deviation. The orders were written redundantly. There's no need for both submarines to call attention to themselves. The *Santa Cruz* will provide sufficient bait."

"I suppose you're right, sir."

"I am. We will remain silent and remain vigilant in doing so. In fact, I intend to reach the delousing with the *Specter* with the *Ambush* having no idea where we are."

"You intend then to not reveal our position to the *Ambush* at all, despite orders to the contrary, sir?"

Gutierrez turned his back and stepped toward the exit. At the door, he stopped and turned back to Fernandez.

"Join me in my stateroom," he said. "It's time for me to share special details of our orders that you have yet to hear."

CHAPTER 7

Commander Nigel Gray awoke from a restful sleep. Unlike most people preparing for mutiny, murder, and treason, he accepted turning his back on everything he'd known as a logical continuation to his tragic life.

His first waking thought drifted to a three-month old memory when he had been seducing barflies in a Portsmouth pub. Instead of finding a woman to help him forget his loneliness, he had found a new foreign friend. A Frenchman had approached him and offered his services in retaliating against a system that had failed him.

The Frenchman had paid significant sums of money to hold subsequent private meetings where Gray had to do nothing but listen. On their third meeting, Gray surprised his companion by asking him to cease his incremental commitment recruiting techniques.

He remembered his words.

"You need me to commit an act of treason. You have no need to justify it or make it seem something that it is not. I am ready to do my part for my own reasons, and I will trust you to offer me a fair compensation. I assume that you have a pricing model for such activities, based upon weapons given to your disposal, adversarial assets neutralized, strategic impact, and the like."

Within days, the Frenchman had offered a plan for Gray's review. When they had agreed upon it and its associated price of treason, the French recruiter revealed himself as Pierre Renard.

The name meant little to him, but somehow the puppet master named Renard felt like a friend–Gray's first. He knew there could be no friendship in such a usury relationship, but the false feeling comforted him.

After rolling off his rack, he placed his bare feet on the deck plates of the *Dragon* as it rolled in the rising seas of the South Atlantic Ocean. He reached and clicked open a metal door, and then he stepped into his private bathroom.

As he brushed his teeth, he diverted his gaze from the mirror to the metal basin. He perceived himself as a nothing, a creature unfit for cohabitation with humans, and he refused to refute that belief by gazing at his reflection.

He clenched his jaw and squeezed his eyes shut as a volcano of emotions rose within him. After a moment, he regained his focus. Then the emotions hit again, restarting the perpetual cycle of his subconscious mind humiliating him with the shame of having been sired by a wayward drunkard and abandoned by a teenage mother through her death in his childbirth.

Denied his maternal bonding, he developed anger, fear, and misery as his earliest preverbal memories. Then a childhood in a dank orphanage on the outskirts of Manchester, where his abnormal intelligence caused him ostracizing and taunting, sealed his fate as a tormented outlier.

He spat and rubbed an electric razor over his chin, pondering society's obligation for him to care about people. Snapshot memories of failed experiments with trusting people, feeling empathy and showing compassion, flashed through his mind. Any yardstick he could grasp to measure the return on such investments came up empty or left him betrayed.

Stepping back into his stateroom, he recalled the odd chain of events that had landed him in the Royal Navy.

When he was sixteen, a larger boy had taken to beating him on the grounds. Friendless, Gray sought quiet, solo revenge.

For years prior to the beatings, he had found an isolated patch of grass between a toolshed and the orphanage's wall as his refuge. The arrangement served all parties. The other children exercised without the distracting temptation to mock him, adult caretakers could ignore their worst problem child, and Gray read books to educate himself in safety.

That changed when the larger boy took to demonstrating his physical superiority.

Using a small garden hoe, Gray had launched his retaliation plan and had started digging a shallow trench in his private unused patch of grass. He worked in spurts, covering the evidence of his efforts and peeking around the shed every five minutes to verify his solitude.

His daily labor included carving a pit into one end of the trench, and it included sharpening sticks, which he hid under the tarp when the bell rang to summon him to his beating en route indoors. His ritual also included leaving raised patches of grass, which he practiced running on each day.

After a week, Gray had finished digging, and he embedded two dozen sticks into the ground under the plastic tarp. He then removed a shoe and ran it over locations on the tarp to create a random set of mud prints. Then he repeated the task with his other shoe. As the bell rang, harkening his beating, he approached the larger boy and kicked him in the testicles.

He turned and ran, and a glance over his shoulder verified that the boy's anger had overpowered his groin pain. Gray sprinted for the shed but heard the boy gaining on him.

Turning the corner, Gray stepped the memorized path over the elevated grass patches hidden under the plastic. He stopped on the tarp, turned, and raised his fists.

As the larger boy corned the shed, Gray stared him down. The boy charged, but as his foot hit the tarp, his leg sank, and the he toppled down into the crinkling plastic and the wooden spikes hidden under it.

A spike cut through the canvass and carved a line from the boy's wrist to his upper arm. Another barb punctured his thigh. Gray lamented that the tarp had provided sufficient armor to save his victim's life where another wooden spear had bruised the boy's belly.

A magistrate had offered him a choice between a sentence in a youth detention center or conscript service in the military. He had chosen the Royal Navy.

Within the service, Gray discovered that following a predictable set of rules spared him from oppression, and he found that people valued his intelligence. Officers had recognized his abilities and had guided him toward an officer ascension program, earning him a commission.

He memorized lessons in leadership, allowing him to execute robotic responses to real world situations, and his tactical brilliance had given him a career trajectory to his present position of executive officer of a *Type 45* class destroyer.

But it was ending. His commanding officer had judged him too harsh and uncaring of those in his charge. Given the consistency of this judgment from his past evaluations, he had no basis to object. Upon the *Dragon's* return to Portsmouth, he would be processed out of the Royal Navy.

Gray buttoned his blue uniform shirt and grabbed a leather binder from his desk. Passing through the door of his stateroom, he noticed the main passageway's soft artificial lighting indicating the after-dinner hours when the crew completed evening maintenance.

His heels clapping steel girders, he climbed to the bridge deck and then turned a corner behind an electronics cabinet. A sailor in working blues knelt before an open metal access panel.

He startled the sailor, who looked up with wide eyes. Gray noted the disappointment as the man recognized him. It was the look he received when he entered the presence of his crewmen.

"Good evening, Petty Officer Smythe," he said. "I am going to conduct a random audit of your maintenance. As you know, I conduct this once per week."

"Yes, sir," Smythe said.

Gray slid his fingers between the zipper edges of his binder and withdrew an audit sheet. He closed the zipper, balanced the binder on his forearm, and spread the audit sheet over it.

"You've isolated all power feeds to your work area?"

"Yes, sir," Smythe said. "This entire cabinet is supplied by low-voltage direct currents no higher than twenty-four volts. My particular work area has only three power inputs. I've secured all of them. You can see the tags hanging here, sir."

Gray noticed the red paper tags hanging from breaker switches.

"I see," Gray said. "Do you have a wiring diagram so that I can verify that you've isolated the proper circuit?"

"Not with me, sir. I returned the hard copy to the electrical division after I set up my work area, but I can get you one."

"Get me one."

"Yes, sir. Immediately."

The sailor shifted his weight and extended a hand against the cabinet to balance himself as he stood. As Smythe darted around the corner, Gray dropped to a knee and reached into the cabinet. He felt for a connector and separated it from a circuit module.

From his binder, he withdrew a small electronic module and snapped it onto the connector. He then remade the connection within the cabinet, his customized module integrated into the circuitry.

He pulled his phone from his pocket and found the private and hidden Bluetooth connection to his rogue circuitry. With his phone mated, he stepped into the main passageway and rounded a corner toward the bridge. He walked through a door and latched it shut behind him.

As his eyes adjusted to low-level light, darkness enshrouded the wide bridge windows. He looked down and squinted.

"Good evening, sir."

"Good evening, officer of the deck," Gray said.

"Can I help you, sir? Would you like a status report?"

"No. I'm merely observing. As you were."

He moved behind a man seated at a digital control panel and looked over his shoulder through the window. The silhouette of the forward gun became distinct in front of the bow, and a ray of moonlight shimmered over wave tops.

He looked at the seated sailor's panel and focused on a temperature gauge that indicated ambient temperature. He then lifted his phone close to his nose and tapped a command giving him an option to select a number. He picked the number seventy-nine, entered it, and held his breath.

Below him, the temperature gauge rose to seventy-nine degrees, and he tapped a command on his phone returning the value to its true reading. As the values on the sailor's panel returned to normal, he excused himself from the bridge and returned to the electronics cabinet.

"I have the schematics, sir," Smythe said.

Gray grabbed them and knelt to the panel. He verified that Smythe had shut off the correct feeds, stood, and gave back the paper.

"Very well," he said. "Proceed with your maintenance."

Gray watched Smythe probe circuit modules with a battery-powered signal generator and oscilloscope. He knew that Smythe's scheduled maintenance excluded reviewing his sabotaged module, but he monitored the work in case the petty officer stumbled upon it.

Twenty minutes later, Smythe finished without incident or discovery, and Gray walked away.

He returned to his stateroom and changed into exercise gear. Into his gym bag he lowered a contraption, built by Renard's Taiwanese army of engineers, that resembled a car battery with yards of exposed cable. Stuffing towels around and under the equipment helped to hide the sharp corners outlined on his bag, but as he strained to hoist it to his shoulder, he hoped that no witnesses would notice its abnormal sag.

Since he knew the depopulated path to follow, he faced the solitary threat of a random wanderer as he descended into the ship several decks, crept quickly, and cast frequent glances in all directions. He worked toward the ship's bow and angled around a corner. Stopping at a locked door, he reached into his bag for a key, slid it into the keyhole, and twisted his wrist.

He popped open the lock, lifted its freed arm from its hole, and let it dangle from its chain. Gray rotated the circular ring that withdrew the metallic tentacles from recesses in the bulkhead, and then he pushed open the door.

A forest of metal launch tubes sprawled across the compartment, gauges and access panels on each offering the only clue that they held Aster surface-to-air missiles. The sterile scent of cleaning agents, steel, and dried paint reminded Gray of the room's infrequent human occupancy. One sailor per day entered the area and walked its length and width seeking temperature, humidity, pressure, and explosive gas gauges that deviated from their norms. He knew that he could hide his sabotaging equipment in plain sight.

After latching the door behind him, he lowered the bag to the deck. He withdrew one white towel, wrapped the bag within it, and nestled it in a recess against the bulkhead. He then opened the door, latched it in place, and satisfied himself that the latched ovular shape of metal hid the towel-covered bag.

Perfect, he thought.

He then marched aft, climbed a ladder and turned. He unlatched a door and stepped into the blue dimness of the combat operations room. The eerie indigo-hued form of the officer seated at the center chair stirred.

"Good evening, executive officer," he said.

"Good evening. Give me the latest data feeds," Gray said.

The officer reached over the chair's arm for an electronic tablet and extended it to Gray, who grabbed it and sat in an empty seat in front of a console.

The news told him that Argentine military activity had increased. Twenty A-4 Skyhawk attack aircraft exercised maneuvers, launched missiles, and dropped bombs over an inland weapons range.

Three of the nation's four aged so-called destroyers, which in Gray's perspective were instead small, multi-purpose frigates, each shot an Exocet anti-ship missile into a barge off the coast of Puerto Belgrano before closing in and finishing their target with naval gunfire.

The British Empire took note of the resurgence in Argentine activity, but when one of the destroyers had to be towed back to port for apparent engine trouble, the empire judged the threat worth monitoring but minimal.

Argentine submarine activity had provided the greatest interest when both *Type Seventeen Hundred* vessels left port on the same day. The nuclear-powered *Astute* class submarine, the *Ambush,* trailed the Argentine submarines *San Juan* and *Santa Cruz* as they practiced attacks on merchant vessels in shipping lanes.

Gray read that the empire's intelligence teams considered the activity to be a flurry relative to the Argentine military's normal tempo but that it remained a blip against the British regional defenses. He agreed, deducing that if every active Argentine war machine made the long journey to the Falkland Islands with its weapons intended for hostilities, the outcome remained obvious–the British defenses were overpowering.

He considered that if the Argentines challenged the existing British defenses, the *Ambush* would sink the submarines, the *Dragon*, the four Typhoon fighter aircraft on the islands, and the numerous surface-based Rapier anti-air batteries would turn back the entire aged A-4 Skyhawk fleet, and the geriatric Argentine surface combatants would falter against anything they faced.

Gray returned the tablet to the watch officer.

"I almost feel bad for the *Dauntless*. Don't you, sir?"

"Why?" Gray asked.

"In five days, we'll be patrolling the Falkland Islands, and they'll be on their way home."

"Yes, we are en route to relieve them of duty per the normal operations plan. Why would you pity them?"

"If these Argentines actually think they can stir the hornet's nest in the Falklands, we're the lucky ones who will have the privilege of reminding them of the Royal Navy's abilities."

Gray nodded and left the operations room.

As he climbed stairs toward his stateroom, he redid the math in his head for an Argentine attack. He adjusted the numbers for his secret knowledge.

He removed the *Ambush* from the equation, and then he removed the *Dragon*. By reducing the British arsenal by those two vessels, he gave Argentina fifty percent odds of succeeding in an attack on the Falkland Islands. Then he shifted the *Dragon* to the Argentine side of the equation, just for a single day, and he calculated the odds as favoring the South Americans.

He decided that under Renard's plan, the Argentines would take the islands.

What happened after that meant nothing to him. Renard had promised him a safe exit from the fray, but he found himself uncaring about the Frenchman's promises.

No matter who supported him, betrayed him, or punched him in the stomach as the bell rang, he would act upon plans of his own. He would dig the ditch, plant the spikes, and find a way to overcome adversity.

Accepting danger, Gray knew he would survive.

CHAPTER 8

Jake rose from his foldout chair and placed his hands on the metal railing encircling the *Specter's* elevated conning area. After a week and a half at sea, he felt the edginess of cramped confines, and his unkempt beard itched.

"How's our trim, Henri?"

"Neutral, Jake. Within a ton, I believe. But I am tempted to pump a thousand pounds of seawater overboard from the aft trim tank to balance us out better. I'll know more when we come to a complete stop."

"Good enough," Jake said. "All stop."

Seated at his panel on the starboard side of the control room, Henri maneuvered a joystick. Jake thought that the Frenchman appeared disheveled versus his norm, an out of place tuft of hair and an oil stain on his collar marring the otherwise impeccable image.

"We are at all stop, Jake" Henri said. "Drifting at three knots."

"Very well, Henri."

He shifted his gaze to the small room's other side and locked eyes with a Taiwanese sailor seated at a control panel. Jake remembered ignoring the man's name when they had met, but after a week and a half inside the *Specter's* steel shell, he decided that each crewman's name deserved memorization.

The young Taiwanese, none of whom had spent extended time underwater, were earning his respect while gaining their sea legs. They ran their daily emergency procedure drills, cleaned the spaces, and kept positive spirits as they integrated with the experienced French team.

He had made his drone operator the primary object of his observation.

Despite his acne, Min Kang reminded Jake of an X-Games athlete–a dirt bike-flipping, skateboard-twisting, snowboard-launching conqueror who had too much ability to realize that he had too much bravado. The youngster walked with a swagger, and Jake suspected that his jet black hair, parted to a side and slicked down with gel, exceeded the length regulations of the Taiwanese military.

"I'm ready, Jake," Kang said.

"You mean the drone is ready."

"We both are."

"Very well," Jake said. "Launch drone one."

"Launch drone one, aye."

Jake admired the subtlety of a drone launch. Unlike torpedoes, which needed high-pressure air to thrust them out of the tubes, drones operated free of safety protocols that required rapid accelerations to unlock. He sensed nothing as the *Specter's* first mechanized spy slipped into the ocean.

"Drone one is launched, Jake," Kang said. "Normal launch, all systems normal, normal control."

"Very well," Jake said. "Send it two miles straight ahead of us at two and a half knots."

"Don't you want to go faster, Jake?" Kang asked. "The drone is designed for five knots without degrading its ability to listen and without being heard by adversaries. You can cut the search time in half."

The youngster's recommendation startled Jake. He stared at the sailor trying to determine if his words conveyed disrespect. Per his training and his grasp of millennium of history, a captain of a warship at sea equated to God. Nobody questioned a nautical commanding officer's direction.

Then he realized that the kid came from a new mold of youngsters who belied the military model that the United States Naval Academy had taught him. Taiwan's newest crop grew up in a world of information overload, and self-expression oozed from everyone's pours as a birthright.

Jake had grown weary of playing God, and he decided to change his tact and respond with the wisdom of understanding.

"Not quite five knots," he said. "We're in no hurry, and the worst thing we can do is be heard or fail to hear something around us. But I agree we can go faster. Drive the drone at four knots."

"Four knots, aye. Thank you," Kang said.

Jake couldn't remember having been thanked for an order, and he braced himself for an odd dynamic leading the blend of his French veterans and the Asian newcomers into a hostile exchange.

"Don't thank me, Petty Officer Kang," he said. "Just use your drones to make sure we know who's out there."

Thirty minutes later, Jake sat on his foldout chair rubbing his eyes. He called out to his sonar expert.

"You got anything, Remy?"

"Nothing, Jake."

The news relieved Jake, although he knew the *Ambush* could slide through the water without the hydrophones of the *Specter* or its deployed drone hearing it.

"Are you ready for the drone to begin its spiral search?" Jake asked.

"Yes, Jake. It's time."

Jake stood and looked at a monitor. Eschewing the Subtics tactical computer system's high-end graphics, he preferred the two-dimensional representation of the world with simple symbols. Far from shipping lanes, the *Specter* and its drone appeared as inverted blue triangles, adrift and alone. He aimed his nose at his drone operator.

"Steer drone one left, five-degrees rudder. Conduct an outward spiral passive acoustic search."

Kang acknowledged, and during the next hour, Jake watched the drone's blue triangle carve an expanding spiral around the *Specter's* stationary symbol on his liquid crystal display.

When the drone had circled outward eight miles from the *Specter*, Jake ordered Kang to send it in a straight line. When it reached ten miles away, he had Kang turn it around and point it back at the *Specter*.

He checked his watch and calculated that the first Argentine submarine, the *San Juan*, would pass between his ship and the drone in six hours. He decided get some rest before the delousing, but as he turned, Remy's shrill announcement froze him in place.

"Metallic transient noise," Remy said.

Defensive instincts dominating his mind, Jake sought data.

"Bearing?" he asked.

"Bearing one-nine-three from the drone," Remy said.

"Show me a line of bearing on Subtics," Jake said.

Jake darted to his monitor and watched a red line appear as the Subtics system overlaid it on the display.

As understanding released him from fear's grip, he exhaled and slumped his shoulders.

"That's us," he said.

"Yes, I think so," Remy said.

When the relief of knowing that another vessel hadn't created the metallic noise ebbed, ire grew in Jake. He roared with a dominance he hadn't showed in years.

"Who the fuck is banging metal while we're rigged for ultra-quite operations and deploying a delouse trap?"

The silence and blank faces confirmed that he had asked a rhetorical question. Henri conveyed comprehension of his meaning by standing, directing a Taiwanese sailor to sit in his place, and scurrying by Jake on his way out of the control room.

"I shall find our culprit," he said.

Jake grabbed the Frenchman by his arm, stopping him cold, and pulled him in so that he could whisper.

"Chances are this was a young Taiwanese kid," Jake said. "Go easy on him. I've already established myself as the bad cop, but if we're both bad cops, it all becomes noise on deaf ears."

"I understand the concept, but what would you have me do?"

"Whoever it is, bring him to me when you find him. Make sure he knows I'm pissed off and that he's going to pay for it. I want him to remember the fear of punishment to avoid making critical mistakes. I want his fear to be an example."

"Yes, Jake. I will find him. I've been at this long enough that I can read the guilt on a man's face."

As Jake heard Henri move through the door behind him, he again looked to his drone operator.

"Okay, Kang," Jake said. "You know what this means, don't you?"

"No, Jake. I'm afraid to ask."

"It means you don't get to directly deploy drone number two. Since we just announced ourselves to anyone within twenty miles, you get to do it the hard way."

"Another spiral out search?"

"Correct."

Kang's face darkened, but he held his tongue as he launched the second drone. Jake stepped down from the conning platform, slid by bodies, and knelt beside Remy.

"Get some rest, Antoine," he said.

The sonar expert slipped his headphone behind his ear.

"You want me to rest now, Jake?"

"Yes. Let your Taiwanese understudy handle this drone deployment."

"You would trust him with this?"

"If there's someone out there who heard our transient noise, he's far away. He's going to be curious and making speed to chase us down. I expect that we'd hear even the *Ambush* if it's coming to investigate us, and I trust your understudy to notice it–and that's if the sound analysis algorithms don't automatically flag the noise."

"I'm fine, Jake. Really."

The lines and shadows stretching across Remy's aging face contradicted his claim.

"I know you want to stay glued to that seat, but I need you rested so that you're one hundred percent refreshed when we ambush the *Ambush*. I'm going to lay down the law on whoever the kid is who made the noise, but really, it didn't cost us anything. We're alone out here."

"I hope you're right, Jake."

"I am, Antoine. Go to bed."

Remy stood, stretched his legs, and offered the seat to the eldest of the Taiwanese naval crew. A slender man with pronounced cheekbones took his place.

"Petty Officer Kang," Jake said, "listen to the world around us, and prove to me that we're alone."

Jake returned to the elevated conning platform and flopped into his captain's chair. He let himself doze off, and when he awoke, he tasted stale copper.

He stretched his legs and then pushed himself to his feet. A glance at the nearest monitor showed the *Specter's* second drone finishing its outer leg of its outward spiral search.

"Anything on sonar?" he asked.

Petty Officer Kang shook his head.

As Jake waited for the second drone to complete its task, Henri escorted a young sailor into the compartment. The forlorn look of shame on the Taiwanese man's face revealed his guilt.

"This is our culprit," Henri said.

"I see," Jake said. "How did you find him?"

"I could tell by the look on his face that it was he who made the noise, and he could tell by my demeanor that I sought him. He came forth without my asking."

Jake stiffened his back and added shrill tenor to his voice.

"What happened?"

Looking to Henri for a queue on how to react, the Taiwanese sailor stayed silent.

"He remembered leaving a wrench on the deck after performing maintenance," Henri said. "He then returned to pick it up to avoid allowing it to rattle. Then he dropped the wrench by accident. Sad irony, really, that he created a noise while trying to assure our silence."

"He's lucky that nobody was close enough to hear us. Six hours later, and he may have ruined our entire mission."

"I'm sorry, Jake," the man said.

"I know you are. I expect that guilt will be your primary punishment, but it can't be your only punishment. Henri will assign you to scrubbing the toilets during every cleaning session for the remainder of this deployment."

The man's face tightened in disgust but softened in realization that his blunder had cost him no more.

"Yes, Jake. Thank you," the man said.

"Back to your station," Jake said.

As the man departed, Jake replayed the punishment in his mind, wondering if he'd swiped too gingerly at the man with his claw of justice. But then he decided that it meant nothing compared to his upcoming performance against the *Ambush*. If he nailed that, the entire crew would respect him as much as the French veterans who had witnessed his past miracles.

"The outward spiral search is complete for drone two," Kang said. "I'm ready to position drone two for delousing."

The sailor's words brought Jake to the present moment, and he glanced at the monitor. The inverted blue triangles appeared where he expected. In an hour, the third triangle representing the second drone would settle twelve miles to the east, setting a perfect triangular trap.

Drone one to the north, drone two to the east, and the *Specter*, with its vast arrays of hydrophones draped across its hull, bunched in its bow, and trailed behind it, would establish the most sensitive mobile listening post in the ocean.

And either the first Argentine submarine or the one following it six hours later would bring the *Ambush* to it.

"Deploy drone two to the delouse point," Jake said.

Having not slept in a bed for a day, he collapsed onto his captain's chair again and toggled in and out of consciousness.

"We're half an hour from the first delouse, Jake."

The familiarity of Henri's voice calmed the rush of anxiety that surprised him as he awoke.

The disquiet in his soul troubled him. Desperation and anger had insulated him from fear in his earliest victories, and his striving for selfless contribution had driven him through any dread he faced in his recent successes.

But this fight felt different. Something new harkened him to it— something beyond his personal motivation that he thought he had forgotten.

Morality.

It felt wrong, it bothered him, and he couldn't fathom a single reason to be aboard the *Specter* other than he had heard a greater authority calling him to do it. His anger lingered a distant world away, and any spirit of charity within him seemed inapplicable to his plight. He wasn't doing this for vengeance, and he wasn't doing it for people he cared about. He was only doing it because he intuited that an imbalance in the world needed righting by his hand.

For the first time since wearing the uniform of a United States naval officer, the noble call to duty compelled him forward, and he couldn't quell it.

But it left him vulnerable to his fear, and he wondered if the charm that Renard thought protected him had vanished.

"Half an hour, you say?" he asked.

"Slightly less," Henri said.

"Wake Remy and get him ready."

"He's already at his seat," Henri said.

"The other sonar men?"

"By his side. We have ears listening to every array."

"Great," Jake said. "Then we wait and listen."

Time oozed like molasses, and nothing happened. Jake stepped down from his conning platform and slid behind the seated bodies hunched over sonar screens. Letting his team listen, he stifled the urge to ask questions and stared at the lines on the Subtics monitors showing the surrounding aquatic sounds.

As his patience waned, Jake saw the tiny telltale twitch in Remy's finger that indicated that he heard something.

"What is it Antoine?" he asked.

The finger and its cousins rose to the headphone on the Frenchman's head, pressing it against his wide, toad-like shape. Remy curled his head down in thought and listening, running the sounds he heard against his inventory of auditory memories. Jake held his breath as his guru drew his conclusion.

"Something on the towed array sonar," Remy said.

Jake envisioned the line of hydrophones trailing behind the *Specter*, their distance from the ship separating them from its interfering noise and their length allowing them to hear lower-frequency sounds.

"What do you have?" Jake asked.

"Low-speed screws," Remy said. "Clean, cut by precision machinery. It's a warship."

"A submarine?" Jake asked.

"Yes. The blades are deep enough that seawater is preventing cavitation. I hear no such bubbling."

"Do you have number of blades? Blade rate? How fast are they going?"

"Based upon revolutions per minute and the number of blades on a *Type Seventeen Hundred* submarine, I calculate six knots."

"Is it the *San Juan*?"

"It has to be."

Jake raised his voice to fill the control room.

"Listen up everyone. We've got the *San Juan* on the towed array sonar," he said. "Check the bearing on your monitors and look for it on our other sensors. As we pick it up on other hydrophones, we'll have tons of data on it to tighten its location, course, and speed. So this is a time to practice our targeting skills before we encounter the *Ambush*. Get on it!"

During the next twenty minutes, the *San Juan's* propeller blades, flow noise, fifty-hertz electric plant, propulsion reduction gears, and the periodic cycling of its trim pump filled the ears of the *Specter's* sonar team and illuminated its Subtics tactical system monitors with lines of bearing connecting the heard to the listening. Jake wondered if the crew of the *San Juan* held any auditory clue to the existence of his *Specter* or if they could only trust in his presence.

"Okay," he said. "The *San Juan* just passed between us and drone one. It's passing over drone two. If the *Ambush* is trailing it, it will be in our hearing range soon. Shift your focus from the *San Juan* to five miles behind it. Listen for the *Ambush*. You know what frequencies to listen for."

Jake labored to breathe as he awaited a confrontation with his greatest tactical adversary. He became lightheaded but hid his trepidation by anchoring his grip on the polished rail that semi-enclosed the conning platform. He bowed his head to prevent any fear being seen.

Seconds ticked like days, and Jake prayed for Remy to announce his discovery of the British submarine.

Then he realized that the *San Juan* had driven out of detection range and that the *Specter* remained alone.

He risked a glance at Remy, who seemed to sense Jake's query and look up at the perfect moment. He shrugged his shoulder and shook his head.

"Nothing?" Jake asked.

"It's not here," Remy said.

"So be it," Jake said. "The *Ambush* didn't follow the *San Juan*. We have six hours to regroup and do this again with the *Santa Cruz*. Everyone except the basic watch section stand down and get some rest. Back here in five hours to get ready."

Henri weaved his way through the moving bodies.

"That tested my nerves," he said.

"Tell me about it."

"This heightens the tension for the next go around."

"No shit. We're either going to find the *Ambush* trailing the *Santa Cruz*, or we'll find that the *Ambush* hasn't taken the bait."

"What then?" Henri asked.

"Given that it's quiet as a mouse but has the speed and endurance to maneuver around us any way it wants, I don't want to find out what happens if we have to face it later on equal footing."

CHAPTER 9

Commander Nigel Gray gazed through the bridge window of the *HMS Dragon*. Port Stanley's nighttime coastline appeared as flat black emptiness save for the sparse lighting of the village spread below him.

It's time to give the Falkland Islands back to their rightful owners, he thought.

Then he laughed at the sentiment's sarcasm.

Be honest with yourself, Nigel. It's time for you to stick your thumb into the Crown's eye and move on under your own terms.

He pondered the payoff Pierre Renard would render for his deeds. His French game master had offered a sum, and Gray had accepted without negotiation, pointing out that the amount interested him less than the mission as long as it provided him the financial freedom to live anywhere while hiding from the angry eyes of the British government–if he survived to spend it.

Though he slogged through a hollow existence, Gray valued his survival instinct. He respected Renard's plan to get him out alive, but Gray the survivor had devised a backup escape.

But first, he had to begin.

He dialed a number and lifted his cell phone to his ear. A glance over his shoulder showed two sailors on the bridge, using the high vantage point to watch over the destroyer and its surroundings. One sailor caught Gray's gaze and nodded.

Gray ignored the man, turned, and let Renard's voice soothe him.

"How is everything, my friend?" Renard asked.

"I miss you, Mary," Gray said.

He waited while the Frenchman translated the phrase's meaning. As planned, Gray intended to seize the *Dragon* this night.

"Excellent! Expect a gift from me within minutes."

The smallest of three payment installments, one million pounds, were landing in Gray's bank account.

"I promise," Gray said. "I shall call you again soon."

"Good luck my friend," Renard said. "God be with you."

He slid the phone into his pocket and looked to the sailors, one of whom braved a rare attempt of levity with his executive officer.

"Found a new lady, sir?"

"You noticed?"

"How long do you think you'll keep this one?"

Gray managed a smirk as he noticed an opportunity to strengthen his alibi, or at least a chance to cast doubt on his guilt, if the sailor and the one standing beside him survived to serve witness.

"Perhaps forever."

The second sailor lowered his binoculars and shifted his gaze toward Gray.

"You, sir? The ship's senior bachelor? I never thought I'd hear of it."

"Neither did I. But I may have to actually accept that I've been smitten by a lovely lady back home. I'm deeply considering keeping this one and settling down upon our return home."

"Well, sir. Congratulations. This could be perfect timing."

"What could be?"

"Your separation from the Royal Navy."

"Ah, yes. Of course. I am quite ready for the next phase of my life. It's quite late, gentlemen. Good night."

He left the bridge, descended into the ship, and returned to the vertical launch system compartment for the first time since hiding his gym bag inside it.

Within the compartment, he glanced at the forest of missile tubes and then shut the door behind him. He withdrew the power source, which had a week ago reminded him of a car battery. Studying it, he wondered if that's what it might be—rectangular, rigid, and heavy.

He lowered it to the deck and flipped over the plastic guards that protected its conductive leads. With metallic clamping teeth on either end, the conductor he withdrew from the bag reminded him of jumper cables, but instead of plastic insulation, a soft magnetic material encased the conductive wire.

And there was only one wire—designed to connect positive to negative with minimal resistance.

Hoisting the wire from the bag, he stepped forward and tossed the cable forward. Its mass dragged it downward, and its magnetic encasing snapped it against the middle of the back of compartment's door.

Gray frowned, detached the length from the door, and lifted it higher. He then ran the cable's magnetically-attached length in a serpentine pattern, covering as much area as the wiring allowed.

A spark flew as he clamped the teeth of one end to the power source. Then, assuring his hands gripped the nonconductive plastic grips of the other end's exposed teeth, he turned his head and watched from the corner of his eye as he completed the circuit.

Electrons crackled in the air as the teeth engaged, and Gray watched the wire turn orange with heat. He lifted the gym bag and used it as an oven mitt on the door latch, creating. a slim opening to the outside passageway.

After sliding through, he closed the door and placed the back of his hand against it. It burned, and he yanked his hand back.

Renard had promised that the Taiwanese power source would keep the door hot for fifteen minutes, and he left it to its purpose as he hurried around the corner. Sprinting up ladders and jogging through passageways, he reached the electronics cabinet behind the bridge, his chest heaving but controlled due to Gray's jogging regimen.

He reached into his trousers and lifted his phone toward his face. The custom Taiwanese-developed application opened, and he tapped in a temperature value he wanted displayed on the *Dragon's* systems—five hundred degrees Fahrenheit. Then he tapped in another reading, followed by three more.

After transmitting the data, he awaited confirmation of his false readings' acceptance by his sabotaged electronic connection. A simple green icon on the phone sufficed.

Through the steel door, he heard a klaxon blare and fill the bridge with its fury. Then silence ensued, followed by a panicked voice on the ship's loudspeaker.

"High temperature—vertical launch system chamber! High temperature—vertical launch system chamber!"

Gray counted to thirty to pretend that he had covered the distance from his stateroom. Then he barged through the door.

"What the devil is going on?"

"Fire, sir! Maybe, I mean. We don't know. There's a high-temperature alarm in the vertical launch compartment."

"What are you doubting?"

"We don't see any smoke."

"What smoke do you expect from a sealed compartment? That's a fire, and it means that we need to get underway under emergency conditions."

"Shouldn't we wait until the damage control team investigates the compartment?"

"No! Assume it's a fire."

Gray stepped forward and grabbed a handset.

"This is the executive officer. There's a fire in the vertical launch system. Probable solid fuel combustion incident. Damage control team, assemble by the compartment, but do not enter. I repeat, do not enter."

He looked to the sailor.

"Which tube is it, or are there multiple tubes?"

"Tube seventeen, sir. Its temperature reading is off the scale. Its neighboring tubes are abnormally high but still safe. The compartment temperature is also high enough to indicate a fire."

"It sounds like seventeen is undergoing a slow burn and has breached its containment. We need to get to sea."

"Half the men are ashore, sir. Only the duty section is aboard."

"Eighty percent of the men are ashore since we just pulled in to port today, and half of them are drunk. There's no time to get anyone back, and I want an evacuation anyway. All but essential personnel for damage control and propulsion."

"Sir?"

"If this compartment blows, God knows what could happen with all that fuel and ordnance. I don't want to risk civilian lives or the lives of sailors unnecessarily."

"What do you want us to do, sir?"

Gray looked to the closer sailor.

"You make contact with the damage control team as they assemble. Let them approach and sense the compartment door for heat, but remind them not to enter. I don't want them fanning any flames."

"Aye, aye, sir!"

He looked to the second sailor.

"You make contact with shore authorities. Inform them that we have a fire in the vertical launch system compartment and are heading to sea in an emergency deployment. We are leaving as soon we can get underway."

"Aye, aye, sir!"

Gray lifted the handset to his lips again and flipped a switch to isolate his voice to his engineering spaces.

"Engineering, Bridge, communications check. Over."

The retort crackled through loudspeakers.

"Bridge, Engineering, communications check is satisfactory. Awaiting your orders, sir."

"Engineering, Bridge, conduct an emergency startup of the propulsion plant. Be ready to get underway as soon as possible."

He flipped a switch to send his voice throughout the ship.

"Attention crew of the *Dragon*. This is the executive officer and the senior officer aboard. The captain is ashore with the majority of the crew. The fire in the vertical launch system compartment is a danger to the harbor. I intend to get underway in five minutes. All nonessential personnel are ordered to evacuate the ship. I repeat, all but the primary damage control party and propulsion team are ordered ashore immediately. Cast off all lines. Disconnect all shore power, fuel, water, and sewage connections. Leave the brows. They will pop off as I drive the ship away."

The first sailor on the bridge lowered a sound-powered phone.

"Shore authorities acknowledge our distress situation. They are asking if we need assistance."

"Tell them to make ready helicopters to rescue our crew as we take the ship to sea."

The second sailor chimed in.

"The damage control team is at the compartment door. They report that the door is hot to the touch. They are spraying the door with water to cool it for entry. They are awaiting your orders."

"Get them out of there. Send them ashore. There's nothing more they can do."

Two minutes passed, and Gray received reports that the *Dragon* had been freed from its moorings. He addressed both sailors remaining with him on the bridge.

"You two, get out of here. If you can't make it off the ship before I get underway, I recommend that you jump."

As the men left him alone, a voice rang from loudspeakers.

"Bridge, Engineering, ready to get underway."

He raised his handset.

"Engineering, Bridge, make turns for three knots."

With imperceptible grace and power, the destroyer slid forward. Gray moved to the control console and tapped a screen that commanded a servo-hydraulic system near the ship's stern to move the rudder, and he watched the bow glide from the pier.

Taps against a screen invoked a nautical chart, and Gray observed a dot moving within the overhead graphical rendition of Port Stanley. Technology allowed him to drive the graceful vessel with a fraction of his brain.

Rotating the rudder again angled the *Dragon* into a wide channel, yielding room to maneuver. He intended to violate the safe local speed limits and trust that he could guide the warship past the shoals to open water.

"Engineering, Bridge, all ahead two-thirds," he said.

"Bridge, Engineering, answering all ahead two-thirds."

Shimmering moonlit water hastened by the *Dragon's* flanks.

"Engineering, Bridge, I need more speed," he said.

"Bridge, Engineering. I need about two more minutes to bring up the second gas turbine. I can give you ahead standard now."

"All ahead standard."

The shimmering water accelerated, and the deck began rhythmic bobbing. Random chatter from shore authorities filled the bridge, asking for statuses and offering help that Gray ignored.

"Bridge, Engineering, ready to answer all bells."

"Engineering, Bridge, all ahead flank."

The *Dragon's* prow spat glimmering spray skyward, and the pitched heaving made Gray balance himself on a console.

"Bridge, Engineering, what's going on up there?"

Since he wasn't giving an order, Gray let protocol slide.

"Listen, lieutenant. I can't tell you when or if the vertical launch cells are going to blow, but if and when they do, there's enough fuel in those missiles to slice this ship in half. I don't want anyone else on this ship except myself when that happens. There's no reason for you or anyone else to remain aboard."

"What about you, sir?"

"When we're far enough from shore, I'll head to the engineering spaces and secure propulsion so that the ship drifts to stop. I don't want it doubling back toward land or heading God knows where without any man aboard."

"How far from shore is far enough, sir?"

"I've no idea. I assume that I'll know the appropriate time and place when I get there."

"Are you sure you don't want volunteers to attempt entry into the vertical launch chamber? There are still enough men back here to fight."

"Negative, lieutenant. Opening the door may accelerate the burning, and there's no amount of water that can help in this situation. Get off this ship now."

"Aye, aye, sir. How do you expect us to evacuate?"

"Shore authorities have scrambled a helicopter. I expect arrival in less than five minutes. I can't verify, though, since our radars are off. You'll have you use your eyes to verify its presence."

"We don't have a helicopter handling team, sir. I don't see them landing while we're at flank speed."

Realizing he hadn't considered that, Gray improvised.

"I expect that you'll have to jump."

Gray noticed a pause in the response.

"I will have the team jump, sir. We're abandoning the engineering spaces. We're abandoning ship. Good luck to you, sir."

"Good luck to you."

A light on the navigation system pulsated, its inertial guidance algorithm claiming a trajectory toward concealed rocks. Gray shifted the rudder again, and as the ship rolled away from the turn, he abandoned the helm and walked about the bridge, energizing its radar systems.

Fuzzy images of electromagnetic signals reflected from the skins of commercial ships appeared on a screen as the surface navigation radar system awoke. His three-dimensional view of objects in the sky awaited the calibration procedures of the *Dragon's* Sampson active electronically scanned array.

He redialed Renard and lifted his phone to his cheek.

"What's the status, my friend?" Renard asked.

"It's done. I'm heading to open ocean with a ship that's all but abandoned. There may be stragglers, but not enough to matter."

"Excellent! The assault team is en route. Are your combat systems ready?"

"Not yet, but they will be," Gray said.

"You will let me know, of course, once they are. This is an essential part of our mission."

"I understand. If you can wait a few moments, I may be able to update you in real time."

"Safer to hang up and reconnect when you are ready to make your next report. I trust my cellular encryption scheme, but always best to speak in short bursts."

As Gray lowered the phone, flickering text on a console announced the illumination of the Sampson system. A swipe of his finger invoked a three-dimensional rendering of the sky around his warship.

He turned and walked away from the console with the intent of heading to the combat operations room. He paused and curled his lips, recalling his radar-panoramic view of the sky around him.

The sky around him, he commanded.

CHAPTER 10

Jake rose from a fitful sleep. Four hours of dreamlessness offered him a brief reprise from exhaustion, leaving him alert but tired. Every breath he took aboard the *Specter* reminded him of the encroaching danger of the British submarine, preventing complete relaxation at all levels of consciousness.

After brushing his teeth, he poked his arms through his undershirt and cinched his belt around his khakis. Tucking in his white dress shirt as he closed his stateroom door, he squinted in the passageway's bright lighting. The short walk to the control room left him in a trancelike state, and he welcomed the steaming cup of coffee that awaited him at the navigation table.

In the room's center, Jake converged with Henri, Remy, and Kang to review the springing of their trap on the *Ambush*. Three-dimensional renderings of submarines, drones, and ships glowed on the table's flat screen, but Jake tapped a section of glass to transform the world into his preferred classic view of simple color-coded shapes.

"The *San Juan* should be thirty miles away by now, to the east by northeast," Jake said. "It's going to wait until we delouse the *Santa Cruz* before snorkeling, but that's just a safety precaution. It's far enough away that it can make all the noise it wants and no longer be a factor."

"I lost sound of it at about ten miles," Remy said. "It's been over three hours."

"I understand," Jake said. "But I'll trust it's staying true to the plan and positioning itself where it should be."

"What about the *Dauntless*?" Kang asked.

Jake tapped the screen to enlarge its scale and bring a red icon onto the edge of vision.

"Per our latest update from our source in the British fleet, it's three days away at its best speed," he said. "It's not a factor either."

After tapping the screen again, Jake shrank the view of the world around the *Specter*.

"We're here, drone one is still to the north, and drone two is still to the east," he said. "The geometry is the same as when we deloused the *San Juan*, thanks to some delicate drone control by Petty Officer Kang."

"You wanted the best, Jake. I make it look easy," Kang said.

Jake had grown accustomed to the youngster's bravado.

"Keep it up," he said. "I'm going to need you alert and perfect when we hear the *Ambush*. I may need you to maneuver them. I may need you to transmit active sonar from them. You'll have to hear exactly what I say and get it right under pressure."

"No problem, Jake. I'm your man."

Jake nodded and changed the subject.

"The outer doors to tubes one and two are still open, right Henri?"

"Correct. There was no reason to close them while we drifted silently. I repositioned us only once while you were asleep to account for the ocean current. I assumed it would be quieter to just keep them open."

"Good move," Jake said. "Keep them open. Now let's talk power. The MESMA system has handled our needs while we've drifted. That leaves us at eighty-two percent battery charge. Enough to sprint from a torpedo if needed."

"Yes, Jake," Henri said. "Power is not a problem."

"So this is an exact repeat of what we just did with the *San Juan*," Jake said. "And we hope that when the *Santa Cruz* goes by, the *Ambush* reveals itself trailing it. The odds strongly favor it since it didn't show up trailing the *San Juan*."

He looked to a digital clock read out.

"We've got forty minutes until the *Santa Cruz* is scheduled to arrive," he said. "Take your places."

He reached his chair on the conning platform and eyed Remy at his sonar station. With the sound-nullifying headset over his ears and his hunched back, the Frenchman assumed his toad-like pose.

Jake leaned his elbow against a console and rested his jaw in his palm. Reflecting that the worst part about combat was waiting for it, he strained his mind for an insight—any last-second idea he had overlooked.

The finality of the pending encounter with the *Santa Cruz* weighed on him. He would either find the *Ambush*, or his mission would fail. In ninety minutes, he'd have his resolution.

He realized he could risk wasting a weapon.

"Petty Officer Kang," he said.

"Yes, Jake?"

"Can you drive a torpedo with the precision of a drone?"

The Taiwanese would-be X-Games athlete rendered a quizzical look.

"It depends what you need. A torpedo moves faster and can't make the turns as tight, but the controls are similar. Of course, you always run the risk of the wire breaking because of the speed, and you also will eventually run out of fuel since the wire is just a control wire and not an electronic power supply."

"Good assessment. I want a torpedo positioned as close to drone one as humanly possible and then shut down to drift with the cable still intact so that I can command it to attack the *Ambush* from there. Can you do that?"

Kang furrowed his eyebrows.

"I can do it. The hard part will be turning the torpedo around to point at us. There's the chance of cutting the wire with such a move."

"And the weapon will start a countdown to shut itself off if it believes it's circling back on us. Just leave it pointing away from us. It can maneuver itself through any necessary turns for chasing after the *Ambush*."

"Sure, Jake. That's easy. I can do it."

"Henri," Jake said. "Warm up tube one to run at slowest search speed, passive search mode. I don't want this thing making any noise other than swimming."

"Are you not concerned about this noise, Jake?"

"I am. That's why I'm doing this. Let's make the noise now, while we're still far away from the *Ambush* and with the *San Juan* between us. If the sound reaches them, they'll think it's the *San Juan*, which might jeopardize the mission but at least keep us from being detected."

Henri acknowledged and obeyed.

"Tube one is ready," he said.

Jake looked to a Taiwanese sailor seated beside Remy.

"Enter drone one's position as the target destination."

The sailor acknowledged the order and carried it out.

"Shoot tube one," Jake said.

As air-driven high-velocity water pushed the torpedo into the ocean, Jake's ears popped, and the flushing whine of the impulse launch system filled the *Specter*.

"Tube one, normal launch," Henri said. "Wire guidance engaged."

"Transfer control to Petty Officer Kang," Jake said.

"I've got it," Kang said.

"Wiggle it left and right to be sure."

The youngster verified control of the weapon. Jake again looked to the man beside Remy, the one who supervised everyone except Remy on the team that listened to the numerous hydrophones at their disposal.

"Make sure someone is listening to what the torpedo hears. It may be our bluntest listening tool, but it's another set of hydrophones."

Jake watched the inverted triangle of the torpedo slide across the screen from the *Specter* toward the first drone. As it reached a mile from its destination, he stood.

"That's good enough," he said. "Let it coast to a stop."

He suspected his timing to secure the weapon was perfect as his sonar guru pressed his headset against his wide skull. Remy curled in his ritual of thought and listening, and Jake held his breath

"I've got a contact on the towed array sonar," Remy said.

"What is it?" Jake asked.

"Low-speed screws," Remy said. "Clean, cut by precision machinery. It's the *Santa Cruz*. Based upon revolutions per minute, I calculate six knots, as expected."

Jake raised his voice to fill the control room.

"Attention, everyone. We've got the *Santa Cruz* on the towed array sonar," he said. "Check the bearing on your monitors and look for it on our other sensors, including the torpedo. Just like last time on the *San Juan*. Tighten up your targeting skills. Get on it!"

During the next twenty minutes, the *Santa Cruz's* sounds filled the ears of the *Specter's* sonar team and illuminated its Subtics tactical system monitors.

"Okay," he said. "The *Santa Cruz* just passed between us and drone one and our torpedo. It's passing over drone two. Expect the *Ambush* to be in hearing range soon. Shift your focus from the *Santa Cruz* to five miles behind it. Listen for the *Ambush*. You know what frequencies to listen for."

Seconds ticked like months as Jake's eyes burned on Remy. He blinked, and the Frenchman's finger rose.

Jake froze as his sonar expert's body again began to curl. Then he sprang to the conning platform's polished rail and stared. The control room fell silent, and everyone stared at Remy.

As his breathing returned, Jake kept his eyes on his hunched sonar guru while half-whispering an instinctive order. In the silence, a half-whisper sufficed.

"Henri, warm up the weapon in tube two."

His order acknowledged, Jake felt his heart leap into his throat as Remy faced him.

"Reactor coolant pumps."

"Bearing? Bearing rate?" Jake asked.

"Bearing three-three-eight. Bearing rate, I need more time to get you something reliable."

"You've got two minutes."

"Drone one has it now," Kang said. "They must be close to the drone."

On the monitor beside Jake, a hyperbolic line representing the arc of hearing from the *Specter's* towed sonar array cut across the ocean. Then a straight line from its drone intersected it.

"Nailed," Jake said. "Don't need bearing rate. That's the *Ambush*, right at the intersection of those two bearings. Enter a course of zero-eight-five, speed of six knots. Now!"

"Done, Jake," Remy said.

"Petty Officer Kang, send the solution to your torpedo."

"The solution is entered, Jake," Kang said.

"Engage your torpedo, maximum speed, active search."

"Torpedo is engaged, Jake."

"I hear high-speed screws and cavitation from our torpedo, Jake," Remy said. "And there's the active search. It's using the preprogrammed Argentine sonar frequency."

Jake swallowed as he considered the terror shooting through the hearts of each British sailor aboard the *Ambush*.

"Petty Officer Kang," he said. "Transmit active from drone two, simulate Argentine sonar frequency. Increase transmitted frequency from base frequency to account for Doppler effect of a fifty-five-knot search speed pointing directly at the *Ambush*."

"Done, Jake," Kang said. "Twenty-two-point-three kilohertz transmitting from drone two."

"Good," Jake said. "Increase sound volume ten percent every thirty seconds and keep the drone pointed at the *Ambush*."

"It's a turkey shoot, Jake!" Remy said. "Our torpedo has the *Ambush* dead to rights. Two miles and closing. Drone number two is transmitting, mimicking the sounds of a second torpedo. The *Ambush* has deployed gaseous countermeasures and active transmission countermeasures. The *Ambush* is cavitating, accelerating to flank speed."

"What else? Have they launched a retaliatory weapon?"

"Not yet, but wait… outer doors are opening. Two of them… one weapon away, and now another."

"Bearing rates to both torpedoes?" Jake asked

"Calculating!"

"Are they going the ways we want? On the right, drawing right fast and on the left drawing left fast?"

"Yes, Jake. Torpedoes from the *Ambush* are moving away from us. I suspect they are shooting exactly where we would hope."

"They've shot back at submarines that aren't there," Jake said. "That's all they could do. They don't hear us, and they shot at our drones."

"New launch transients!" Remy said.

"A weapon?"

"No. Something smaller. I think it's a three-inch launcher."

"Damn," Jake said. "That's a cool captain. He's sending a doomsday message to let the Royal Navy know the details of his death before he goes down."

Jake flexed every muscle in his torso to stifle any rising emotions that would betray his mission.

"Torpedo is range gating!" Kang said.

"We've got them," Jake said. "The trap was perfect!"

"Impact in twenty seconds!" Kang said.

"Launch transients!" Remy said. It's a third weapon from the *Ambush.*"

"To the east?"

"Yes, vaguely. It's so hard to tell, Jake."

"I know. I assume this one's a vengeance shot against the *Santa Cruz.* I hope its captain is paying attention."

"Not a concern," Remy said. "*Santa Cruz* is accelerating. With its distance, it should be safe."

"Which way is the *Ambush* running?"

"Southeast. They think they're trying to evade two torpedoes. That's the best way for them to run."

"Detonation imminent!" Kang said.

Jake braced himself for the fury of roaring ocean that he had been trained to anticipate but knew wouldn't occur today. Today's detonation would be miniscule. As he held his breath, the report from Remy rendered his solitary comprehension that his weapon's warhead had exploded.

"Detonation has taken place," Remy said. "Limpets deploying."

"Count how many attach to its hull."

"I'll do my best, Jake. There will be a lot."

"You're recording this, right?"

"Yes," Remy said. "Limpets are attaching."

Jake pictured twenty-five buoyant limpets rising into the hull of the *Ambush* and attaching themselves with magnetic force.

"Limpets are going active," Remy said. "At least half of them have attached. Maybe more."

"Play it out loud in the compartment," Jake said.

Remy flipped a switch, and the ocean's haunting reverberations filled the control room. Amidst the natural sounds, clamping thuds and their ensuing electronic tweets rose in a chorus of ensnarement.

With the underbelly of the *Ambush* riddled with chirping parasites, the magnetic limpets announced the submarine's presence to any nearby undersea warfare system.

If forced to stave off the *Ambush*, the *Dragon* would have an easy time of it, as would any Argentine warship, submarine, or anti-submarine aircraft.

Jake considered his mission complete and decided to evade before the commander of the *Ambush* attempted a desperate or bold retaliation.

"All ahead one-third," he said. "Make turns for three knots."

As a speed gauge revealed the *Specter's* imperceptible crawl, stress drained from his shoulders. He stepped backwards and slumped into his captain's chair.

"Cut the wires to drones one and two," Jake said. "Keep the outer doors open."

Henri acknowledged the order, and a glance at a monitor showing the tactical information of the *Specter's* Subtics computer system confirmed his hope that the *Ambush* continued its retreat.

"Increase speed to five knots," he said.

"Making turns for five knots, Jake," Henri said. "Do you wish to close the outer doors yet?"

"No. I'll risk the flow noise versus creating a mechanical sound of closing the doors. We're far enough away that they won't hear the flow noise, especially since they're still cleaning the shit out of their pants. Don't you agree, Antoine?"

A sideways glance to Remy, who crouched in attentive listening, alerted him to a new danger. The control room's staff had been watching Jake for guidance on celebrating, but necks turned in unison and became a spectacle of a dozen muted men gawking at the frozen Frenchman.

Jake tiptoed to the senior Taiwanese sonar operator beside Remy, tapped his shoulder, and whispered.

"Do you hear anything?"

The man shrugged his shoulders and shook his head, and Jake resisted the urge to interrupt him. Then, after restricting himself to a series of shallow breaths, he heard the surprising news.

"Torpedo in the water," Remy said. "Bearing one-two-eight. Minimal bearing rate, but it's far enough away that I would expect the bearing rate to be small."

"Shot at the *Ambush*?" Jake asked.

"Probably. It's so far away I can only guess."

"Guess, then," Jake said. "If there's nobody else out here, who else could it be?"

"It's not the *Santa Cruz*. It has run safely to the northeast and evaded the *Ambush's* third torpedo. But I agree, Jake. It must be targeted at the *Ambush*."

Jake opened his mouth to ask a following question, but Remy raised a finger to hush him.

"The *Ambush* has zigged to the southwest," Remy said. "That confirms my belief that the weapon did not come from the *Santa Cruz*. It's running in a different direction, as if the weapon came from the east."

The realization of possible foul play and clandestine objectives overcame Jake in a tide of tingling numbness. He crouched before Remy.

"Shit, Antoine."

"What, Jake?" Remy asked.

"Are you getting any identifying features from that torpedo? Blade rate, number of blades, active search frequencies?"

"I'm getting it all, but it will be useless information until I can reconstruct the path of the torpedo. Torpedoes have multiple search frequencies, and the Doppler shift based upon its speed and direction will take time for me to narrow it down to what type of torpedo it might be. Perhaps hours."

Jake stood and turned to the room's central navigation plot.

"Henri, get a relief at your control station and join me here."

Within seconds, the Frenchman leaned over the hard-coated liquid crystal display plotting table with concern in his face.

"What are you thinking?" he asked.

"Watch," Jake said.

He manipulated the course and speed of a symbol, turning it as if the captain of the vessel it represented had omniscient advanced knowledge of the attack that had just unfolded. When he finished, the symbol appeared at a distance from the *Ambush* equal to the edge of its torpedo range.

"Dear God," Henri said.

"Hostile torpedo fuel is exhausted," Remy said. "The *Ambush* has evaded."

"How close was it, Antoine?" Jake asked. "I know you don't know for sure yet, but give me your gut feel."

"I think the crew of the *Ambush* will need to clean their underwear again, Jake."

"That's what I figured. Asshole!"

"Agreed," Henri said. "Treachery. We must warn Renard."

"Right," Jake said. "Prepare a written message for his personal encrypted text letting him know what the hell just happened. Obviously, we're not playing a fair game with our Argentine friends."

"Shall we maintain five knots speed?"

"Yes," Jake said.

"I assumed so," Henri said.

Jake reduced his voice to a whisper.

"And no faster," he said. "We now need to assume that we're in the middle of something out of control and need to maintain our stealth. For all we know, someone has orders to find us and sink us."

Jake glared at the icon on the screen that represented the assailant that had launched a lethal weapon at the *Ambush*.

"You son of a bitch," he said.

The text below the icon labeled the assailant as the Argentine submarine *San Juan*.

CHAPTER 11

Within the combat operations room, Commander Nigel Gray tapped the final command into the Sampson fire control system, ordering the *Dragon* to engage any high-speed airborne target within ten miles

When he climbed back to the bridge, the lights of Port Stanley dotted the horizon, and his motionless destroyer drifted in the waves. Stepping onto the bridge wing enveloped him with cool humidity, and a rearward glance revealed a rescue helicopter plucking crewmen from the water.

Seeing no human silhouettes remaining on the fantail, he returned to the warmth of the enclosed bridge. He assumed himself alone, uncaring if a random sailor or two had failed to abandon ship and confident that his incoming colleagues would nullify any resistance that straggler crewmen could mount.

A glance at the Sampson system's three-dimensional rendering showed what he hoped–aircraft arrived from the west. They flew at low altitude and in tight combat formation, representing the bulk of Argentine airborne firepower.

He knew that early warning radar systems from the Royal Air Force's Mount Pleasant installation would also see the incoming threat, and he expected their response.

But first, his ship's reaction startled him.

An alarm whined, and lights blinked on the Sampson's display screen. Before he could comprehend the warning, the system unleashed its automated response.

Metallic clunks resonated through the hull as vertical launch tubes opened. Two bursts of bright brilliance blinded him, and the bridge windows shook. Trailing orange plumes, two Astor missiles climbed into the night, accelerated to multiples of the speed of sound, and angled downward toward the shore.

Breathless and blinking the brightness from his retinas, Gray scrambled across the deck to watch the weapons trace lines of fire through the darkness, erupt in conical conflagrations, and cut down a pair of Royal Air Force Typhoon fighter aircraft that attempted to take off from Mount Pleasant.

Unable to see the victims, he trotted back to the Sampson display and glanced at it. Pulsating icons representing the British jets receded into slaughtered nothingness. With only four fighters dedicated to protecting the Falkland Islands, he noted that his treason had halved his nation's local air forces.

The annoying and incessant radio requests for status from port authorities halted, and Gray felt solitude in his semi-deafened silence.

He ambled to a radio control panel and shifted his frequency to a secure military channel. After tapping in a memorized encryption code, he heard a new voice speak his code name with a Spanish accent

"Guardian, this is Hail Storm. Over."

Ten seconds passed, and the hail arrived again.

"Guardian, this is Hail Storm. Over."

Gray lifted a handset and answered.

"Hail Storm, this is Guardian. Over."

"Guardian, Hail Storm, we are approaching. Secure your system in five minutes. Acknowledge. Over."

"Hail Storm, Guardian, I will secure the system in five minutes. Over."

"Guardian, Hail Storm, acknowledged. Out."

Respecting that the Argentine squadron refused to attack with the Sampson system energized, Gray hurried into the depths of the destroyer to shut it down.

Inside the combat operations center, he looked to an infrared scanner's readout. The lack of white-hot jet engines confirmed his hope that the Royal Air Force grasped that an attempt to launch its final two Typhoon fighters equaled suicide.

As he shut it down, the Sampson system showed the Argentine squadron fifteen miles away. Moments later, plumes of infrared white revealed the courage of the remaining two Typhoon pilots. Free of the Sampson system's menace, the jets traced plumes down a runway and then rose into the night.

As their aircraft escaped his infrared system's field of view, Gray gave the British pilots a nod of respect and a silent wish for speedy and painless deaths.

Instead of returning to the bridge, he crept deeper into the belly of the warship and sought its diving locker. He stepped into it and pulled down a wetsuit, fins, and scuba gear.

Months of practice for this day allowed him to don the gear without thought. He folded his uniform on a bench, and the suit enveloped him in his undergarments like a glove. After pulling the hood over his head and drawing the zipper to his neck, he hoisted the tank's traps over his shoulders.

He slid the facemask over his head, draped the flippers over his shoulders, and grabbed his clothes. A detour to his stateroom allowed him to stow his uniform and retrieve a watertight bag that contained keys and cash. Slinging the bag over his shoulder, he headed for the bridge.

Barefooted, he felt the coolness of the deck plates as the windows came into view. The lights of the port had moved to the corner of the bridge's panorama, highlighting the aimlessness of the *Dragon's* drifting. He stepped onto the bridge wing, inhaled the cool moisture, and prepared for the show of fireworks.

The first orange streak speared the darkness and pounded the top of a hill with a conical burst. As the explosion's rumble reached his ears, he recognized the elimination of the first targeted Rapier anti-air battery.

The sky and ground erupted in a fury of exchanges. Bands of color traced laser-like paths of destruction, and bursts of brilliance on land and in the low-altitude air suggested an initial even battle.

Then the airborne bursts ebbed as the Argentine bombs and missiles found their marks, halving the British air defenses. In what Gray assumed to be a second wave of Argentine aircraft, the tide shifted toward the attackers.

He dialed his phone, lifted it to his cheek, and awaited Renard's voice.

"Hello, my friend," Renard said. "All is well, I trust?"

"Yes," Gray said. "Everything is going as well as could be hoped. The attack appears to be going well."

"Indeed. I've heard reports that you managed to take down the first two Typhoons. Well done!"

"I see very little air-to-air exchanges. Do you know how close our colleagues are to controlling the sky?"

"I've heard that the Typhoon aircraft have performed admirably, splashing four or five Argentine assault craft. Fortunately, numbers are prevailing, and one Typhoon has been eliminated, leaving only one. Another two or three Argentine aircraft have succumbed to ground fire, but the ground defenses are being neutralized. The sky will soon be ours."

"Then you'll soon be dropping the paratroopers to secure my ship?"

"Of course. They will be dropped in the third wave and join you shortly. Once the shore batteries are silenced, the technician team will be dropped in a fourth wave."

Gray swallowed.

"I'm about to take a decision that will be irreversible and crucial to our relationship."

"I am concerned. What is troubling you?" Renard asked.

"I intend to forego my bonus and leave you before the Argentine forces land on my ship."

The Frenchman's tone became agitated.

"Perhaps you suffer from lack of trust in me?"

"It's not a matter of wanting to trust you," Gray said. "You've acted trustworthy. It's a matter of not being allowed to trust you for my survival. Given your line of business, I cannot allow one-hundred percent trust, nor dare I assume that your Argentine colleagues would honor your intentions with me."

"I see. You believe that since the infiltration team has been trained to handle the rudimentary operations of the ship without you that I consider you expendable."

"The thought crossed my mind."

"You are my insurance policy against the unexpected. I wish you would stay. You have my word on—"

Renard's speech gave way to a silence Gray found eerie.

"Your word?" Gray asked.

"I'm receiving an important text," Renard said. "Will you excuse me?"

"I'd prefer to stay on the line."

"Very well. Give me a moment."

With Renard taking his time to read his message, Gray lowered his gear to the deck. He grabbed a pair of night vision glasses and stepped onto the bridge wing.

Scanning the night, he saw a large aircraft approaching at a medium altitude–an altitude conducive to jumping. Assuming it to contain paratroopers, he lowered the glasses, returned inside the ship, and snapped at his phone.

"I don't have all day!" he said.

He put his phone against his ear as Renard responded in a peacemaking tone.

"My friend, if you have decided that your safety warrants that you flee now, then so be it. I cannot stop you, nor should I. Do you have an escape plan?"

"Yes."

"Very well. You will forfeit your bonus, but our score is otherwise settled. I will not come for you, and I will do my part to assure that others involved in this mission keep their distance from you. I wish you luck."

"Why do you need to make such an assurance?" Gray asked.

His question found no answer but silence, and he accepted that he operated alone.

Peering through his night vision glasses, he turned his head toward the shoreline and confirmed his expectations. His fishing vessel, the one a premium payment had secured from a Chilean-descended islander sympathetic with Argentina's plight, awaited at anchor less than four miles away.

Though moonlight shaped the craft into a somber silhouette, a red navigation aid illuminated the shoal areas behind it, giving Gray a target for his swim.

He sealed the phone inside his watertight bag and carried his equipment below. The twisting passageways of the destroyer seemed surreal in their emptiness, and for a moment, he heard the ship's metal frame whisper accusations of betrayal.

Shaking his head clear of his conscience, he pushed a door open and stepped onto a weather deck. With his mask over his face, he bit down on his breather, testing it. Tasting metallic oxygen, he climbed down ladder rungs until he slipped into the water.

A flip toward his belly aimed him toward shore, and he kicked himself forward. Adrenaline compelled him until he became accustomed to the water and slowed himself to the pace he had practiced in a pool.

As he stopped to tread water and find his bearings, the *Dragon* seemed a football field away, and the red light beaconing him shoreward had receded below his short horizon. Keeping the destroyer in his hindquarters for reference, he ducked his head below the surface and swam.

His next check showed the destroyer slipping below his horizon, but he still held no visual on the navigation aid. He pushed himself straight down into the water and then kicked himself upward. With his added height above the water, he saw the red illumination he sought.

Before he dove again, traces of missile engines sliced the night sky, and the thunderclap of explosions echoed over the water. Trickles of plumes climbing from the ground signaled the weakening of the defenses.

Then an extended chain of thunderclaps rang atop the waves, telling Gray that the final air attack was taking place. He recognized the sounds as Argentine Skyhawks scattering bomblets across the runways at Mount Pleasant, denying their use by any British aircraft that might attempt to land and replenish the island's air defenses.

Adjusting his course toward the light, he ducked his head below the surface and swam. When he stopped again, his beacon appeared visible at first glance. Risking a moment of curiosity, he swung his body around to bid farewell to the *Dragon*.

As if spurred by his interest, the destroyer came to life. A single Astor missile, bathed in the light of its exhaust, cut a high arc into the night and then angled toward the horizon. The weapon escaped Gray's view and disappeared into silent oblivion.

The odd event told Gray several things. It told him that the assault was over, since the destroyer's defenses had been unleashed. It also told him that a British Typhoon fighter aircraft had survived the attack, chased the withdrawing Argentines to eek whatever revenge it could, and then risked a return home to avoid having to eject in the open ocean.

The attempt had exposed the supposed Typhoon to the reengaged *Dragon* and its lethal air defenses, which someone with technical training had reenergized. Since he had expected a first paratrooper wave void of technical people capable of turning the system on, he sensed his expendability and a commensurate betrayal.

This observation, combined with Renard's agreeable tone after receipt of a text message, redoubled his effort to escape. Death as a traitor awaited him ashore, and death as an expended resource awaited him on the *Dragon*. The survival instincts that had motivated him to secure a fishing boat as a backup escape route were proving true.

He kicked harder, straining his groin, legs, and lungs, stopping for brief course-correcting observations. Focused, he covered distance with motivation, reached the boat, and climbed in. The scuba tank became a lead brick on his back until he could drop it to the deck.

Balancing himself against a chair, he felt hot acid coursing through his rubbery legs. Hobbling, he climbed to the pilot house, and he fumbled through his watertight bag for an ignition key. The diesel engine started, and he energized the winch to hoist the boat's anchor.

Trusting that he could slip into the fishing areas unnoticed, he nudged the throttle. Beyond anything, he hoped for stealth, and he exercised patience slipping into the waters east of the Falkland's archipelago.

When the artificial lights of civilization became distant, he risked speed and rounded the southeastern tip of the island chain. As he later pointed his vessel west, he dared to assume he had escaped.

He expected the two-day journey to Punta Arenas, Chile, to prove taxing and dangerous with treacherous seas. But he believed in his maritime skills.

As the image of a stronger boy with wanton bloodlust tripping into his hidden defenses on an orphanage playground danced in his head, he wondered if his treason amounted to anything. Had he chosen the correct side? Could his choice have ripple effects to make a difference?

Such ponderings bounced in his head, finding no foothold for judgment. He decided instead to succumb to his instincts, drive the ship toward safety, and continue his life as a survivor.

CHAPTER 12

Olivia McDonald awoke to the sound of a chirping phone and a dry taste in her mouth. The empty bottle of Châteauneuf-de-Pape Grenache on her nightstand betrayed her tailspin toward lavish hedonism.

The lump under the covers beside her stirred, and she squeezed her eyes shut to recall the name of her boyfriend of the month. Her inner psychologist warned her to stop bedding men, but rationalizing voices silenced her conscience. Why stop when gorgeous men with Adonis bodies flocked to her for her beauty, power, and success?

She lifted her phone to her itching eyes and realized she had missed a call from Pierre Renard. Startled, she slid out from under the satin sheet and tiptoed into her apartment's kitchen.

Hours ago, Renard had called her to announce the attack on the Falklands. In her inebriated state, she had managed to liberate herself from her lover and send an urgent message, the majority of which she'd drafted ahead of time, up her chain of command.

The Frenchman's recent unanswered call perplexed her.

Guzzling Gatorade to recover from her hangover's dehydration, she ran down her mental checklist of possible items on Renard's mind. A chance to wrap a thin thanks around boasting of his successful campaign? A manipulative request for more weapons? Or possibly bad news she couldn't fathom?

To brace herself for any news, she sat on the edge of her living room couch. The voicemail from Renard revealed urgency in his tone and a request to call him back immediately.

She drew a deep breath and tapped his number. His voice carried anxiety.

"Thank God you called me back," he said.

She feigned levity.

"I'm sure you would keep calling if I didn't," she said. "I also wouldn't put it beyond you to send a ninja to my apartment to wake me up if I ignored you."

"Perhaps I would. Forgive me for forgoing pleasantries, but I must be curt."

"Sure."

"I suspect that I've made a grave error in judgment."

Renard never made errors in judgment–not since he picked the wrong side in a Sudanese civil war eighteen years ago and armed a massacre of innocents. His dossier and their relationship–she dared consider it a friendship–told a story approaching two decades of perfection in his selection of clients.

"What happened?" she asked.

"I fear that President Gomez has betrayed me."

"How?"

"Jake believes that one of Gomez's submarines launched a war shot torpedo at the *Ambush*."

A sickening feeling rose in her stomach, adding to her nausea. Her authorization to arm the Argentine air attack on the Falklands left her exposed, and her career would implode if Gomez turned the Falklands into an incendiary bomb.

"Are you sure?"

"I could use your help getting the recording of the encounter analyzed at an American acoustics lab," Renard said.

"I appreciate the free intelligence."

"It is part of our deal. But regardless of what your labs might find, we don't have time to await their analysis. We must assume that Gomez meant to destroy the *Ambush*. It's also unlikely coincidental that he's restricted my access to Argentine tactical information. Right after the paratrooper wave, he rescinded my access to his tactical net declaring that I no longer had a need to know. We now must assume that he's operating outside of my control."

He paused, as if encountering his forgotten human fallibility.

"I should have sensed this sooner," he said. "I suspect I was blinded by greed."

"More like ego."

"Insightful and direct. I've always admired that about you."

"I'm sorry. I know that criticism doesn't help."

"But it does. I need my full wits about me, no matter how painful my awakening. Damn my ego. I consider myself so crafty that I believed I could hunt down any prey as my client and have my way with them. Apparently, I need to rethink this."

"Nobody's perfect, Pierre."

She scrunched her face as the platitude escaped her lips.

"I appreciate you trying to console me. You're not very good at it, but I trust that your effort is sincere."

"Consoling people isn't my strong suit," she said. "Let's get back to Gomez."

"If he's willing to sink the *Ambush*, I can only speculate what else he's planning."

She recalled Renard's plan with the *Ambush*. The Taiwanese-designed limpets would nullify the submarine's stealth until its crew could pry them off, and that required either surfacing or getting help from a third party. With Argentina controlling the sky, the *Ambush* was alone and helpless.

"What would Gomez gain by sinking it?" she asked.

"Per my plans, nothing," Renard said.

"Let's talk it through. What agenda would sinking the *Ambush* support?"

"I've been so preoccupied with reacting to the attempt that I hadn't considered why he would order it. I just assumed he was being bullish and aggressive."

"Softening the Falkland air defenses and taking down a few fighter planes can be forgiven during a negotiation," she said. "His dossier supports him being aggressive but not stupid. If he went after the kill with the *Ambush*, he either assumed that his show of power would make the British cower in negotiations…"

"We agree that he's not that stupid. I've seen haughtiness and ego blind men to the obvious, but he sees the world clearly enough. The British are anything but cowards, and I'm sure he's well aware of it."

"Then he's not planning on a negotiation."

"Dear God," he said. "He's not. Damn it! I've been a fool!"

"What?"

"He's planning an invasion."

A spike of shame and fear impaled her as her career and life of wild success slipped away. She wished for Renard to say something to placate her, but the prolonged silence tormented her. Wanting to cry out, she choked back her suffering and squeaked out a shrill but coherent response.

"You have an idea to counter him, don't you? You always have an idea to clean up your messes."

"Correct."

"What do you need from me?" she asked.

"You will recruit his political adversary to our side."

"Ramirez? The Provisional President of the Senate?"

"Yes. Had I not meddled in Argentine affairs, I suspect that Senator Ramirez would win the next presidential election. If we are to contain this mess I've created, we now need Ramirez to step up."

"Step up and force an emergency vote of no confidence in Gomez?"

"Indeed, at least to secure his automatic rise to the national presidency by succession. But he must also take action outside any procedure of governance. He needs to move faster. Immediately. Troops mobilized tomorrow."

"Troops? A coup?"

"Just enough to convince the British that Argentina is undergoing civil unrest that will be solved in their favor without their involvement. They need to be convinced that Ramirez will take over the country and that he is the president they wish to deal with for an optimal outcome with the Falklands."

She mentally pitted Gomez versus Ramirez. The former had the brutishness to pound the Falkland Islands with an iron fist, damn the British retaliation. The latter, a younger career statesman, could set the country on a path to peace and economic recovery. But she didn't see him having the moxie to take the presidency by force.

"Gomez is creating enough rope to hang himself after he screws everything up," she said. "Ramirez could just wait until the next elections if he wants the presidency."

"We can't wait. Ground forces, especially their marines, are loyal to Ramirez, at least enough of its leadership to prevent an invasion force from storming the Falklands if he ordered it. We need him now."

"I understand that, Pierre, but what's his motivation? What does he get out of helping us?"

"A country with its military intact and the oil reserves around the Falklands. If he lets Gomez play this out, the British will spare no lives in quelling the invasion, and there will be no negotiating a transfer of oil reserves, including those they have yet to find."

"You think that's enough to motivate him?"

"Possibly. If he's shrewd enough. But he may need extra convincing."

"Like what?"

"You could also offer him price increases on imports from Argentina to America, at least for six months while his presidency stabilizes."

"You know I don't have that power."

"But one of your friends soon will."

Her thoughts turned to Gerald Rickets, her mentor, who had led the CIA and then served as the Secretary of Defense prior to seeking the nation's highest office. Originally wooed to the Republican ticket, Rickets had found a stronghold as a centrist Democrat.

Each thought of Rickets reminded her of pain and redemption. As amends for risking her life while breaking a sex slave ring and subjecting her to a rapist who gave her HIV, he had assured her choice assignments for her advancement. But guilt had limits.

"If you mean Gerry, he's busy running for president," she said. "And I'm running out of favors he owes me."

"If you have one favor remaining with him, I recommend that you exercise it now."

"Say that I do. There's no guarantee that Gerry wins the election."

"You and I share the good fortune of being respected by his opponent. I saved his friend's life, and we've both proved instrumental in keeping Jake alive for years. You can secure the promise from both sides."

Rickets' opponent, Admiral John Brody, had mentored Jake Slate as a submarine officer prior to his rise to Chief of Naval Operations. He now held the position as his party's frontrunner to face Rickets in the national election. In Olivia's reckoning, Brody owed both her and Renard a debt for preserving Jake's life in past conflicts, but she questioned Brody's perspective on the matter.

"You're asking a lot of me."

"You can be convincing."

"I'll give it a shot. This is no time for me to be timid."

"You can call them from the plane. You'll need to charter a flight immediately to Buenos Aires."

Despite her liver's efforts churning alcohol into acetate, she felt the room spinning.

"This is happening so fast."

"You must make haste. You must move immediately. There is no other way. I fear that the invasion force may leave at any hour."

"I'll check satellite reports for activity," she said. "But I had an alert set to warn me if anything abnormal happened on troop movement. So nothing yet."

"Why would Gomez wait?" Renard asked.

Suspecting that the military veteran president had a concrete reason, she pondered his apparent delay.

"Morale," she said.

"Morale?"

"Yeah. He doesn't want the foot soldiers to head toward the islands until they see the pilots return."

"Interesting," Renard said. "Go on."

"The last time their fathers' generation tried invading, they underestimated the British resolve and got beaten badly. Gomez doesn't want to just send them on his orders. He wants the pilots to return and share their spirit and confidence. He wants the foot soldiers buying beers for a bunch of swaggering, triumphant aviators and wishing they could taste their success."

"That's brilliant."

"Well, it's just a theory."

"No, it's not. I am sure that if you see where the Argentine air forces have landed, you'll see a massing of ground troops. It will not be a coincidence."

"I'll check."

"Regardless, you do need to hurry."

"I'll get moving."

"One more thing," Renard said. "You'll need to convince Ramirez that you are committed to assuring his support from both U.S. presidential candidates."

"Should I get signed notes from both of them?"

"That would be splendid, but don't see you achieving that. I had something more subtle in mind."

She feared the conversation's climax.

"Like what?" she asked.

"Do as you were trained. You are an analyst, you are a field officer, but first and foremost, you are a seductress. Use your wiles, woman, and save your career."

"You want me to jump on a CIA-chartered plane, fly to Buenos Aires, and then jump on a man until he agrees to overthrow his country by force?"

"I'd rather call it agreeing to save his country from disaster."

"You know what I mean."

"Indeed. And if any woman is capable of such a deed, it is you. He respects your intelligence and power."

"You're giving me too much credit."

"Don't be modest. Every world leader with an interest in the international intelligence community knows who you are."

"Even if that's true, then I'm just a paragraph and a headshot in a dossier for him."

"No. I imagine that he'd find a fair-skinned red-haired beauty such as yourself to be a cherished prize. The CIA trained you to be irresistible, and this is an ambitious man you will find easy to manipulate. You must and will place him into the mood to conquer."

"And you want me to get him revved up by letting him conquer me?"

"No, not letting him conquer you. Making him conquer you. Force the issue. Confuse him. Relax him. Enthrall him. Control him. It's a two-day trip to the islands for the invasion force. You've got tomorrow to outline a plan with him, charm him, and make him feel like a king before he must turn that force back."

"You expect him to roll off me in the middle of the night, pound his chest, and call a general or two before midnight?"

"I'm trying to respect your privacy by not picturing it in my mind, but yes. Isn't that how they taught you to manipulate men?"

She reflected on how easy it would be. She reflected on how it would salvage and re-launch the career she had lost at the beginning of the conversation. She reflected on how powerful she would feel, and how wanted she would feel by the handsome, successful man she knew Ramirez to be.

Before she could let morality or cowardliness turn her, she needed to set her adventure in motion. But first, she owed Renard a jab.

"Have you lost count, Pierre?"

"Of what?"

"Of how many times you've used sexy women as tools against men?"

"I've never kept count, but since you ask, I would guess that it's somewhere around. Well…"

"You've lost count."

"Touché."

"You knew I'd agree to this, didn't you?"

"After my miscue with Gomez, I'm unsure of anything. But I was optimistic, yes."

"Why?"

"Fear, desperation, ambition, challenge, and lust for both power and hedonistic pleasure. I think that covers all bases."

"Did you ever consider that he would do it if I just asked him nicely?"

"No I hadn't" Renard said.

"Well?"

"I imagine it's possible that he'd agree without seductive pressure, but why take the chance?"

"Damn you for being so manipulative," she said. "But I must admit that it's okay for a girl to mix business and pleasure."

CHAPTER 13

Commander Gutierrez pounded his fist on the console. "Damn!"

"You knew this was a desperation shot, sir," Fernandez said. "Long range against a target that was already evading at flank speed. You couldn't have expected a hit."

Gutierrez agreed with his executive officer, but he had allowed himself to hope.

A week and a half earlier, President Gomez had been clear with him and Commander Martinez during a private conversation in his wardroom. Although the Frenchman had professed a surgical campaign of restraint designed to engender a favorable negotiation with the British, the Argentine military leaders were to deviate from this path.

From the moment the *Specter* deloused the *Santa Cruz*, the Frenchman, his plans, and his agents were expendable. From that moment, every British vessel became a target of opportunity, including the *Ambush* and including every warship that the Royal Navy would send toward the Malvinas.

Gutierrez appreciated his president's style. Warriors set history's course by winning campaigns in battle–not politicians by yammering at bargaining tables. Sinking the *Ambush* would take his nation one step closer to military success, and it would assure his status as a hero.

Fernandez appeared unwilling to support that agenda, his coy smile revealing his complacent approval of the *San Juan's* torpedo attack against the *Ambush*, despite its failure. Bothered by his executive officer's lack of bloodlust and ambition, Gutierrez responded with a grunt.

"It was a well-placed shot, sir," Fernandez said. "If not for their speed, it would have hit."

"That means nothing," Gutierrez said. "Any British submarine we face will have the speed and endurance of a nuclear power plant."

"We've at least shown that we can track an underwater target and launch a credible shot at one. That's a strong signal to the British that we're prepared to fight for our territorial rights. We've created a deterrent."

"Really? We needed the aid of limpets placed by a mercenary. Were we able to hear anything else from the *Ambush*?"

"High-speed coolant pumps, blade rate, cavitation, and broadband flow noise."

"No, you imbecile. I mean before it accelerated to evade torpedoes. Were our systems and our sonar operators capable of hearing anything from that ship before it started sprinting for its life?"

"No, sir."

"Then my only chance against the *Ambush* is to sink it while it's hindered by limpets."

"The latest message traffic says there are two Orion anti-submarine aircraft en route to sink the *Ambush*. With the British air defenses on the island nullified, our aircraft will have free reign. With our latest targeting data and the sounds of the limpets to guide them, they will have no trouble finding the *Ambush* and sinking it."

"They won't find it if I destroy it before they get there. They are still an hour away. I need to get closer and attack again, before the *Ambush* can find a way to rid itself of those limpets."

"That's impossible, sir. They must be at least thirty nautical miles away by now. And we're working against a grave speed disadvantage. They can sustain twice our speed."

Gutierrez looked to his aging monitor. Lines of monochrome sound thinned as the *Ambush* carried its wailing chorus of limpets to the edge of the detection range of the *San Juan's* hydrophones.

"If the captain of the *Ambush* has true courage," he said, "he will stop running."

"Do you really expect him to turn and fight? The limpets place him at an acoustic disadvantage, even against a ship as old our as ours. I would consider that suicide."

"Well, then. Let's have a test. What would you do in his place? What should he do?"

"He should sprint to the nearest friendly port. He's eleven hundred nautical miles from the South Sandwich Islands. That's less than two days for a ship as fast as the *Ambush*."

"Why?"

Fernandez showed a spark of intelligence that Gutierrez expected. He knew his executive officer to be thoughtful, though lacking aggressiveness.

"By continuing to sprint, he'll evade all our naval vessels, including us. If he can reach port, he'll have shore-based air protection, even if they're just shoulder-mounted point defenses. Plus, the geography of hills and an enclosed harbor would add additional protection against attacks by Orions."

"The Orions will reach him before he can reach the South Sandwich Islands."

"True, sir, but the aircraft still face the burden of deploying sonobuoy fields and resolving the *Ambush's* location accurately enough to drop a torpedo."

"They have enough time to do so."

"The British may have scrambled fighter aircraft from Ascension Island."

Gutierrez tapped buttons on his monitor to call up global distances. The Ascension Islands that had helped the British in the campaign thirty-five years earlier lay thirty-four hundred nautical miles to the north, midway between the land masses of South America and Africa.

"I grant you that the British may be capable of mounting such a protection mission, but at top speed, their jet fighters could cover the distance in roughly six hours. They would need refueling support, which isn't stationed yet. So that's at least eight hours from being able to protect the *Ambush* from our Orions."

"You asked me what I would do, sir. You didn't ask me about the odds of success."

"If the captain of the *Ambush* is a true warrior, he will discount his acoustic disadvantage against us. He can still hear us, and he still has a speed advantage. If I were him, I would turn and fight my way back to Port Stanley."

"Even with the *Dragon* working against him?"

"I would rather go down fighting us, the *Specter*, the *Santa Cruz*, and the *Dragon* than wait for aircraft to sink me."

"I see, sir."

"But first, I would attempt to remove the limpets."

"And that's where you plan to attack, sir?"

"Yes. Set a course to chase down the *Ambush*."

"The course is already set, sir," Fernandez said. "But we have five minutes left on our battery before we risk inverting cells."

Gutierrez had let his fierceness for the *Ambush* blind him to his battery status.

"Damn! Prepare to surface the ship. We will pursue on the surface while snorkeling."

"That will limit our speed to thirteen knots."

"I know that, you halfwit. Make it happen."

Ten minutes later, the deck rolled below Gutierrez's feet, and he steadied himself against the periscope. The *San Juan* bobbed on the surface and charged its diesel engines while pushing its way through swells toward the *Ambush*.

A radio message informed him that the P-3 Orion aircraft that had taken off from Argentina's coast would reach the estimated position of the *Ambush* in less than an hour. Since the wailing of the limpets had faded from his sensors, he could only speculate about the British submarine's location and behavior.

Turn and face me, he thought.

Gutierrez grew frustrated as time's lethargic dripping brought the Orion aircraft closer to the *Ambush* but moved the target farther from him. Absent acoustic data of the British submarine's whereabouts, he assumed it opened distance from him at a flank-speed sprint.

As he entertained thoughts of conceding the British submarine to his nation's aviators, an alarm startled him.

"Torpedo seeker!" Fernandez said.

Scenarios about the source and intended target of the torpedo vied for plausibility in Gutierrez's mind. The idea that took root angered him.

Someone–a naval vessel, a satellite, any sensor–had fed the location of his surfaced *San Juan* to the *Ambush*. That meant that the *Ambush* had slowed and come shallow, possibly surfaced, allowing it to download radio traffic.

"Secure snorkeling! Submerge the ship! Take us to forty meters!"

As the deck angled downward, he lowered the periscope and silenced the torpedo seeker alarm. A monochrome display showed the weapon's active search frequency and confirmed his belief that the torpedo was British.

"Left ten-degrees rudder, steady course zero five zero."

The San *Juan* rolled and dived into the turn.

"All ahead flank!"

He watched Fernandez labor against the ship's incline to reach him. His executive officer's eyes were open wide.

"How is this possible, sir?"

"I'll explain when there's time," Gutierrez said. "How much battery is left?"

"Minimal at flank speed, sir. We had barely reached one-tenth of a charge before submerging. Five minutes. Perhaps six."

"That's enough," Gutierrez said.

"For what?"

"To get out of the accursed thing's way."

Over the next five minutes, the lines of bearing to the incoming weapon veered to the right.

"It's close," Gutierrez said. "But it's passing safely behind us. Slow to ahead one-third."

"New battery life calculation, sir. Six minutes left at this speed, sir," Fernandez said.

"Very well," Gutierrez said. "Make your depth fifteen meters. Line up to snorkel."

A monochrome monitor showed the torpedo drifting through the *San Juan's* baffles and emerging on its port side. Then the lines disappeared.

"The incoming weapon has ceased transmitting," Fernandez said. "Sonar was able to hear its high-speed screws after we slowed, but the screws have stopped. The weapon has shut down."

Gutierrez stepped to the periscope, rotated its hydraulic ring, and watched it slither upward.

"Make your depth thirteen meters," he said.

When the optics broached the surface, stars dotted the horizon.

"Raise the radio mast," he said. "Send a message stating that we just evaded a hostile torpedo launched by the *Ambush*. Then get a download."

As he awaited radio traffic, he had the snorkel mast raised, and the quad diesel engines groaned to life.

He heard Fernandez move beside him.

"Why don't we fire back, sir?"

"It's an impossible shot," Gutierrez said. "The *Ambush* is too far away. The *Ambush* was only able to shoot at us because we were moving toward it at thirteen knots. But with it moving away from us at thirty knots, it would be a futile tail chase, especially since our weapons have less range than theirs."

"I see, sir. It would be a waste of a torpedo better used on the British task force."

"You are mastering the obvious. Give me news. What is the update on the search for the *Ambush*?"

Keeping his eye to the lens, he heard Fernandez flip papers on a clipboard.

"The first Orion has arrived on station and has started dropping sonobuoys. No contact yet."

"It's only a matter of time. This battle belongs to our aircraft now. I will no longer waste my time considering it. What other news?"

Fernandez flipped paper.

"Interesting note here, sir. The British prime minister has already denounced our attack and has asked the admiralty to establish a task force to retake the islands."

"History repeated," Gutierrez said. "This new task force exists only in words now, but it will be reality soon, and I expect every vessel in their fleet will rally toward the Malvinas. The one that interests me is the greatest prize–the *Queen Elizabeth*. Is there any mention of it?"

"The carrier, sir? It's hardly seaworthy."

"But seaworthy it is. There will be a debate within the British admiralty about pressing it into service early, but I expect their need for air power will force the issue."

Fernandez rustled papers.

"Here, sir, at the end of the broadcast. It's not news but an intelligence assessment forecasting that one squadron of British Lightning jet fighters has progressed enough in its training to be useful for carrier-based flight operations. The carrier doesn't have its full weapon systems readied, but it's expected to be the center of the task force to take back the Malvinas."

"That gives me a prime target," Gutierrez said.

"There will be plenty of them, if the British actually form this task force and approach the Malvinas."

"Do we have a rallying point for us and the *Santa Cruz* yet?"

"Yes, sir. Two hundred nautical miles north of the Malvinas. The *Santa Cruz* will be twenty miles to the west of us."

"The British will send submarines ahead of the bulk of the task force. There may already be another submarine in the area."

"Our intelligence says otherwise."

"Our intelligence on submarines is always suspect. We must move carefully–slowly, silently, and with diligent ears on our sonar systems. Review the search plan with the sonar team for *Astute* class submarines and update it with the noises we heard from the *Ambush*."

"I will see it done, sir. But what of the *Specter*? Should we also be listening for its discrete frequencies?"

"That's a waste of effort that should be focused on British submarines. I don't see any reason that the *Specter* would stay in the area. It served its purpose, and its team has been paid. They are mercenaries and have no interest in staying."

"I'm just thinking of contingencies, sir."

"If the Frenchman wakes up tomorrow and has any delusions that President Gomez still needs his services, I trust our president to deal with it. I'm sure he knows how to threaten lives, families, or whatever it is that politicians do to get their way when talks fail."

"And if that fails, sir? If the *Specter* remains?"

Gutierrez waved his hand.

"I don't care how advanced the *Specter* is. Its crew is a mix of mercenaries from countries that don't give a damn about the outcome of this campaign. These are my home waters, Fernandez, and I assure you, I give a damn about winning. If their American commanding officer is foolish enough to stay, I will make him soon wish that he did not."

CHAPTER 14

Seeking the nearest exit, Pierre Renard marched through the lobby of the Four Seasons resort. He was indulging his flight instincts, scheming while moving, planning where to run. But his focus failed, and his mind's eye saw smoke rising from the twisted metal of bombarded Rapier anti-air batteries, aircraft erupting into flames, and submarines sprinting for torpedoes in directions unknown.

Unsure if he needed to flee, and uncertain if running would garner unwanted attention, he slowed and slipped into the evening. He followed a gaggle of young ladies he tagged as daughters of rich Americans into the bar, and rapid service produced a tumbler of Courvoisier's finest imperial cognac.

The upscale leisure wear of patrons and their alcohol-fueled joviality caught his attention and shifted his awareness to the living city's late evening. He let himself watch people to anchor himself in place and time. As festive conversations danced in his ears and smiles abounded around him, he discerned no evidence of the Falkland Island attack's imprint on humanity's rhythm.

He sniffed and sipped, and heat billowed in his mouth. The fluid warmed him but left him edgy. Failing to relax, he reached for his phone and called Olivia McDonald.

She would ground him, he hoped. But when she answered, she sounded hurried.

"Yeah, Pierre?"

"Are you airborne yet?" he asked.

"I'm getting a ride to the airfield. What's on your mind?"

He needed to ask countless questions, but he feared looking weak.

"I... I'm not sure."

"You're on an encrypted line. Say whatever's on your mind."

"You go first. I'm less in the mood the talk than to listen."

"Who are you, and what did you do with Pierre Renard?"

"Cute. Humor me."

"Sure. Gerry Rickets got me in with Senator Ramirez," she said. "I'm meeting him for lunch, and he's clearing most of his day for me after that. I didn't even have to bother Admiral Brody. Rickets took care of it. Apparently, Ramirez thinks Rickets is going to become the next American president."

"I knew you'd find a way."

He slid his glass on the counter and fumbled in his blazer for his cigarettes.

"Pierre?"

"Yes. Yes, I'm still here."

"I can tell when somebody needs to talk. Keep talking."

"Will you be sending me a bill for this therapy session?"

"Probably not. But I never thought I'd have to be your conversational crutch. You're taking this rejection by Gomez hard."

He changed his mind on the cigarette and lifted his fingers from the crinkling pack.

"I'm not sure I can yet qualify it as a rejection," he said. "I rendered him services, he accomplished his mission, and he paid me my standard fee. I should be celebrating a successful client engagement. Why do I feel so damned violated?"

"Because you've become used to people keeping you on as their advisor until you're done advising them. This time, Gomez kept you on until he was done being advised."

"I see," he said. "I've been a fool to think he would let me serve as his negotiator at the bargaining table. He used me instead to ignite a war. My God, what have I done?"

"You did the right thing, Pierre. I wouldn't have helped you if I thought otherwise. The Falklands issue has been a volcano for years, and it had to erupt some time. Now's as good a time as any while we can tie it to a hothead president."

He reached for his cigarettes again but willed his hand back into his lap.

"Perhaps. But what do we do now that I've opened Pandora's Box."

"We stop Gomez. Is he expecting you to contact him again?"

"He said he'd summon me tomorrow morning to debrief me, but I believe that was lie. I don't expect to hear from him again. But I will have to attempt to contact him and go through the motions since he doesn't know that I know of his attempt to sink the *Ambush*."

Her tone turned somber.

"I have bad news. Anti-submarine aircraft are going to get to the *Ambush*."

"Dear God. Can anyone stop it?"

"I'm afraid not, Pierre."

"I did this," Renard said. "I doomed innocent men on a submarine to a ghastly fate."

"You've done it before. You'll recover from it."

Although meant to soothe, her words stung. The count of faceless corpses weighing on his conscience approached one thousand, but each prior episode of devastation had served a greater good. The *Ambush* would be the first vessel sacrificed to his failing. His breathing became rapid and labored.

"How long do they have?" he asked.

"The first Orion is already dropping sonobuoys," she said. "I've asked Ramirez to stop them, but he's not sure what he can do."

"Has he called for an emergency election for a vote of no confidence in Gomez?"

"He's gathering commitment for the vote and expects to have enough support to call for it in the morning."

"Then he must behave as if he already is the president. He must reach out to his loyal military followers and call off the attack on the *Ambush*."

"He's doing what he can."

"He must do better!"

"Hold on," she said. "Let me hang up and make a call to get an update. I need to get on the plane now anyway."

He lowered the phone into his pocket and sipped cognac. Forgetting himself and yielding to nervous compulsion, he then tipped the glass back and swallowed the stinging heat.

When Olivia called, he lifted the phone to his cheek and heard turbojet engines whining in the background.

"Yes?" he asked. "What news?"

"An admiral loyal to Ramirez was able to pull back one of the Orions. Apparently, the admiral knows the pilot and was able to get his attention. But the second Orion is ignoring hails outside of the chain of command."

"Misapplied military discipline," Renard said.

"At least that's only half the danger, right?"

"That's like saying one dagger in the heart is less fatal than two," he said. "It only means that the single Orion may need more time to find its target."

"I'm sorry, Pierre."

"Would the Argentines send one of their own aircraft to counter the Orion? Are there any pilots loyal to Ramirez?"

"No," she said. "Ramirez can influence ground troops and small portions of the maritime forces, but Gomez owns the air. We're lucky he got one of the Orions to turn back."

"Are there other Orions coming?"

"No, that's it," she said. "They scavenged parts from their remaining aircraft to get the first two airborne. If that last remaining Orion is turned back, the *Ambush* will escape."

The bartender approached Renard, who gestured for a refill.

"Is there nothing the British can do?" he asked. "Are there any combat aircraft in the area? Patrol craft from Ascension Island that could engage?"

"There's nothing close enough from Ascension. Technically, there's a Typhoon remaining from Mount Pleasant, but it's helpless. It's completely out of missiles and almost out of bullets."

"There's a British Typhoon remaining in theater? You jest."

"No. I'm not kidding. One survived. The pilot is credited with shooting down five Argentine Skyhawks and may get credit for more by the time they sort it out. But he can't do anything without weapons."

A low flame rose within Renard's pit of despair.

"The Orion hunting the *Ambush* is carrying a standard anti-submarine load out, is it not?"

"I can't vouch for the load out."

"Let's assume that it is. That means minimal to zero air defense. That could work to our favor. What's that Typhoon doing, specifically?"

"He's at low altitude to hide from the *Dragon's* radar and waiting for his fuel to run out before he ejects. They've sent ships to pull him from the water after he jumps."

Renard's mind jumped into hyper-drive and raced toward a perceived opportunity.

"Can I speak with him?" he asked.

"Who? The pilot?"

"Yes, I have an idea."

"What sort of idea? I can't just patch you into the British communications channel and let you chat with him."

"Of course you can," he said. "What you mean is that you won't because of my role in these hostilities."

"How would I introduce you?"

"As your naval combat advisor."

"But you're not."

"I will be, once you agree to it."

"Say I agree to it," she said. "What's your approach?"

"You and I need to understand the minimal amount of damage that an Orion aircraft can withstand before it becomes uncontrollable."

"The British have already assessed this. They have experts, and they know that the Typhoon's remaining bullets are useless against it."

"Perhaps, but if you compound the bullets with the fuselage of a Typhoon aircraft moving at several hundred knots, then I'm sure you can bring down an Orion."

"You want me to patch you into a secure Royal Air Force military channel to talk a British pilot into a kamikaze mission?"

"Not quite," he said. "But almost. And maybe. I'll need an Orion expert engaged in the conversation as well to help assess the approach."

"You're asking a lot."

"We don't have time. Will you patch me through? Will you trust me, Olivia?"

In the silence, he thought he heard her heart beating.

"I'll set it up," she said. "When I call you back, don't use your name or any of your aliases. In fact, use the code name Angel."

"Angel?"

"Because you're playing God, and if you're going to talk a man into killing himself, it would be useful to hint at a happy afterlife."

"Very well."

"And look for documents from me, too. I'll get you specifications on the Orion aircraft. When I call you back, be ready."

The second cognac arrived, and he savored its biting aroma as it wafted over his tongue. A text message arrived showing images of the P-3 Orion aircraft and its vulnerabilities.

Short of chopping it in half, disabling multiple engines, or breaking off a formidable amount of a wing, the aircraft had one weakness. The Typhoon pilot would have to attack its rudder.

When Olivia called him back, he drew in a breath and prepared to deliver a sermon.

"This is Officer McDonald online with Major Thomas Greene, the commanding officer of Mount Pleasant's Royal Air Force Base and Doctor Julius Taylor of Lockheed's Advanced Engineering department. Can you hear us Angel?"

"Indeed I can. Greetings all."

"This is Major Greene," Greene said. "Officer McDonald tells me that you plan to talk one of my pilots into a Kamikaze mission against a P-3 Orion? Is this true?"

"I don't mean to condemn the man," Renard said. "But I if I can convince him that his life is worth stopping that Orion, then I believe we can create an attack that will at least persuade the Orion to disengage."

"I understand that the *Ambush* is compromised," Greene said. "I can do the math, and I understand that one pilot is worth a hundred men's lives. But I would never give the order for him to sacrifice himself."

"Would you sacrifice yourself, major, if it were you in his place?"

The silence told Renard that he had struck a chord.

"No man knows how he'll face his mortality until the very moment," Greene said. "But I would like to think that I would."

"Then let me give your pilot a chance to do the right thing. If he doesn't try something and learns that he might have saved a submarine, the guilt may haunt him forever."

"I understand," Greene said. "But before I do, you must convince me that he can succeed. I believe that's why you have Doctor Taylor on the line."

"Doctor Taylor has advised the CIA in the past," Olivia said. "He assisted in the reconstruction of the Hainan Island Incident when an American Orion was brought down by a collision with a Chinese fighter jet in two thousand and one. He's our expert and understands the vulnerabilities of the aircraft. Doctor Taylor?"

Taylor's voice was soft and thoughtful.

"Although a jet fighter's mass is much less than that of a P-3 Orion, the Hainan Island Incident proved that a jet fighter can bring down an Orion by impact alone."

"I already assumed that a kamikaze attack would work," Greene said. "What I want is to give my pilot a chance to do this without suicide."

"If he could disable two engines on the same wing and damage the rudder, the aircraft would become unstable," Taylor said. "If he leaves a working engine on either side, the pilot may be able to compensate for a failed rudder by steering the craft by varying thrust to either wing. But with a damaged rudder and the inability to apply thrust to one of the wings, the craft will become unstable."

"He has only forty rounds remaining in his cannon," Greene said. "Is that enough to take out two engines?"

"I don't know," Taylor said. "It would depend on how well placed the shots are. One bullet is enough to take down an engine if it severs the fuel line. In aerial combat, I can only imagine this will require a lot of skill and a lot of luck. But this is way aircraft used to shoot each other down for decades. So it's certainly possible."

"And then the rudder?" Greene asked.

As the conversation paused, Renard grasped his opportunity.

"This is where we'll need to call upon your pilot's courage and skill. I know your pilot is an ace, major, because he just overcame at least five adversaries in combat. He should be capable of disabling the Orion's rudder with his fuselage. I know that a Typhoon can handle that impact, at least enough."

"Enough for what?" Greene asked.

"Enough for him to bail out if he hits a flat spin after impact."

"What if he doesn't hit a flat spin, Mister Angel?" Greene asked. "What if he instead rolls or tumbles? That Orion is at low altitude, and my pilot would not have time to recover."

"Then let me convince your man that if he must die that he would be doing so for a noble purpose. I hate to insist, major, but time is short."

"Hold on, Mister Angel," Greene said. "Doctor Taylor, remind me of the fate of the Chinese pilot that collided with the P-3 Orion in the Hainan Island Incident."

"He lost control of his aircraft and died," Taylor said.

"This will be a high-risk endeavor," Renard said. "But it must be done. Will you let me speak to your pilot?"

An eternity seemed to pass as Renard awaited his opportunity.

"His name is Lieutenant Anderson," Greene said. "Lieutenant Ian Anderson. I authorize you to advise him to bring down the P-3 Orion that is hunting the HMS *Ambush*, by any means necessary and at his disposal, including sacrificing himself if necessary."

CHAPTER 15

Renard lifted his refilled glass of cognac to his lips and stopped. Reconsidering his need for clarity, he returned the drink to the counter as his phone's speaker shot forth its distorted rendition of whining jet engines.

"Lieutenant Anderson," Greene said. "Report your status."

Renard noted adrenaline in the young man's shrill voice.

"Altitude, one thousand feet," Anderson said. "Air speed, two hundred and fifty knots. Seven percent fuel remaining."

"How are you holding up, lieutenant?"

"I want a full fuel tank and weapons load out so I can go after the bastards that did this."

"You've already downed five of them. You've done your duty today. You've fought with honor and valor."

"That doesn't make up for the friends I lost."

"What would you say if I told you I have more victims for you?"

"I'd say you want me to engage those P-3 Orions. I'm willing to do what it takes to save our submarine, but I don't see how I can take down two of them."

"One of the Orions turned back already. You now only have to deal with one of them. You can save the *Ambush*."

"Bloody hell, sir. I'm sure I could do it with a kamikaze strike, but I'd much prefer an alternative solution if possible."

"There's a man on the line, code named Angel, who will explain the attack. I will interject if I disagree with anything he says, but he is working with a Doctor Taylor of Lockheed who understands the Orion's vulnerabilities completely."

"Good evening, Lieutenant Anderson," Renard said. "I am Angel. Time is of the essence. Major Greene has calculated a flight plan to vector you toward the Argentine Orion without exposing yourself to the *Dragon*. Have you received this flight information?"

"Yes, sir. I've got it."

"Then head after your target."

"Roger, sir. I'm turning toward heading zero-seven-eight, altitude five hundred feet, air speed six hundred knots."

Renard heard the Typhoon's engines howl.

"Nobody is asking you to sacrifice yourself, Lieutenant Anderson," Renard said. "I believe you can do this and live. But this is dangerous work, and if you wish to save a hundred of your countrymen, you must be willing to risk your life."

"Royal Air Force pilots have been doing it since before I was born, sir. Risking my life is what I do."

"Excellent. You're coming in below the Orion, and your first point of attack will be engines on the same wing."

"Does it matter which wing, sir?"

"No," Renard said. "You choose. The intent is to disable each engine on the same wing. You'll have to aim your cannon at the turboprop engines."

"I will do that, sir," Anderson said. "But I suspect that an Orion can still fly with its two other engines."

"Indeed it can," Renard said. "But not so if its rudder is damaged beyond use."

Renard let the pilot digest the meaning.

"I see, sir. I assume that's where you expect me to run out of bullets?"

"Let me invite the input of Doctor Taylor from Lockheed," Renard said. "Doctor?"

"Yes, lieutenant," Taylor said. "Your twenty-seven-millimeter rounds should be capable of disabling the rudder, if you have any rounds remaining from attacking the engines. However, if you need to use the fuselage of your aircraft as a weapon, it's better for you to use it against the rudder than the engines."

"I understand, sir."

"If you're using bullets, your optimum angle of attack against the rudder is from the Orion's beam at equal altitude to the Orion," Taylor said. "If you must use your fuselage, you're best to approach from above and from the Orion's forward quarter. A glancing impact should be sufficient, if you can maneuver your aircraft with such accuracy."

"I can maneuver as well as any pilot, sir!"

"Excellent," Renard said. "Also remember that attacking a submarine requires complex and precise flight patterns by an Orion. Any damage you inflict might be enough to at least buy the *Ambush* enough time to escape."

"I see it!" Anderson said.

"The Orion?" Renard asked.

"Yes, sir. And it's only using three engines."

"Which one is off?" Renard asked.

"Number three," Anderson said. "The outboard starboard engine."

"Could this be some sort of fuel conservation effort, Doctor Taylor?" Renard asked.

"I don't believe so," Taylor said. "They'd want to use all engines for optimum control during anti-submarine operations. That engine must be inoperable or risky to operate."

"This may be our lucky break," Renard said. "This may be an artifact of the squadron's limited access to spare parts and funding."

"I hope so, sir," Anderson said.

"Lieutenant Anderson," Renard said. "On your first pass, concentrate fire on the engine beside the one that's not running. Don't expend all your rounds. See if you can disable the other engine on the same wing. Engine number one, starboard inboard."

"I'll put fifteen rounds into it and see what happens."

Background noises seemed subdued versus Renard's expectations. He had expected more fury from the climbing Typhoon, but its powered and accelerated ascent sounded graceful through his phone.

"Engaging with cannon," Anderson said.

Renard heard the chirping staccato of bullets followed by Anderson's voice, which was strained as he withstood the acceleration of a tight turn.

"I hit the target and overflew the Orion. Coming back around for another pass."

"Any damage?" Renard asked.

"I see smoke from number one engine!" he said. "But it's still running. Number three engine is still idle."

"Let's see how long engine number one holds on with extra strain," Renard said. "Put ten rounds into its rudder."

"Hold on, Mister Angel," Greene said. "Those bullets are best used making sure the engine dies."

"I agree," Taylor said.

"Gentlemen, I know what logic would dictate, but I feel it. This Orion isn't going to remain in the air much longer. Do you not agree Lieutenant Anderson?"

"Yes, sir. I've got a feeling about it too. Plus, I'm in position now to hit the rudder. I'll save fifteen rounds for engine number one if I need to make another pass at it."

"Excellent man! Do it!" Renard said.

"I concur," Greene said. "You're trained to make these judgments based upon what you see. Shoot straight."

As Renard heard staccato chirps in his phone, he realized he had tucked himself into a corner at the edge of the bar's counter to avoid being overheard.

"Damn!" Anderson said. "Half my rounds missed. The rudder is still intact."

"But you put holes in it, did you not?" Renard asked.

"About five."

"That will lessen its effectiveness and strain its structural mounting," Renard said. "Now another pass on engine number one."

"It dropped something into the water with a parachute."

"That could very well just be another sonobuoy," Renard said. "Even if it's a torpedo, we'll trust that the *Ambush* can evade."

"I'm coming from below again, making a pass at engine number one. Engaging with cannon!"

When he heard the last bullet fire, Renard realized that the Typhoon had become unarmed.

"Heavy smoke from number one engine!" Anderson said. "The propeller is still turning, though."

"Damn!" Renard said. "Come back and give their rudder a beating with your jet wash!"

"No, sir," Anderson said. "I can't do that."

"I don't understand," Renard said.

"I'm almost out of fuel. I have enough for one more pass. I'm not going to leave this to chance."

Renard knew that everyone wanted to wish the young man well, but nobody could find appropriate words. The whine of engines vanished, indicating that Anderson decided to protect everyone's ears from the sound of the impact.

"Are you there, Lieutenant Anderson?" Greene asked.

"I fear we've lost him," Renard said.

"Lieutenant Anderson?" Greene asked.

Renard braced himself for Greene to reprimand him for sacrificing his pilot to a failed mission, but he instead heard the major take on an inquisitive tone.

"Hold on," Greene said. "We're receiving a distress signal here. I need to deal with it. I'll call you back if I need you, Officer McDonald."

"What could that be about?" Taylor asked.

"Evidently not our concern, doctor," Renard said. "I thank you for your support. I'm sure Officer McDonald will share with you whatever she can about the outcome once it's known."

"Of course, I will, Doctor Taylor," Olivia said. "I thank you as well. I'm going to secure this line. Angel, I'll contact you when I learn something."

The line went dead, and Renard walked back to his chair. He lowered his phone to the counter and, against his upbringing, he gulped his second drink of the night.

After decades of shaping national boundaries, he had forgotten the feeling of helplessness. He struggled to recognize it, but when he did, its presence bothered him. Thoughts of calling his wife for support rose and died as he remembered their agreement to protect her from all awareness of his work.

When the bartender approached, Renard dropped a bill on the counter that far outweighed his tab. He turned and fled for the street where he sought a concierge's aid in hailing a taxi.

Ducking into the vehicle's back seat, he realized that he lacked a destination. When the driver queried him, he responded in passable Spanish that he sought any hotel of his choosing across town that cost a fraction the rate of the Four Seasons.

As the driver nodded and motored him into the busy street, the Frenchman leaned his head against the rear window. Beautiful people filled the sidewalks, flowing with the city's natural beat between dance clubs, bars, and restaurants. With his adrenaline level subsiding, he allowed himself to envision a life of leisure, strolling the world's finest cities and enjoying his fortune with his family.

During that moment of desire, he fell asleep.

Renard dreamt.

He appeared in his favorite childhood place atop Mont Sainte Victoire in France's southern Provence region. The summit made famous by Paul Cezanne's impressionist renderings had gained an observatory and living post since Renard's childhood climbs, but his dream respected his early memories by showing him a peak void of all clutter save his favorite statuesque symbol, the Cross of Provence.

The shining summer sun yielded to storm clouds, and Renard tumbled through space and time until solid steel confines held him in stasis. His subconscious mind told him that the American Trident missile submarine USS *Colorado* served as his dungeon.

The walls closed in, and fire engulfed the compartment. Gasping for air, he felt his life ending until a door materialized and brought hope. But when the door opened, Jake Slate walked through it with a dagger sticking from the shirt of his naval uniform. The smoke had cleared, but Jake, his eyes wide with pain and anger, instilled terror in him.

"You got me into this!" Jake said.

"I have only tried to help you," Renard said.

"You exploit people!"

"I help those who need and deserve it."

Wincing as both his hands grasped the dagger, Jake withdrew the bloodied weapon from his belly and lifted it over his head.

"Who made you God?" he asked.

Renard raised his palms to protect himself from the downward stab, but he knew his arms would give under the former naval officer's strength.

Remaining captive to his dream, the Frenchman appeared in the passenger seat of a car made unidentifiable by the black smoke rising from its engine compartment. Beside him, Jake somehow drove the vehicle with his hands clasped on the hilt of the dagger that had rematerialized in his gut.

The Frenchman felt the car achieve impossible speed.

"Where are we going, Jake?"

A sly expression supplanted Jake's visage of pain and fear.

"I've told you before in countless dreams."

"I don't understand."

"We're going to die."

The vehicle disappeared, and Renard felt himself falling beside a canyon wall. As the desolate ground rose to impact him, he found himself inside the control room of a warship that resembled a blended memory of several classes of submarines. Old friends he had recruited from the French Navy, Antoine Remy, Henri Lanier, and Claude LaFontaine, knelt, their arms bound behind them.

"What's going on?" Renard asked.

In silence, his colleagues bowed their heads.

Jake appeared behind them, wearing khaki pants and a white dress shirt instead of his naval officer's uniform. He pointed a pistol at Remy's head.

"Let's do this," Jake said.

Crimson splatter exploded from Remy's forehead. Jake then disappeared and reappeared behind the other two kneeling Frenchmen, putting rounds through their heads before Remy's corpse hit the deck.

"Why, Jake?"

"It's better than the fate you've sentenced them to."

"We've together survived the Chinese, a rogue Pakistani submarine, and a hijacked Israeli submarine," Renard said. "Why do you accuse me of sentencing them to horrors?"

"Because you're playing God again," Jake said. "And this time you screwed it up."

Renard awoke to the sound of his phone ringing. As he placed it to his ear, he scanned the streets and saw empty sidewalks. Ahead, he saw midgrade hotels and realized that he would spend the night in a safe and quiet part of the city beyond the reach of President Gomez.

"Hello," he said.

"I've got a status from the Falklands," Olivia said.

"Yes. I'm all ears."

"Lieutenant Anderson damaged the Orion enough to stop it. The *Ambush* is safe."

"This is excellent news."

"In fact, the Orion requested an emergency landing at Mount Pleasant. Apparently, the Argentine crew trusts the British enough to treat them humanely."

"And why wouldn't they?" Renard asked. "Both sides shared medical assistance in the prior conflict. They are not bitter enemies but people caught on opposite sides of an argument."

"This could erupt, or this can end peacefully, depending what I can get Ramirez to do."

Something burned in the pit of Renard's stomach that felt like unfinished business.

"What of Lieutenant Anderson?" he asked. "Do you know if he survived? I'm not sure how I would react if I talked him to his death."

"Good news, Pierre. The Argentine Orion crew confirmed the parachute. There's a good chance you'll be able to sleep tonight."

CHAPTER 16

Jake lowered a cup of coffee to the table and surveyed the *Specter's* wardroom. As a formality, he had invited the senior Taiwanese member, a short and plain-looking engineering chief petty officer, to join his group of French colleagues. But the charismatic Kang served as his countrymen's ambassador to Jake's inner circle.

Each of the six men that filled the room's chairs sat in silence digesting Jake's oration of the latest radio download. Renard had sent confirmation of Gomez's betrayal, but his French mentor's failure to foresee his client's behavior hurt more than the duplicity itself.

He had considered Renard invincible. His clients never dismissed him, and they never operated outside of his will. But now that it happened, Jake expected a stronger response from the Frenchman, who remained indecisive.

"That's it?" Kang asked. "He wants us to wait for instructions in the morning? We can't wait that long. We need to take action now."

"I agree," Jake said. "But first things first. Our mission together officially ended three hours ago when we put limpets on the *Ambush*. I was supposed to be on my way home to my wife tonight, and if I can convince myself that cleaning up this mess is someone else's problem, I stick to our original schedule and point our bow toward Rio de Janeiro just like Renard planned."

Jake's provocative words combined with his banishment of cigarettes from the wardroom caused Claude LaFontaine's wiry frame to quiver in a combination of protest and nicotine withdrawal.

"Whatever it is that you decide," LaFontaine said, "I demand that you be honest with your intentions. You cannot leave us in the midst of a campaign."

"I left you in Taiwan because I had a bout of selfishness," Jake said. "I've already admitted that was wrong, but in my defense, I knew you'd be okay, which you were. But there's too much uncertainty here for me to leave this ship. I'll stick around until our business together is done."

"I believe you, Jake, if for no other reason than the water is too uncomfortably cold for you to swim to shore without a wetsuit."

Jake appreciated the levity of the Frenchman's half-joke.

"I'll consider that a practical vote of confidence," Jake said. "Good enough. So now that I'm stuck here with you guys wondering what the hell I'm supposed to do, we need to agree if we're still a crew."

"Count me in," Kang said. "Count all of us in from Taiwan. We need all the training we can get."

"That goes for us, too, Jake," Henri said. "Pierre has made all of us millionaires many times over by these missions. Some of the new recruits may do it for the money, and I've given them my word already that Pierre will compensate them fairly for extending this mission. But the rest of us do it because this is what we do."

"So, I have a full crew."

"Indeed, you do," Henri said. "The challenge is to define our mission."

"Let's start with staying alive," Jake said. "We don't know if anyone is coming for us, but in this mess, I expect both sides to shoot first and ask questions later. Let's review potential threats, starting with the *Ambush*."

"I don't think it will come for us, Jake," Henri said. "It has more interesting targets. It has to stop the Argentine submarines, the troop ships, and even possibly the *Dragon*. We should be of no concern to it."

"Good points," Jake said. "But I'm not entirely convinced. We pissed it off and showed that we are a nuisance. The Royal Navy may order it to kill us for spite. But we at least have until morning to worry about it since it's going to need at least until midmorning to pry off the limpets and get back to our general area. For that reason alone, the *Ambush* is not yet a factor."

"What of other British submarines?" Henri asked.

"I'm sure they're sprinting here, but it will take them days, if we trust the intelligence reports."

"Intelligence reports on submarines always include conjecture," Henri said.

"I know, but it makes sense that the *Ambush* was the only one in the area. By itself, it's all the Royal Navy needs to control the local waters. I'm actually concerned about other submarines."

"Other South American navies?" Henri asked.

"No. They're smart enough to stay out of this. It's the Americans that worry me. There's probably an American nuke out here watching everything. But there's nothing we can do about it, and it will be content to watch. In fact, if there really is an American boat out here, I'm sure it has orders to not get involved."

"So what, then, Jake?" Henri asked. "Do we make an approach on the *Dragon*? Do we give the British a fighting chance to control their airspace again?"

Jake considered the possibility of using the *Specter's* missiles to cripple the destroyer and spare the British the full loss of its investment.

"No," he said. "If an attack on the *Dragon* can help the British cause, I'll leave that to the *Ambush*."

"Do we instead position ourselves to the west to interdict Argentine troop transport ships?" Henri asked. "They are sure to be coming if they are not already en route."

"No. There will be plenty time to do that after waiting to hear from Renard in the morning. Plus, I'm not ready to get trigger happy and send thousands of men to watery graves–at least not until I have a better idea of what's going on."

"Then that leaves the Argentine submarines," Henri said. "We're tracking the *Santa Cruz*, but the *San Juan* is beyond our hearing. We can't track them both unless they move closer to each other."

"I would agree with you if it weren't for our limpet torpedoes," Jake said. "Now that I think of it, that's our next move. We'll put limpets on the *Santa Cruz* and then we'll search for the *San Juan*. We'll be able to hear the *Santa Cruz* across the world with those limpets on it."

Henri lifted a cup to his mouth and sipped as he stared into space. After a moment, he frowned.

"The limpet idea is flawed," he said. "The *Santa Cruz* needs to only surface and send divers over the side to pry them off, just as we expect the *Ambush* to do now that it's no longer being pursued. Then we would have all but wasted a weapon."

"I don't think so," Jake said. "I've got a trick up my sleeve if they try that."

Henri stared at him.

"I think I know what you mean, Jake. If it's what I'm thinking, I'm unsure that I agree."

"Let's put limpets on the *Santa Cruz* and then let Commander Martinez figure out his next move. Trust me that we'll have the proper response to anything he would try."

From his perch on the elevated conning platform, Jake surveyed the *Specter's* control room. His blended Franco-Taiwanese crew displayed a routine of competent teamwork in preparing a firing solution to the *Santa Cruz*.

As he prepared to launch a limpet torpedo, he watched Remy curl forward in intense listening. Jake delayed his order to launch the weapon and watched his sonar expert's toad-shaped head twist in his direction.

"The *Santa Cruz* is accelerating," Remy said.

"Get me blade rate," Jake said. "Get me its new speed."

"From the initial sound of it, not very fast. My initial estimate of blade rate says eight knots."

"Very well," Jake said. "Update the solution to the *Santa Cruz* from four knots to eight knots."

"Done," Remy said. "That reduces our torpedo's spare fuel from forty percent to twenty-three percent."

"Any sign of changing course?"

"If there's a change in course, it's only slight. No more than thirty degrees. I need a minute to analyze that."

"You've got Doppler on a discrete tone, don't you?"

"Yes. The strongest is the fifty-hertz electric bus."

"Assume a new speed of eight knots and analyze the Doppler shift you're hearing on the fifty-hertz tone. That will tell you how much they've turned. The bearing rate will nail it as being a turn to the left or right. Take your time. There's no hurry."

"You mean I have two minutes instead of one?" Remy asked.

"Don't push for more because I know you don't need it. When that submarine has finished turning, I'll show you a little patience in wanting to know its new course."

While Remy analyzed his data, Henri stood from his control station and walked to Jake.

"Do you wish to reconsider shooting?" Henri asked.

"Why?" Jake asked

"Because a target that was moving at a speed to hold its position without being heard has just accelerated to its optimum cruising speed. It could be going somewhere interesting and worth following in secret."

"Where could it possibly be going other than to rendezvous with the *San Juan*?"

"My point precisely. Why not see if you can trail the *Santa Cruz* to the *San Juan*?"

"Good point," Jake said. "But let's stick with the plan. The *San Juan* is loud enough that we can find it any time it tries to move. The only time it stands a chance against us is if we're moving and it's not. I'd rather just remove the *Santa Cruz* from the equation and take my chances one-on-one with the *San Juan*."

"You'll be announcing to Commander Gutierrez of the *San Juan* that you're remaining in theater with an agenda working against him."

Jake ran his hand through his hair and thought about it.

"Good," he said. "Let Gutierrez sweat. If he knows we're out here and working against him, it may throw a monkey wrench into his plans. Let's see how he deals with fear. Let's see if it forces a mistake."

"These decisions are why you're in charge."

Henri returned to his station.

"Do you have a solution yet, Remy?" Jake asked.

"Yes. The turn was twenty-five degrees to the starboard."

Jake studied his screen and verified that the new direction of the *Santa Cruz* held no special significance. It cruised to nowhere in particular, meaning that Henri was probably right about it repositioning itself closer to the *San Juan* for delousing, underwater communications, or other benefits of collocation.

A voice in his head told him to withhold his limpet weapon and to instead trail his target to a potential rendezvous. But he silenced that voice with a counterargument of taking decisive action.

"Shoot tube one," he said.

Jake's ears popped as the flushing whine of the torpedo launch system filled the *Specter*.

"Tube one, normal launch," Henri said. "Wire guidance engaged."

"Transfer control to Petty Officer Kang," Jake said.

"I've got it," Kang said.

Jake watched the inverted triangle of the torpedo slide across the screen from the *Specter* toward the *Santa Cruz*.

"Do you think they'll realize that it's a limpet weapon?" Henri asked. "I can't imagine their terror when they hear its screws and mistake it for a kill shot."

"I wouldn't worry about it," Jake said. "Even at just eight knots, that thing won't hear the torpedo until it's right on top of it, which, by the looks of it, is about four minutes."

"Do you wish to change course, Jake?" Henri asked. "They may get lucky and hear the torpedo in time to fire one back at us. A puncher's chance, I believed is the term you've used in the past."

"Good point," Jake said. "Let's get on a lag line of site. Left ten-degrees rudder, steady course zero-two-zero."

Jake felt a gentle lurch as the submarine turned. The symbols representing the torpedo and its target converged, and Remy announced the *Santa Cruz's* reaction.

"The *Santa Cruz* is accelerating to flank speed," he said. "Cavitating. Dropping active decoys."

"Did it shoot a countering weapon yet?" Jake asked

"I just picked it up," Remy said. "Launch transients. Now high-speed screws. Torpedo in the water!"

On his monitor, Jake checked the line connecting the *Specter's* torpedo to the *Santa Cruz*. Since he expected his target's commanding officer to shoot back down the bearing of the *Specter's* weapon.

"How long to confirm the course of the torpedo?" he asked.

"Probably thirty seconds," Remy said.

"Our torpedo is approaching the decoys," Kang said.

"Guide it through," Jake said.

"I have a course estimate for the *Santa Cruz's* torpedo," Remy said. "It's right where we expected it, passing safely aft."

"How long until detonation?" Jake asked.

"Twenty seconds," Kang said.

Moments later, Remy described the detonation.

"It sounds like a perfect hit," he said. "Most of the limpets are attaching and activating."

"Very well," Jake said. "We've tagged our target, and now that the *Santa Cruz's* crew knows it was a limpet torpedo, they can all clean their underpants."

Henri locked eyes with him. Jake sensed the question before the Frenchman voiced it.

"What weapon would you like loaded into tube one?" he asked.

"An Exocet."

"I'll send for my relief at my station and see to it personally that the missile is loaded."

"When you're done with that," Jake said. "Set up the normal evening watch section. Everyone needs to get some rest tonight."

In his stateroom, Jake reclined in his rack and tried to push the what-if scenarios from his mind. He grabbed a novel about earth defending itself from an alien race with a space-based navy and opened to its middle pages where he had left off.

The story's hard science left him wondering if mankind were close to discovering fractional light-speed travel, power sources that don't consume carried fuel, and weapons of destructive force beyond his reckoning. The novel made the assets of the *Specter* seem prehistoric, but the concept of an alien race intrigued him more than the science.

Jake looked away from the book and pondered that writers had flirted with extraterrestrial life since the dawn of imagination. If alien intelligence existed, they must know something crucial about the universe. He wondered if such a race were found, whose earthly wisdom would it confirm, and whose would it contradict.

He glanced at the bible on his foldout desk and decided to let the question remain in the realm of fiction. Proof of any truth would always elude him, and at some point he would have to pick a belief system based upon faith.

He swallowed as he acknowledged that his present belief system allowed him to beat a man to death out of anger.

A knock at the door startled him.

"Come in," he said.

Kang's head appeared.

"Jake," he said. "The *Santa Cruz* is surfacing."

In the control room, Jake watched his best men shuffle to their stations. Some rubbed sleep from their eyes.

"Won't you offer Commander Martinez a warning?" Henri asked.

"The limpets were his fucking warning. If he thinks he can just surface and pry off limpets after I tag him, he's delusional. I'm not playing that game."

"A verbal warning, perhaps?"

"I'm not revealing my position with a radio broadcast."

"Launching an Exocet missile will reveal our position."

"I'd rather give up one piece of information about our whereabouts than two. Plus, I'm not in a forgiving mood with this guy since he thinks he can just stop and undo my work. If he didn't get the memo with the limpets that he needs to bow out of this theater and head home, he deserves my wrath."

As his words echoed in his head, Jake realized he risked replicating the same behavior that led him to kill a man with his fists. But he also knew that the real world demanded action in real time, denied the luxury of complete philosophical reflection. He believed his actions were just.

"Load the solution to the *Santa Cruz's* into the Exocet."

"It's loaded, Jake," Kang said.

"Henri, take us to thirty meters, speed three knots."

As the *Specter* began its imperceptible climb and deceleration toward optimal parameters for the submerged launch of an Exocet missile, Henri came close to him and whispered.

"You may sink the *Santa Cruz* and kill them all," he said.

"It's a chance I'm willing to take," Jake said. "I have to."

"You don't believe that you're going to sink the *Santa Cruz*, do you?"

"The missile will target the conning tower, and most of the blast energy will be expended outside the pressure hull. Even if it does breach the pressure hull, it's only going to kill the men in the control room. The damage should be manageable enough to keep the *Santa Cruz* afloat."

Henri sighed and returned to his station, leaving Jake with the burden of the decision.

"Shoot tube one," Jake said.

The flushing whine of the launch system shot the missile from the tube.

"Tube one, normal launch," Henri said.

Jake realized that he had fired his first missile from a submarine and that there was nothing he could do but wait for the impact. Given the missile's speed, the report came quickly.

"Loud explosion from the bearing of the *Santa Cruz*," Remy said. "I'm sure that was the Exocet."

"Do you hear any evidence that it's sinking?"

"Not yet, Jake."

"Water ingress?"

"I can't tell. I don't hear it."

"Do you want to drive in closer for a visual inspection through the periscope?" Henri asked.

Jake took the clue from Henri. The fate of the *Santa Cruz* existed beyond his control now, and no amount of questioning or monitoring of it would change the outcome.

He had played God one more time, and his conscience would bear the burden, whatever its weight in dead bodies.

"No," he said. "What's done is done, and no matter the fate of the *Santa Cruz*, it is no longer a factor. Let's drive out of here and begin a search pattern for the *San Juan*."

CHAPTER 17

Olivia wiped her mouth after launching another throat-full of vomit into the toilet.

Hoping her spasms had ended, she brushed her long auburn hair aside but threw up again. She gasped and collapsed against the bathroom's metal wall, balancing her weight on her heels.

"Damn it!" she said.

Her world spun, and she mocked herself for mixing vodka and Ecstasy.

The only way to know you're in control, she thought, *is to push the limits.*

She reached for the washbasin and pulled herself to her feet. As she closed the bathroom door behind her, her stiletto heel buckled under her first hazy steps, but her ankle withstood the torsion. She recovered and slowed her gait over the aircraft's thin carpet. Bending, she stiff-armed the couch, rolled her frame into its softness, and reclined.

The throbbing of her sprained tendon seemed out-of-body, and the world spun as her assistant appeared over her.

"We've got nine hours before landing, ma'am," he said. "Perhaps you should get some sleep."

She had counted on the down time before ingesting her favorite chemical indulgences. With a pillow and wool blanket, she curled herself into the couch and passed out.

The nudge at her shoulder rousted her to consciousness before she felt ready to return to the living.

"Wake up, ma'am," her assistant said. "Flash message from headquarters."

"What time is it?" she asked.

"Still early. Not yet four o'clock."

He placed her phone in her hand, and she lifted it to her face. Her interest in the update stifled her nausea, and she read the news that she feared.

"Shit," she said.

She scrolled through her contact list to Renard's number but then reconsidered calling him. He could do nothing to help her, nor could anyone in her network.

"What is it ma'am?" her assistant asked.

"Argentine troop movement has begun toward the Falklands," she said. "Troop ships, freighters pressed into service to carry troops, and even fishing ships."

"Fishing ships?"

"Decoys," she said. "In case the *Ambush*, or any submarine for that matter, tries to sink the landing force."

"Will that really work?"

"According to what Renard has taught me over the years, yes. Most ships give off so much noise that it's hard to tell one from another without looking at it. And if you get close enough to look at it, you're letting all the other ships get by."

"How many ships? How many troops?"

"Over fifty ships and five thousand troops. Some of the troops will be air dropped, too. They'll probably take the western island, which is practically unguarded."

"How long ago did the landing force leave?"

"About the same time we took off, I'm sure right after Gomez realized that the *Ambush* survived. They'll be there in about twenty-five hours. What's left of the Argentine Navy is escorting it. That's only six frigate and corvette-sized ships, but it's enough to shoot guns and torpedoes at any British vessel that they'd find."

"Does the report say where the *Ambush* is and how long it would need to arrive in time to stop the landing force?"

"It can't stop the landing force," she said. "The best it can do is cut it in half. Argentine forces will land."

"How can that be so?"

She realized that by befriending Jake and Renard years ago, she had learned and taken for granted submarine basics that few people understood.

"A frontline submarine can carry only about forty weapons. If they're all torpedoes, that's at best forty ships sunk, but what usually happens when a submarine tries to take out a large amount of ships is that the first explosion sends all the ships into crossing patterns, and then each torpedo hits whatever target it finds first."

"So torpedoes hit the wrong targets and are wasted."

"Right," she said. "Then there's reload time of at least five minutes per weapon, since you can have only six to eight tubes, depending on the type submarine."

"I didn't know how complex it was. I thought a submarine just had its way with surface vessels."

"It's a matter of too many targets to hit all at once. Plus, the submarine needs to avoid being attacked. It needs to reposition itself to avoid a lucky shot from anything shooting back at it, and God forbid that there are helicopters looking for it. A couple of the Argentine warships have them and will have a credible chance of fighting back."

"Okay, ma'am. I'll keep this all in mind."

"Get me some water," she said.

He brought her a bottle and she gulped. Her mouth felt dry and tasted rancid.

"The latest report is that the *Ambush* needs another two hours to remove the last limpet," she said.

"To me, that sounds like the *Ambush* will be available to attack the incoming troops."

"It can if the British want it that way. If I do the math in my head, the *Ambush* needs another five hours to get back to where it was first attacked, and then another hour to get to the west side of the Falklands. The incoming landing force will be twenty hours out by then, or roughly three-hundred miles."

"How'd you figure that out?"

"You always assume commercial traffic moves at fifteen knots," she said. "At least that's how Slate and Renard do it. I imagine that the freighters and fishers could go faster, but not much. So if the incoming force is moving at fifteen knots and the *Ambush* is at thirty plus knots, let's round up and say fifty knots of closure."

"Five hours for the *Ambush* to reach the western side of the islands," he said. "And then another six before it can start attacking. We will at least have time for your audience with Ramirez to take place before then."

"That's the first thing I'll talk to him about," she said. "But no matter what the *Ambush* does, I need to let headquarters know that Argentina will place boots on the ground in the Falklands, just in case they didn't already figure it out themselves."

She leaned back on the couch and chugged the water.

"Send a message to headquarters summarizing what we just talked about."

"Yes, ma'am. Is there anything else we can do about this?"

"At the moment, nothing," she said. "I'm going to get some more sleep and be ready to deal with Senator Ramirez when we land."

As she drifted to sleep, a thought nagged her. She wondered why Gomez would delay sending troops long enough to allow the *Ambush* to be a factor. Perhaps he assumed the *Ambush* would be destroyed by now, she reckoned as she lost consciousness.

The impact of landing jostled her from her sleep. She felt dehydrated and queasy, but thanks to a regimented jogging and martial arts program, she felt equal to the day's task.

While the jet taxied, she gave herself a rapid sponge bath of her selected body parts and then changed into a low-cut blouse with a skirt cut high enough to show her thighs. A glance in the mirror confirmed her professional seductiveness.

As the flight attendant opened the door, the southern hemisphere's summer heat filled the cabin. She grabbed a bottle of water and started drinking to fend off thirst.

Anxiety kicked in during the limousine ride to the senator's home, and she absorbed only partial glances of the city's European-inspired architecture.

She called Renard.

"Good morning," he said. "It is still morning, is it not?"

"About eleven o'clock."

"I tried calling you a few hours ago, but apparently your phone was off."

"I needed the rest."

"You're still planning lunch with the senator?"

"Of course. Did you hear about the troop movement?"

"No," he said. "But it doesn't surprise me. May I conclude that the landing force is of sufficient size that several thousand troops will reach shore, regardless of the *Ambush's* actions?"

"Correct."

"Have you considered why Gomez waited to send his landing force?"

"When we talked about it last night," she said, "I just assumed it was for boosting morale among the troops."

"Sharing the confidence and jubilation of the returned pilots. Yes, I remember your theory. I thought it was accurate. But now you doubt yourself?"

She tilted back her bottle and signaled to her assistant seated beside her for a replacement.

"Yeah," she said. "He isn't the type of guy to leave things to chance. He must have allowed for the possibility that the *Ambush* would survive."

"Do you know his plan?"

"Sheer numbers, by the looks of it," she said. "Fifty ships to move five thousand men. Many of them fishing ships for decoys."

"Interesting. Such a plan should work."

"Not if I can talk Ramirez into pulling them back."

"I wish you luck," he said.

"What about Jake?" she asked. "I assume you've talked to him? One of our satellite's infrared sensors picked up a submarine burning on the surface."

"That was indeed him," Renard said. "I spoke with him just before I attempted to call you. He used limpets on the *Santa Cruz*, and then when Commander Martinez surfaced to remove the limpets, Jake ended the encounter with an Exocet missile."

Her mind raced to frame Jake's attack in her favor.

"Okay," she said. "Neither of us have access to a casualty report, but if the *Santa Cruz* is still floating, I can assume that Jake did a good job minimizing the body count. Ramirez will have to respect that."

"Indeed. I've asked Jake to seek the *San Juan* and to attack limpets to it as well. His limpet attack paired with the threat of a subsequent Exocet missile is a brilliant way to neutralize a submarine with minimal damage."

"Has he had any sign of the *San Juan*?"

"Not yet, I fear. Not since it ran after the *Ambush*."

"Call me if you hear anything from Jake."

"I will. Are you sure you don't want me to join you during your audience with Senator Ramirez?"

"Not yet. Let me feel him out first."

"Remember your seductive wiles. Use every asset you have to turn him to our cause."

"I'll get the job done."

Senator Ramirez represented the Buenos Aires province and lived in the city in an upper middle class ranch. He surprised Olivia by marching out of the door of his personal residence as the limousine he sent for her pulled up to the portico.

The car stopped, and the driver let her assistant our first. When she took her turn greeting the senator, she noted his trim posture and handsome features.

His square jaw moved without perturbing the slight grin that revealed his apparent belief in his invincibility, and dark, unblemished skin covered his sharp features. Intelligence beamed from his dark eyes, and his voice sounded graceful and strong like silk, reminding her of a classically trained tenor.

"The pleasure is mine," he said. "May I have a moment in private with you?"

"Of course," she said.

She sent her assistant ahead into the house as Ramirez gestured for the limousine to drive away.

"Come here," he said.

Tentative, she smiled to keep him at ease. Every moment she had with him needed to arouse or entice him to keep him off balance. She obeyed and stepped closer to him.

He surprised her again by extending his arm around her waist and pulling her into an embrace. He pressed his lips against hers and immobilized her, but he held his tongue within in his mouth. He then ran his face through her hair and whispered.

"In case anyone is watching," he said. "I need to give the impression that you are my mistress."

She whispered back to him.

"You're doing a fine job of that, senator. How did you know that I wouldn't protest?"

"Because I've read your dossier just as you've read mine. Despite your rise in the administrative leadership, you're still a trained seductress. The cleavage you're revealing, your shapely thighs calling to me, your eyes commanding me to yield to you. I know the tricks."

"I meant no offense. But can't a girl enjoy herself by mixing business and pleasure? How many daughters of cops from Connecticut get to kiss the future most handsome and desirable president of an industrialized nation?"

"There's no need for flattery, and no need for seduction. True, I cannot deny my weakness for women, but my tastes are my own to decide. Do not force the issue, especially when my country's future is at stake."

"Of course not."

"Good. When we head inside, you will shower away your pheromone-laden perfume and change into clothes that hide your curves and skin. I'm certain that I have your size somewhere in my guest wardrobe. My assistant will see you to the shower and then to the lunch table where we will discuss the matters you came to discuss."

He released her, and she felt like she had landed on the wrong end of a negotiation. She recovered her dignity by reminding herself that she had at least earned Ramirez's attention.

"Follow me, please," he said

When she passed into the house, he closed the door. A servant approached, but Ramirez raised a finger to pause him.

"Now that we're beyond potential prying eyes and ears, let me address the first issue that I'm sure you wish to discuss."

"And what's that?" she asked.

"Please," he said. "We don't have time for games. Give me a gesture of trust by sharing your most immediate concern with me."

"The troop movement."

"I appreciate your candor," he said. "And now you shall have mine. I could have stopped the troop movement to the Malvinas, but I opted not to. Do you care to guess why?"

The news startled her. She thought he had tried and failed. She feared that he was as hawkish as Gomez, but then she let herself assume he had a better motive. She wracked her mind for that motive, found it, and voiced it.

"Credibility?"

"With whom?"

"Your military leaders, your political rivals and supporters, your voters, and the British Prime Minister."

"Well said. You are indeed insightful. That was the complete answer, and I believe that we have a basis of understanding for the day's discussions."

"So, would you like me to freshen up now? A little less leg and cleavage?"

"Yes," he said. "But while you are away, I ask you to consider a very important argument very carefully."

"I'll be glad to. What is it?"

"Part of your obligation during our discussions, Officer McDonald, is to demonstrate something vital to me. Since I see nothing standing between myself and the presidency, I would like you to prove to me that I need you."

CHAPTER 18

Jake leaned forward in his foldout captain's chair and rubbed his eyes. When he lowered his hands and blinked, he noticed that Henri's tennis shoes looked free of grime, as if the will of their wearer made them as impeccable in appearance as himself.

"This is going to take forever," he said.

"Patience," Henri said. "The crew is looking to you for it. You're old enough now to understand the value of the virtue."

Jake leaned back and looked up to Henri, who appeared crooked with his hip planted against the railing that encircled the conning platform.

"We cut holes in the water with our hull all night, and not a peep from the *San Juan*."

"You said it yourself. That old ship is loud when it moves, but it's as silent as a ghost when it crawls. You can only keep searching for it and wait for it to make noise. No submarine can remain silent forever."

Jake glanced beyond Henri and saw Remy curled toward his sonar station. But instead of looking ready to spring with the discovery of an adversarial target, the Frenchmen buckled under pending sleep's weight.

"Remy's not going to pull off a miracle today," Jake said. "I think you're right, Henri. We're not going to find the *San Juan* until it makes a move loud enough to be found. It's going to require a slow and steady search."

Henri twisted his torso toward his countryman, and his gaze seemed to animate Remy, who stiffened.

"I have something at a high bearing rate," Remy said.

Brushing by Henri, Jake covered the distance to the sonar expert in seconds. High bearing rate meant something was moving fast, was nearby, or both. He looked over Remy's shoulder at a monitor that showed a line of broadband noise, comprised of multiple high frequencies.

"What sort of noise?" he asked.

"Flow noise," Remy said.

"What sensors do you hear it on?"

"Towed array and flank array."

"How fast?" he asked.

"Three degrees per minute, to the left."

"Assume a range of eight miles and calculate speed."

"Twelve knots."

"Let's test it. You got enough data on this geometry?"

"Yes, Jake. You can turn."

From the corner of his eye, Jake saw Henri retake his seat at the ship's control station.

"Left ten-degrees rudder," Jake said. "Steady course three-four-zero."

Henri acknowledged the order, and the deck tilted with the *Specter's* turn. Jake kept his eye on Remy's monitor, but he knew that the wealth of knowledge defining the new target's identity and comprehending its behavior lived in the Frenchman's ear.

Seated at the monitor beside Remy, Kang listened to the ocean as the Frenchman's apprentice.

"I hear cavitation," he said.

Remy's toad-head turned in lethargic disbelief. He slid one of his earpieces to his neck.

"You hear cavitation?" he asked. "And I don't?"

"Yeah. It's on the correct bearing."

Remy craned his neck upward and shrugged.

"Young ears," he said.

"Don't forget his great teacher, my friend," Jake said.

He felt the deck level under his feet.

"Steady on course three-four-zero," Henri said.

"Very well, Henri," Jake said. "Remy, you've got ninety seconds to give me your best solution."

Remy slipped his headset back over his ear.

"Signal strength is dropping," he said.

"Whatever we hear, it's driving away from us now," Jake said. "The bearing rate is less than I had expected in this geometry. Our target is still moving to the west, but our own motion is hardly contributing to the bearing between us."

"It's far away, Jake."

"How far?"

"I'd say more than twenty miles."

"Enter twenty-three miles into the system and let's see how it tracks. What speed does that correlate to?"

"Thirty-four and a half knots."

"Well, shit," Jake said. "If this solution tracks, we know we've found something fast enough to be worth finding."

Remy tapped his screen, and a cross section of the ocean appeared showing lines curving over distance and depth based upon the speed of sound across varied temperature, pressure, and salinity. He pointed at lines curving through the *Specter's* present depth of one hundred meters.

"For all sound frequencies, this could be reaching us from a surface vessel or from a submerged vessel. The sound isn't bouncing off the ocean bottom to reach us at this distance. It's coming to us via direct path propagation."

"So it could be a surface warship or a submarine. It's sure not the *San Juan*, though. Not at that speed."

"I've got blade rate," Remy said.

"What speed does it correlate to if that's the *Ambush*?"

"You think it's the *Ambush*?"

"What else could it be?" Jake asked. "There's nothing else out here that moves that fast."

"Blade rate correlates to thirty-three and a half knots if this is the *Ambush*," Remy said.

"Pull the range in to twenty-two miles."

"The solution looks good," Remy said. "You're right, Jake This is the *Ambush*, sprinting to the west as fast as it can."

Jake felt like taking a risk.

"Energize our active bow sonar," he said. "I want to target the *Ambush* with as much power as we can transmit, in the tightest acoustic beam we can form."

"Seriously?" Remy asked.

"Trust me."

"What frequency?"

"The lowest we have. I want to make sure it reaches them."

Remy tapped his screen.

"Sonar is ready to transmit active."

"Transmit," Jake said.

The entire ocean seemed to vibrate around Jake as acoustic energy shot forth from the *Specter's* bow-mounted hydrophones, oscillated throughout the submarine's hull, and raced at fifteen hundred meters per second toward the *Ambush*.

"If they didn't hear that," Jake said, "their sonar system is broken."

"What are you trying to accomplish?" Henri asked.

"Communication," Jake said. "Beyond that, I'm not sure."

"I've lost blade rate," Remy said. "No more cavitation."

"It's moved out of our hearing range, or it stopped moving?"

"Give me a moment," Remy said. "Okay, flow noise is decreasing. I believe they've stopped their screw."

"Prepare another active sonar ping," Jake said. "Same settings as the last one."

"Ready, Jake."

"Transmit."

The ocean shook again.

"Have you considered that you may be inviting a hostile torpedo?" Henri asked.

Jake twisted at his waist to look at Henri.

"The thought crossed my mind," he said. "But I'm going to trust that a British submarine commander has more class than that."

"Hull popping," Remy announced.

Jake recognized the announcement as the expansion of the *Ambush's* hull under lowering pressure as it rose in depth. He turned back to his sonar expert.

"They're going shallow?" he asked.

"Yes," Remy said. "But all I can hear is the hull popping. The flow noise and blade-related noises are gone. I had their reactor coolant pumps, but I can't hear it now."

"I can," Kang said. "Just barely, but I can hear them."

"Young ears," Remy said. "I suppose I should be grateful that he's with us."

"Doesn't matter at the moment," Jake said. "If it's slowing and going shallow, it may want to communicate via radio."

"Take us to snorkel depth?" Henri asked.

"Yes," Jake said. "Quickly."

As the deck angled upward, Jake returned to the elevated conning platform where he tapped a capacitive touch screen to command the periscope's ascent. A subroutine then sent the optics into a rapid full-circle swivel, and a panoramic image of the sweep filled two adjacent monitors beside him.

The first pass had taken place with the periscope submerged, and the panorama contained hues of dark blue water.

"Steady at snorkel depth," Henri said.

"Very well," Jake said.

As the *Specter* lurched in the surface swells, he commanded another full-circle optical scan, and the world above him appeared in his screens as a panorama of light blue sky. The waters above him showed solitude, the *Ambush* remaining beyond visual range.

"Raise the radio mast," Jake said. "I'm lowering the periscope."

"Radio mast is raised," Henri said.

"Very well," Jake said. "Let's see if our new friends want to speak to us."

A minute ticked by.

"They're not talking," Jake said. "Maybe they're waiting for us. Line me up to transmit high-frequency voice."

"Lined up," Henri said.

Jake pulled a handset from its latch, raised it to his mouth, and keyed the microphone. He made a concerted effort to avoid using the *Ambush's* name.

"This is private submarine, *Specter*. Communication check, Over."

Another thirty seconds ticked away.

"Are you sure we're transmitting, Henri?"

"Yes, Jake. I'm afraid so."

"This is private submarine, *Specter*. Communication check. Request communications. Over."

Another thirty seconds.

"What's it doing Remy?" Jake asked.

"I can't hear anything. It's gone quiet."

"I don't suppose super-ears Kang hears anything?"

The young petty officer shook his head.

"Remember to listen in all directions, defensively," Jake said. "We may have announced our presence in unwanted directions."

"There's nothing, Jake," Remy said. "I've been checking. We are alone except for the *Ambush*, and there's no more sign that it's still out there."

"If its commanding officer wanted to talk, he's had enough time," Jake said. "Forget it. Lower the radio mast and take us back to one hundred meters, Henri."

As the deck dipped, Remy curled forward and pressed his headset into his skull.

"Hull popping," he said. "I've got the *Ambush*. It's going deep and accelerating. Blade rate correlates to its maximum speed again."

"Right ten-degrees rudder," Jake said. "Steady course zero-nine-zero."

As the ship turned, Jake announced another command.

"All ahead standard," he said.

"Coming to all ahead standard," Henri said. "May I ask why?"

"In case you're right," Jake said. "In case there's a torpedo coming our way, and we just don't hear it yet."

Five minutes later, Remy confirmed an ocean void of manmade sounds, and Jake realized that the *Ambush* had departed without lashing out at him.

"All ahead one-third," he said. "Make turns for four knots."

He collected his thoughts and decided that they were incomplete without input from his mentor.

"Henri, bring us back to snorkel depth," he said. "And line up our global satellite phone to call Pierre. Patch him through to my stateroom phone. While I'm gone, get a relief at the ship's control station and take the deck and the conn."

In his stateroom, Jake curled forward in his chair and pressed a handset to his cheek.

"So what do you think?" he asked.

"You made a bold decision, my friend," Renard said. "I don't know if I would have risked transmitting active sonar, but since you remain alive, I assume that you made the right call."

"I think the *Ambush* went shallow to send a message telling the Royal Navy that it found us and probably to download a situation report. But no desire to talk to me."

"It's unfortunate that the *Ambush's* commanding offer chose not to speak to you, but your attempt to communicate brings us useful news at an appropriate time. You've confirmed that the *Ambush* is transiting west to intercept the Argentine landing forces."

"So the landing is for real?"

"Yes, indeed. Olivia is meeting with Senator Ramirez now to negotiate what she can, but I expect that troops will land, regardless of anything the *Ambush* might attempt."

"My mission is the same, then? Keep searching for the *San Juan* and do to it what I did to the *Santa Cruz*?"

"Precisely. I'm afraid that the *Ambush* will remain at best neutral to your cause. You've surprised it twice, and I'm sure that you've aggravated its captain to the point where a third such encounter might earn you his wrath. Although you may share a common target in the *Santa Cruz*, stay away from it, and don't again seek to illicit its support."

Jake shifted his weight and leaned back.

"So I'm still alone out here, chasing a ghost?" he asked.

"Such is often the fate of a submarine commander."

"You know that I've only got one limpet torpedo left, right?"

"Use it well, then."

"The commanding officer of the *Santa Cruz* seemed like a total jackass, but I don't want to take killing lightly anymore. If I need to sink the *Santa Cruz*, I'd like to know it's the right thing before I do."

"You can rarely be completely certain that you are correct when killing. We are both haunted by many ghosts that will cause us to question the fates to which we condemned them."

Jake recalled the outcome of his last brawling rage.

"I'm not sure I can trust my instincts anymore."

"That is unfortunate, Jake, because you must. Until I can grant you a better picture of this situation, you have no choice but to do so."

CHAPTER 19

Modest sweat lifting the toxins from her skin, Olivia let the hot water careen over her back. The heat brought temporary relief from anxiety and fatigue as blood coursed through her.

Cleaned of perfume and the stench of travel, she crept out of the stall and wrapped herself in an absorbent robe. The garment trapped the warmth and dried her. In a mirror, she noticed the first line of a crow's foot jutting from the corner of her eye, and she distracted herself from the disappointment by focusing on her hair.

She rubbed water from it with a towel and then attacked its wetness with a hair drier. Satisfied that evaporation would remove the residual moisture, she tied her auburn strands into a pony tail.

The bathroom door opened to a private bedroom where clothes hung ready for her within an armoire. The ease with which the senator and his staff rendered private hospitality caused her to question if his dossier fell short in estimating the number of women he had bedded.

Her hedonistic nature became enticed with joining the herd of partners who could claim carnal knowledge of Argentina's next president. She found him handsome, and her trained eye had noticed him moving with an assured confidence that would translate into skillful lovemaking. Her seductress training would also allow her to leave him with vivid memories she could bank on invoking if she needed a favor from the future South American leader.

As she dressed, a full-length mirror reflected her image. The dark clothes looked general and plain, but even with her skin hidden behind them, she respected her trim frame and athletic curves. But the senator had accomplished his goal of denying her the visual distraction of her sexuality.

Preparing for lunch, she mentally verified her goals. The top priority was her earning credit with the CIA for establishing a peaceful resolution to the conflict she helped ignite. Since she had supplied Renard with weapons, she could claim no middle ground. She either catapulted herself to the agency's executive ranks by guiding it to a peaceful and stable outcome, or her career went down in flames if the Falkland Islands erupted in a military conflagration.

Her secondary objective was Ramirez. Assuming she succeeded in earning advancement within the agency, she wanted him as an ally for assuring future stability in South America.

Ramirez controlled everything, and she needed to be persuasive during lunch. She silently cursed herself for allowing her hangover to cloud her head.

She reached for her phone on a nightstand and saw that she had missed a call from Renard. She called him.

"What's going on, Pierre?"

"I must speak to you urgently," he said. "Are you in a place of privacy?"

"I'm in the senator's guestroom. I'm not sure if I'm being bugged, but I'll take my chances."

"Jake found the *Ambush*. It was sprinting west, and the only logical conclusion to draw is that it intends to interdict the Argentine landing force."

Hopes of a peaceful settlement vanished.

"Jake wasn't able to stop it?" she asked.

"He chose not to. He tried to communicate with it to no avail, but he let it pass without hostility. Though it leaves you in a compromised position, I commend his judgment in sparing the *Ambush*."

"No, I get it. He did the right thing."

"No question."

"So it's the *Ambush* versus the escorted landing force. Hundreds, if not thousands of lives will be lost in the next six hours if I don't stop it."

"It gets worse," Renard said.

"How could it possibly get worse?" she asked.

"I believe that Gomez has armed his landing force with naval mines," Renard said. "The mines that I helped him acquire for blockading the islands will instead be used against the *Ambush* unless you can convince the British to call the submarine back. It's heading into a trap."

"How do you know that?"

"It's just a theory. But consider that Gomez has the mines in his possession and was willing to accept the risk of facing the *Ambush* with his landing forces."

She tried to picture fishing ships rolling mines off their decks against a submarine shooting torpedoes at them, but the image made no sense.

"You're losing me. How would this work?"

"Air dropped mines. Consider that the Argentine forces can see where their aircraft are laying mines, and they have the luxury of communicating among themselves. There may be accidents, but their aircraft could lay mines in front or aside of the landing force, and the landing force could maneuver around them. Not so for the *Ambush*, which has no knowledge of the mines' locations and no idea where the aircraft are."

"If this is true, I'm not sure that Ramirez knows about it or will reveal that he does," she said.

"Assume that it's true and that he knows. You must consider this in your discussions with him."

"I'm already at a disadvantage," she said. "He told me not to bother seducing him, and he made me shower away my perfume and put on subdued clothes. He also told me that he could've stopped the troop movement but didn't so that he could maintain his credibility all around."

"Damn. Then your immediate mission is clear. You must broker a peace before the *Ambush* reaches the landing force."

A knock on the door disturbed her, and she lowered the phone.

"Come in!"

Her assistant stuck his head into her room.

"Lunch is ready. The senator and his staff are waiting."

"Give me five minutes. Wait outside."

"Yes, ma'am."

When the door closed, she answered Renard.

"That's at best a long shot," she said. "Neither side has motivation to back down. If the *Ambush* pulls back, the full landing force hits the beach. If the landing force delays, it gives the British time to send reinforcements."

"Trust your abilities, young lady. My recent error with Gomez aside, history has proven me an excellent judge of people's characters and capabilities. I know you can navigate this challenge."

A waiter slid Olivia's seat under her buttocks and then draped a napkin across her lap. He placed before her a garden salad with crisp lettuce and sliced tomatoes that appeared picked from the vine earlier in the day.

Since the senator had granted her the privileged guest seat at the table's far end, she sat opposite the nation's future president, seated at the head, and she held a clear view of the other guests' profiles.

Her assistant, a recent graduate of Harvard's Kennedy School of Government, sat to her left. For his intellect, she had hand picked him to join her growing staff. She ran the faces of the remaining guests against memorized images of Ramirez's staff as the senator made curt introductions.

To her right, sat Ramirez's economic advisor. The next chairs held his foreign policy advisor and his military advisor. The final chairs, which flanked the senator, held his chief of staff and one person she didn't recognize–his presidential campaign manager.

"You don't recognize my campaign manager, do you?"

"No," she said. "But that's expected. You weren't planning on announcing your campaign for president for another month, I assume. No need to have a publicly recognized campaign manager."

"You've complicated his life by forcing my hand to take the presidency from Gomez via emergency succession. But you may have also made his job that much easier. Time will tell, and we have more immediate things to discuss."

The senator stabbed his fork into his lettuce and took a bite.

"You mentioned the troop movement, senator," she said. "I believe the landing force is our immediate topic of interest."

"Like I said, I have no intention to turn back the landing force. I see no reason to do so. Do you?"

She hurried through a mouthful of salad and swallowed. Doubting her argument's chances, she launched it out of obligation to establish her starting point.

"It would demonstrate to the British that you actually have control of your nation's military."

"I've been candid that I do not control every naval asset."

"But you told me that you could stop the landing force."

"I can. Enough of the ground troops aboard the landing ships are loyal enough to me to take control by force."

"Then I don't understand."

"I've shared this information with you," he said. "I did not share it with the British prime minister."

"You're talking directly with him?"

"Of course I am. How else did you expect me to take credit for saving the *Ambush* from the aircraft attack? How else did you expect me to position myself as the future president in his eyes?"

"I was intending to have the American ambassador intercede on your behalf with the prime minister," she said. "You said you're seeking credibility, and there's an advantage in having a respected third party recommend you to represent your nation."

"It's never too late for the American ambassador to intercede on my behalf."

She tagged his comment as a point in her favor. He wanted the triangulated support of the Americans in convincing the British to deal with him, and she controlled that access.

"If the prime minister doesn't know that you can stop the landing force," she said, "he may order the Royal Navy to try to stop it."

"You mean with the *Ambush*?" he asked. "The vessel I just took credit for sparing? Give me credit for skills in negotiation."

"You don't mind me asking? What have you and the prime minister agreed to?"

"No, I don't mind you asking. I'm rather confident that we've struck an agreement that aligns with the exact outcome that you came here to convince me to pursue."

The server cleared her half-eaten salad and replaced it with a stew of vegetables, beef cubes, and broth.

"I can only imagine," she said.

"Candor, Officer McDonald. I believe you're shrewd enough to recognize that you have no secrets that I need revealed and that you hold no power of which I am unaware. Share what you know, state what you want, and trust me that we can reach an accord that suits both our agendas."

"Fine," she said. "The private submarine that harassed the *Ambush* and crippled the *Santa Cruz* is loyal to me. It heard the *Ambush* sprinting toward the landing force less than an hour ago. I don't believe that the *Ambush* can stop all your troops from landing, but despite any defense you can put together, it can kill hundreds or even thousands of your men. I would like to avoid this."

"I agree," he said. "A hostile encounter between the landing force and the *Ambush* would be catastrophic."

He sipped his stew and swallowed. He then extended her suspense as he washed his food down with a sip of Malbec wine.

"I assume, then, that you have an agreement with the prime minister to prevent this?" she asked.

"Of course. I have enough contacts within our military forces to predict that Gomez intended to send the landing force. My staff and I have considered the possibility of a British submarine standing between that landing force and the islands for weeks, and we've been able to draft an agreement that I expected the prime minister would consider seriously."

"What did you offer him?" she asked. "What did he say?"

"It's very simple," he said. "He allows the forces to land. They hold the western islands while his forces remain entrenched in the east. I take control of Argentina and its military, and I rattle my saber at him. Meanwhile, he sends a task force to the islands, and he rattles a saber at me. We then reach an agreement that prevents the loss of many lives, makes each of us appear magnanimous, and allows each of us to appear strong in claiming political victories."

Accustomed to privileged information, she hated being three steps behind Ramirez. She needed to know what he knew.

"How? What agreement could that possibly be?"

"I will buy the islands from him."

"Just like that?"

"Yes. Just like that. Since I don't have enough money to purchase the islands, I won't be buying them with cash but instead allowing Britain to lease the islands for fifty years free of charge. Call it owner financing, if you will."

"The prime minister has agreed to this?"

"Directionally, yes. The lease will give the island's inhabitants and both nations two generations to adapt, and it will give his nation time to reap the reward of the petroleum reserves it has found to date. Any new reserves discovered will be shared. We haven't yet discussed how to conduct joint exploration for new reserves, but I'm confident we can agree. He seems to be very direct and uncaring about trivialities."

"You've offered him nothing else?"

"I needed to offer him something he could claim as a territorial gain. I'm conceding a small patch of land in the Tierra del Fuego province that he can use as a base for whatever military or Antarctic exploration needs he desires. But without my nation challenging him for the Malvinas, his military needs in the region and the costs for supporting them become a mere fraction of their present state. This is an obvious gain for both sides."

"You're sharing the details with me because you want me to get consensus from Washington?"

"Yes. You will tell your leaders about the agreement I've reached with the prime minister so that they agree to support me as the new leader of Argentina prior to taking the role through the emergency election process. That will still take days, and I need support from Washington immediately."

Her head spun, but she digested the plan's simplicity. She wanted to ask why he needed her, instead of having his ambassador to the United States handle the communications. But then she remembered he had challenged her to prove her value to him.

The *Specter*.

"There are two problems in your way," she said. "The *San Juan* and the *Dragon*. I'm going to guess that you already have a solution to deal with the *Dragon*."

"Correct," he said. "The destroyer is staffed by a small team who can barely operate its basic systems. It's still close to shore and defenseless against any submerged attack force. The only challenge is to minimize damage to the destroyer itself in doing so, but the prime minister assures me that there are British warriors stationed in the Malvinas Islands who have the appropriate skills."

Something about the British destroyer's fate bothered her.

"Hold on," she said. "If you retake the *Dragon*, won't the forces loyal to Gomez know about it?"

"I expect that they will."

"Won't that force Gomez to order the *San Juan* to sink it?" she asked. "If the *Dragon* returns to British control, the Royal Navy would own the air again. Your side would have no power in negotiating a settlement."

"Correct," he said. "The prime minister and I discussed the possibility of using the *Dragon* as bait to expose the *San Juan* to the *Ambush*, but it is too risky to both the *Dragon* and the *Ambush*, and I prefer to avoid destroying a submarine staffed by my countrymen."

"That leaves you with the sticky problem of the *San Juan*," she said.

Then it dawned on her.

"And I'm your link to the *Specter*, which is only submarine that can stop the *San Juan* without killing its entire crew."

"Congratulations," he said. "You have just stated why I need you."

"Plus, the prime minister doesn't want to use the *Ambush*, or any his submarines, against the *San Juan* since the outcome would be the loss of at least one crew, which would complicate your effort to resolve this without stirring up emotions from either nation while you're both trying to resolve this peacefully."

"Correct again. The limpet weapons used against the *Ambush* and the *Santa Cruz* are clever, and they can solve this cleanly. Do you know if the *Specter* has any such weapons remaining?"

"I expect that it does, but I'll have to double check."

The server replaced her untouched stew with a filet mignon accompanied by steamed asparagus and a baked potato.

"How much time does the *Specter* have?" she asked.

"Excellent question," he said. "Five days. After that, the prime minister will lose confidence."

"That sounds reasonable," she said. "The *Specter* is already doing exactly what you planned for it to do."

"I told you our agendas were in alignment."

"Pardon my pessimism, but what if the *Specter* fails?"

"Then British swimmers from the Malvinas will retake the *Dragon*, and the prime minister will have enough submarines in the area by then to both protect the *Dragon* and to conduct a thorough search of the surrounding waters to find and sink the *San Juan*."

"That's a fate we need to avoid, isn't it?"

"Of course," he said. "But it's the best alternative should your commander of the *Specter* fail. But you're quite an accomplished woman, and I expect that you surround yourself with only capable people. Let's plan on his success."

Noting an admiration in his stare that hinted at a possible future relationship, she allowed herself to fantasize beyond the crisis about a future where she held great power in the CIA and influenced the heart of Argentina's young, charismatic leader.

"Why don't you enjoy your meal?" he asked. "We haven't yet discussed the progress on the emergency election. I'm sure that you would like me to assure you of the process that will instate me as the nation's legitimate leader."

"Yes, I'm quite interested."

She tried to savor the taste of the pinkish meat, but her mind raced to the distant sea far to the south.

"Wait," she said. "If the *Ambush* isn't racing to engage the landing force, why did the *Specter* catch it sprinting toward it?"

He smiled a knowing and captivating smile that secured his place in her heart as a man worth knowing intimately.

"Because the *Ambush* wasn't sprinting to chase down the landing force. It was sprinting to entice the *Specter* into revealing its location."

"I don't understand. I thought it sprinted away from the *Specter* after their encounter."

"It did, Officer McDonald. But that was a ruse. It turned back and is now using its superior crew training, propulsion abilities, and advanced sensors to trail your *Specter* and guarantee compliance with our plan."

Olivia felt herself slipping into a hole of disbelief about the magnitude of her informational disadvantage.

"I believe that's unnecessary," she said. "The *Specter's* owner has assured me of his intent to neutralize the *San Juan*."

"The prime minister has made it clear that he's unwilling to take that on faith. He was also clear about the *Ambush's* orders, now that the tide has turned and it has the upper hand on the *Specter*. I recommend that you make the *Specter's* commander fully aware of his new situation."

"I'll convey whatever message you need conveyed."

"I will get you the exact statement from the prime minister after lunch, but the summary for your commanding officer of the *Specter* is that he has angered enough people in the Royal Navy that he would be wise not to test the judgment of the *Ambush's* commanding officer. The British don't carry limpet weapons, and of all the assets available to resolve this conflict, the *Specter* is the most expendable."

CHAPTER 20

Commander Gutierrez lied to his executive officer.

"This is within my mission's parameters. There are certain informational privileges that a commanding officer enjoys."

"I understand, sir," Fernandez said. "But is it necessary? Defensive mining is one thing. Offensive mining is an entirely different thing. This is killing the very civilians we desire to bring under our rule."

"What of it? Too few people will die to matter, and this is a tactical necessity to divert the attention of those who hunt us."

"Can't you at least verify with our admiralty that this is the correct action?

Gutierrez raised his voice.

"I need nobody's authority but my own!"

Faces in the control room of the *San Juan* turned to Gutierrez and then shifted back to their charts, plots, and monitors. He leaned over the conning platform's metal railing, looked down over Fernandez, and lowered his voice.

"I'm not risking an active radio transmission. We are in dangerous waters with a need to remain undetected, and you know damned well that any radio transmission, however directional the beam, is always at risk of being detected and revealing our position."

"I do know, sir. Of course, I do."

"Even if I could communicate with our admiralty, I suspect spies loyal to Ramirez in our communications networks. I could be informing an enemy and inviting bogus orders."

"Then we are in an environment of autonomy, just like sailors of old."

"Yes," Gutierrez said. "Like ancient sailors of old. I had my orders when we set sail, and now I must carry them out without further guidance. It is doubly challenging since Martinez allowed his incompetence to get himself and a quarter of his crew killed. He deprived our cause the asset of his submarine."

"You trust that report, then? You believe that the *Specter* really attacked the *Santa Cruz* and that it's not propaganda to force us into foolishness?"

"I trust the report because I would have done the same if I commanded the *Specter*. I also trust that you're not insinuating that my decision to mine Port Stanley is foolishness."

Fernandez cleared his throat.

"No, sir. Of course, not. I meant my comment only in the general sense. I will set a course for Port Stanley, immediately."

"Use a transit speed of six knots."

"That will take us a day to get there, sir."

"The British task force is still forming. I can be patient. Set the course and take us there. I will take my rest now."

Having been awake for a day and a half, Gutierrez headed to his stateroom and slithered onto his rack. Fatigue drew his mind toward sleep, but he wanted to reset his body's clock to allow his heightened alertness when his ship would lay mines.

His wall clock indicated the local time as the mid-afternoon, and decided to force himself to stay awake. He picked up a sound-powered phone to order a cup of coffee. Two minutes later, a sailor arrived balancing in his palm a serving tray that Gutierrez told him to leave on his desk.

After the sailor departed, he rolled to his feet, stepped to his desk, and pushed aside the tray. He unfurled a nautical chart and flattened it with paperweights at its corners. Sipping coffee, he reached for a pencil and then drew crossed lines at the *San Juan's* location to the east of Port Stanley.

He eyeballed distances in hundred-mile tranches and kept tabs of time in his mind. A day separated him from the port, and then he needed two more days to reach his loiter point to the north where he would await the British task force.

The *Ambush* and *Specter* could be anywhere in his future vicinity, he reckoned, as could any other submarine that the Royal Navy sent ahead of its task force. Predicting the moves of his potential adversaries would be impossible, and he hoped that the diversion of mines at Port Stanley would buy him hiding time.

Beyond the distraction, he relied upon his ability to keep the *San Juan* quiet to stay alive and allow him to interdict the British task force. A student of his nation's naval history, he remembered how close an Argentine submarine came to thwarting Prime Minister Thatcher's task force three and a half decades earlier.

His predecessor had evaded the Royal Navy and launched torpedoes at its warships, but a mistake in maintenance had made his weapons impotent. Instead of allowing the sloppiness that prevented the past submarine from protecting the Malvinas, Gutierrez trusted his iron grip of discipline. No man would dare fail him for fear of shame and reprimand.

One submarine. One torpedo. That's all he needed to cripple the Royal Navy's new aircraft carrier and prevent British air operations around the Malvinas. One act of patience to hide from his hunters as the task force approached, one act of seamanship to drive his way to the carrier, and one envenoming strike to give his nation and his president control of the air.

This would, in turn, give it and him the water, the land, and the surrounding offshore oil reserves. The final outcome would be his personal rise in power to command the strongest navy in his country's modern history.

The upside of losing his sister ship to an Exocet missile, he decided, was that all honor and glory would be his. Martinez, the now-deceased bungler, couldn't get in his way or send a lucky torpedo that would rob him of his glory.

He expected support from air dropped mines in drifting fields that his nation's aviators would lay behind him. But history wouldn't remember pilots who dropped mines and flew home, no matter how many British ships perished by their deeds. It would, however, remember the submarine commander who risked his life to draw close to his prey and assure that his fangs found the high-value targets.

But he first needed his detour to his distraction near Port Stanley. To get there, he hoped that his slow transit speed would minimize the *San Juan's* noise and hide him from the *Ambush* and *Specter*. He also knew that the bold move of approaching the Malvinas defied the expectations of his hunters. They would be searching for him elsewhere, and he expected to lay mines in relative solitude.

Confident he had outsmarted his adversaries in choosing to transit to the Malvinas, he let his mind drift to the larger picture.

He reassessed the promises of a distressed president. To protect Gomez's power and to assure his future in the admiralty, Gutierrez needed to rally his country to war. The successful surprise air strike and the pending troop landing would serve as a temporary advantage, but the nation would rescind its support for Gomez if it believed in the inevitability of the British task force's arrival to retake control.

But if just one submarine could challenge that task force, bolstered by a mine field behind it, hope would spring. To bridge the gap in time before the task force arrived and he could spring that hope, Gutierrez would offer his nation an attack on shipping at Port Stanley. He would show his people that Argentina had a navy, and that it had venom.

His head fell forward and then snapped upward as he fended off sleep. But he yielded to necessity, slithering into his rack and allowing himself to drift to sleep.

A knock on his door rousted him from a deep sleep, and he recoiled in his bed. His reckoning of time had distorted, and he felt disorientated. He heard the knock again.

"Enter!" he said.

A young sailor appeared.

"Sir, the executive officer reports battery level at twenty percent and requests permission to snorkel."

"Tell him to line the ventilation system for snorkeling, to come shallow to forty meters, and to wait for me."

After brushing his teeth and slipping into his jumpsuit, Gutierrez walked to the *San Juan's* control room.

"Slow to four knots," he said. "Raising the periscope."

He pressed his face to the optics as the smooth cylinder glided upward. Walking the periscope clockwise, he took in the midafternoon's sunlit brilliance. He then lowered the periscope to improve his stealth, and he made a mental note to raise it again every fifteen minutes for a scan of the water's surface.

"Raise the radio mast," he said. "Get me a download."

Minutes later, Fernandez announced the receipt of transmissions sent from his home base.

"Lower the radio mast. Raise the snorkel mast."

Fernandez handed him a clipboard and a printout. He flipped through pages to news about Gomez's troops reaching the western shores of the Malvinas. Meeting no resistance, they had established a beachhead and controlled the western section of the region.

He muttered to himself.

"We've conquered the sheep of the western Malvinas. But at least the campaign is moving forward per plan."

He flipped to another page and read about the British task force, which had been defined to the exact ships by name. As he had expected, the task force included eighty percent of the Royal Navy's combatants.

The *San Juan* had deployed with eighteen torpedoes, and after his shots at the *Ambush*, he had sixteen remaining–enough to cripple the contingent of British warships that his navy's intelligence pegged at arriving within his vicinity in twelve days. Unlike its predecessors, the modern Royal Navy had prepared a reaction plan to rally a task force for the invasion. It needed less than two weeks for the first installment of its ships to assemble and arrive.

"Commence snorkeling," he said.

The diesel engines rumbled to life, and Gutierrez trusted the *San Juan's* old but intelligent German engineering to capture enough of their groan and keep the electricity-generating machines' cyclical chopping dissonance away from listening ears. But while his ship made noise, he chose this time to reload his tubes.

"Lieutenant Commander Fernandez," he said. "Load tubes one through four with mines. Set a delay of twenty-four hours for each mine. Actually, pull out your pocket memo and take notes. We may as well conduct all our noise-making evolutions while reloading the tubes."

The executive officer withdrew a pad and pencil.

"Yes, sir. I'm ready."

"Have the cook prepare dinner and have the men use and flush all toilets for the next hour. Once that's done, blow the content of all sanitary tanks overboard. Run the water still, and allow each man two minutes in the shower. If any man wishes to use the exercise equipment, he may do so until you've finished reloading tubes. I want each man recharged and refreshed. Now, read me back your list."

Fernandez recited his notes, and Gutierrez dismissed him. Ninety minutes later, the clunking noises of chains and rigging gear—artifacts of an antiquated torpedo room—subsided, and Fernandez returned to the control room to report that the *San Juan's* tubes held its mines and that the crew had completed all its other noisy activities.

A sailor stepped forward with a report of the specific gravity of the battery's electrolyte that equated to sixty percent charge. Based upon his experience, he expected another two hours of snorkeling. He reminded himself to remain patient.

He made eye contact with Fernandez and curled his finger. When he appeared below him, Gutierrez leaned over the rail and waved his arm across the control room.

"Have them all rehearse the mine laying procedure. Include personnel in the torpedo room. I want it fresh in their minds."

Fernandez scurried from sailor to sailor, ordering them to withdraw operations manuals from cubby holes. As men balanced books open on their laps and slid sound-powered phones over their heads, the executive officer exited the compartment to instruct sailors in the torpedo room to ready themselves for rehearsal.

Nearly two hours later, Gutierrez grew weary walking his team through its fourth rehearsal, but he ordered them to repeat the procedure again. During the fifth repetition, he received a report telling him that the battery had reached full charge. He ordered the *San Juan* deep and returned to its transit speed of six knots.

When the fifth rehearsal of the mining procedure ended, he saw the first man of the evening shift arrive in the control room to relieve his counterpart. As the compartment filled with the next watch section, he saw one of his two junior officers walk through the forward door two steps ahead of Fernandez, who was returning from the torpedo room.

"Lieutenant Commander Fernandez," he said. "Our young lieutenant here can manage the watch team on his own for a few hours. Join me for dinner in the wardroom."

Seated in the chair where he had received promises weeks ago from President Gomez, he poked his fork into a three bean salad. To his right, his executive officer sipped coffee.

"I will soon command a squadron of submarines," he said. "There could be as many as six ships. I will need commanding officers I can rely upon."

Fernandez concealed any emotions the words had stirred.

"It will be a welcome problem to have more submarines than qualified men rather than to have the inverse problem, which we have suffered for decades."

"If he hadn't killed himself by his own stupidity, I would have placed Commander Martinez behind a desk until his retirement. So I consider him no loss. But he also got his executive officer killed in the Exocet missile strike, and that was the loss of a capable man."

"I agree, sir. I didn't know him well personally, but he always impressed me during our training together."

"Until I can recruit and train others, this leaves you as my only future potential commanding officer. I ridded myself of your predecessor because he was slow witted, but you have a sharp mind and think with clarity under pressure during our drills."

"Thank you, sir."

"My concern is your experience in real combat. I commend you for keeping your calm and showing your nerve thus far, and I expect you to continue doing so."

"Of course, sir. Always."

"But I will want to see you lead men in combat before I hand you command of a submarine in my squadron."

"How's that possible, sir?"

Letting the questing linger, Gutierrez ate another bite of bean salad and washed it down with a sip of coffee.

"Unless it is the aircraft carrier, the third British warship that we attack in the task force will be yours. I will give you temporary authority to launch weapons, and I will watch over you as you lead the attack."

Fernandez's face flushed, and the corners of his mouth rose.

"I'm honored, sir. I won't disappoint you."

"I know you won't. I know you're capable. After all, I selected you to my crew, and I don't make errors in judgment."

Four hours later, Gutierrez sat in his foldout chair on the elevated conning platform. The *San Juan* drifted with its shaft stopped, and a wall clock told him that the sun had set thirty minutes ago.

He risked raising the radio mast, exposing it to radar energy and visual sightings, in order to update his Global Positioning Satellite data. He wanted to verify the *San Juan's* location on the inner edge of the navigable channel leading to Port Stanley.

"We've got the positioning data, sir," Fernandez said. "Do you want a radio message download?"

"No. Lower the mast."

"Radio mast is lowered, sir."

Gutierrez hurried to a plotting table where sailors stooped over a chart of the channel. As Fernandez cited the satellite-generated coordinates, a sailor slid a transparent straightedge to the chart's lines of latitude and then drew a hash near his eyeballed estimate of longitude. He then rotated the edge ninety degrees and drew a hash that showed the *San Juan* inside the channel.

He looked up to Fernandez.

"Open the outer doors to tubes one, two, three, and four. Prepare to lay mines."

Fernandez orchestrated a dance of humans, sound-powered phones, and operations manuals in an exact replica of the rehearsals. Then he disappeared through the forward door en route to the torpedo room.

The *San Juan's* senior enlisted sailor, a stocky man with a large jaw and a ring of gray hair outlining his balding scalp, wiggled the breastplate-balanced speaker of his sound-powered phone to his lips. He then looked to Gutierrez.

"Sir, the executive officer reports from the torpedo room that the outer doors are open to tubes one, two, three, and four. Each mine is set with a twenty-four-hour delay after wakeup. The ship is ready to lay mines."

"Very well," Gutierrez said. "Deploy tube one."

The impulse launch changed the air pressure within the vessel and made Gutierrez's ears pop.

"The executive officer reports that tube one is deployed."

"Very well. Drain tube one. Keep it empty."

Staying patient, he let his ship drift with the current for ten minutes. He considered raising his radio mast again, but he opted to trust his inertial navigation system to calculate his position. As the flowing waters pushed him closer toward the channel's center, he made eye contact with his senior enlisted man.

"Deploy tube two," he said.

His ears popped again, and he missed half of the report from a sonar operator.

"Repeat that," he said.

"Sonar contact bearing zero-five-five. Loud screws and loud flow noise. Probably a merchant freighter."

"I need a distance estimate."

"Five miles, sir, but it's a guess. There's no bearing rate, since it's coming right at us."

"I know it's coming right at us, you idiot. We're in its accursed channel. Use the increase in sound strength as it approaches to warn me before it overruns me."

Ten minutes later, the inertial navigational fix showed the *San Juan* passing the center of the channel and drifting to its far side.

"Deploy tube three," he said.

With his third mine laid, Gutierrez studied the chart. A sailor swiveled a straightedge toward the crosshair that marked the *San Juan* and ran a pencil along it. He then made ticks corresponding to sixteen knots of speed, a conservative estimate of the incoming freighter's speed.

Two minutes to impact–less if the solution proved a sloppy estimate. Gutierrez looked to his sonar operator for insight.

"It's getting loud, sir."

The shallow channel disallowed him diving under the vessel, and a collision could damage his hull or prove fatal as a giveaway of his location to his hunters. He decided that three mines sufficed, and he would save the fourth.

"All ahead two-thirds," he said. "Secure mining operations."

He returned to his elevated conning platform and looked to a monochrome monitor. The direction to the merchant's sounds started to change as it approached, passed behind him, and steamed away in a near miss.

"Slow to all ahead one-third," he said. "Right full rudder."

After the turn, the deck steadied, and the *San Juan's* bow pointed at Gutierrez's mines.

"All stop," he said. "Sonar, line up to activate mines, minimal transmission strength."

"Lined up, sir."

"Transmit activation sequence."

The sailor depressed a button, and Gutierrez heard nothing. But he hoped that the hydrophones on the mines heard the specific command sequence of varied frequency sonar pulses from his ship.

"Activation sequence transmitted, sir."

"Report when the mines respond."

"I've got one response! Now two. And three. All three mines are active, sir."

Fernandez returned to the control room.

"You're happy with just three mines, sir?"

"Yes," Gutierrez said. "One might have sufficed. The others are redundant to assure that something in this channel blows up twenty-four to thirty-six hours from now."

"Where to now, sir?"

"Six knots, course zero-five-five. I have no destination in mind yet, other than getting as far from here as possible."

CHAPTER 21

His back against his stateroom's bulkhead, Jake crouched on his heels. He had read the news a day earlier, but his anger lingered, keeping him ready to swipe his paw at the next target that moved.

A day after receiving the message, Jake had left the printed sheet of encrypted letters untouched beside his portable scanner on his desk. His laptop's optical character recognition software had read the message's symbols, and then his decryption software had rendered them in plain English on his laptop screen.

He remembered cursing under his breath as he read the note that Olivia had relayed to him from the British prime minister.

It stated that the *Ambush* had fooled him and had maneuvered behind him. A world-class submarine that outmatched his *Specter* in every measurable parameter trailed him, and his sonar team remained oblivious to it. His initial impulse had been to warn his team and formulate a plan to break away from his British hunter.

But reason set in, and realized that the *Ambush* was not his hunter but instead his overbearing babysitter–provided he performed his mission and prevented himself from provoking it. He likened the *Ambush* to an infantry officer holding a pistol to his back as he charged a hostile hill. As long as he continued forward, he'd be okay.

Charging forward meant navigating to a rallying point several miles north of the Falkland Islands at a given time and date and then starting a search pattern–one that the Royal Navy had defined for him in explicit hour-by-hour detail–and then continuing that search pattern with the *Ambush* trailing him turn by turn.

He had given the search pattern to his crew, and they were making the *Specter* follow it. But he couldn't force himself to explain that the Royal Navy had defined the search route and taken over their destiny. Shame forced him to stuff the news inside himself, and for more than a day, he suffered alone knowing that he had allowed his crew to become the bait to draw out the *San Juan*.

Frustration rose within him, and he thumped the back of his head against the bulkhead.

"You dumb ass," he said.

He allowed one more fantasy of breaking contact from the *Ambush* to play out in his head. He would increase the *Specter*'s speed slowly and open a half mile on the *Ambush*. Then he would command his submarine to its flank speed, deploy active noisemakers to create a wall of bubbles, and blind the British submarine's sonar. Finally, he would turn and slip away to freedom.

Every time he played the scenario in his mind, the *Ambush* launched a spread of six torpedoes. Each time, Jake died.

The message from the prime minister stung as he recited the words from memory in a bad British accent.

"Your limpet torpedoes were a clever addition to this conflict. I understand that you have one such weapon left, and I encourage you to use it against the *San Juan* as you did against the *Santa Cruz*. For the Royal Navy lacks such weapons, and my orders to the admiralty give the commanding officer of the *Ambush* great leeway in determining your fate."

Knocking his head against the bulkhead again, he mumbled.

"Dumb ass."

He consoled himself by verifying again in his mind that he had followed all the British orders. He followed the prescribed course and speed. With the MESMA system running, he could maintain the eight-knot search for the five-day duration without snorkeling. The Royal Navy had pegged his ship's capabilities and pushed him to maximize them.

They had even set up a protocol where the *Ambush* could order him shallow to raise his radio mast for communications.

Avoiding the crudity of transmitting amplified human speech through the water, which could invite unwanted listeners, a three-ping sequence from the British submarine's sonar system served as the signal for Jake to ascend for further instructions. The pings would be measured in milliseconds of duration–mere clicks.

While Remy's otherwise watchful eyes fluttered in deep sleep, Jake had set up an automated alert in the Subtics system to identify the active frequency of the *Ambush's* sonar signal. For more than a day, the *Ambush* had remained silent–and so had Jake about the trailing submarine's presence.

Now he needed to share.

His inner circle joined him in the wardroom.

"Gentlemen," he said, "I've withheld news from you that I received in the download almost a day and a half ago. It's time for me to explain what's going on. We've been pressed into service by the Royal Navy."

The wiry Claude LaFontaine protested.

"Pierre would never allow that," he said. "He's too proud."

Before Jake could defend himself, Henri interjected.

"You said we were pressed into service. Did you mean against our will? Against Pierre's will?"

"The bizarre thing in this mess," Jake said, "is that the Royal Navy is commanding us to do exactly what we want to do and what Pierre wants us to do. They want us to hunt the *San Juan*."

"Well that makes sense," Henri said. "It's just a formality then? To give the Royal Navy a sense of control after being caught off guard."

"Not exactly," Jake said.

He wiggled in his chair, failing to ease a newfound discomfort. Eyes burned on him as he sought the correct words.

"Go ahead, Jake," Kang said. "How bad can it be?"

The youngster's enthusiasm encouraged him.

"Turns out, we didn't catch the *Ambush* rushing to intercept the Argentine landing forces. It was rushing to trick us into attempting to communicate with it."

Blank faces.

"Guys, I need to spell it out for you since it's so strange. The *Ambush* pretended to drive away, but it really turned around and has been following us for a day and a half."

Of all the sullen faces, Remy's turned the most ashen.

"You let the *Ambush* trail us for a day and a half already, and you didn't let me know? How was I supposed to set up a sonar search plan to listen for it? How did you expect me to hear it when I don't know to seek out its particular noise signature?"

"I didn't, Remy. I didn't expect anyone to do anything different. One reason I didn't tell you was so that we could all experience this for a while and realize that this changes nothing. The *Ambush* is really just our babysitter. We are still committed to doing what we agreed to do, together, regardless of any political games back in civilization."

"What if we decide not to follow British orders?" Henri asked. "What if we attempt to break contact and run?"

"The *Ambush* would attempt to sink us," Jake said. "And it would probably succeed."

"Didn't you think this was worth telling us?" Henri asked.

"I'm telling you now."

"I meant when you found out."

"It was hard for me to keep the news to myself, but I thought it was the right thing."

'How can it be the right thing?" Henri asked. "We've known each other for years. You could have trusted us with the information."

The bulkheads closed in on Jake until LaFontaine shook his long index finger at his colleagues.

"I know why he did it," he said. "He's too gracious to say it, and so I will say it for him. It's because this is an embarrassment to all of us, and he absorbed the shame for us."

"You weren't even there," Henri said. "You live in the engineering spaces. You're saying this is an embarrassment to those of us involved in the tactical decisions."

"It's hardly an accusation," LaFontaine said. "It's merely a statement of truth. Jake may have made the decision to risk revealing ourselves to the *Ambush*, but from what I heard of it, the protests were minimal. We as a crew stood behind him. We need to accept it. You need to accept it."

With the length of the submarine normally separating the Frenchmen, Jake's first witnessing of them arguing caught him off guard. But with their strong personalities, he found their disaccord obvious in retrospect, and he was grateful that they sat on opposite sides of the wardroom table.

He was also grateful for his fluency in French as anger drove the adversaries to their mother tongue.

"Don't be a son of a whore," Henri said in French. "Get your hide back to the engineering spaces.'

"Don't tell me how to behave," LaFontaine said. "I will speak my mind. You're just as wrong as he is, and you should thank him for bearing the burden of the defeat."

"Shut your snout."

"I will not. Stand behind him and figure out a way out of this mess. You're as guilty as he is."

Jake interceded in English.

"There's nothing to figure out!"

Silence. Jake continued.

"The *Ambush* has us by the balls, and there's not a damned thing we can do about it. But it's only forcing us to do what we agreed to do. It changes nothing. We keep hunting the *San Juan*."

"And if we fail?" Henri asked. "The Royal Navy is sending a task force. They can't wait forever. What if we don't find the *San Juan* before the Royal Navy grows impatient waiting for us?"

"I really don't have any idea," Jake said. "All I know is that it would get messy. I imagine that every British submarine on the planet would be within five hundred miles of the Falklands, shooting at anything that moves. I'm hoping we can prevent this."

"Are we done here?" Henri asked.

"Henri?"

"I mean no disrespect. We've been through too much together for me to challenge you. But given the circumstances, you'll have to excuse me so that I may process this."

Jake pushed his chair back and rose to his feet.

"No disrespect taken. My standing orders still stand. We continue to follow the search pattern I prescribed. I'll be in my stateroom if anyone wants to talk more."

LaFontaine, shaking with a combination of irritation and nicotine deprivation, stopped Jake in the passageway.

"I thought I'd be the last person to defend you."

"No shit. Thanks for that, by the way. I thought Henri was going to rip my head off."

"I suppose I'm the slowest in our submarine family to forgive but the fastest to protect."

"I guess so," Jake said. "Let's see if I can keep our family protected. Any ideas on what I should be doing?"

"I run the engineering spaces, Jake. I'm sorry, but the rest is up to you."

Reflecting his next move in his stateroom, Jake leaned his chair back and propped the crown of his head against the bulkhead for balance. When a knock on his door startled him, he lost his balance and arched his back to regain it, slamming the chair legs against the deck.

"Come in," he said.

Remy's toad head jutted through the door.

"Is now a good time?" Remy asked.

"The world would have to be ending for me to not have time for you, Antoine."

Jake kicked his guest chair in Remy's direction, and the sonar expert squatted in it.

"You know that Henri is just being himself, right?"

"Yeah. Putting up with his periodic protests is a small price to have him on our team. And for that matter, I count my blessings that you always manage to stay calm. I'm lucky to have you."

"I credit my faith in God," Remy said.

"I wish it was that simple for me," Jake said. "You didn't come here to preach, though, did you?"

"About God? No. About our chances of success? Yes."

"I didn't tell the guys, but we do have a time limit. We have a little more than three days left."

"That compounds my concern, Jake. This search for the *San Juan* may be in vain, at least with passive sonar."

"You think we should go active?"

"You need to consider it."

"Well, shit, Antoine. That may require divine inspiration, or at least divine protection. That would be announcing our presence to the *San Juan* and begging it to shoot a torpedo at us."

"Not exactly, if you trust our secure active mode."

Jake considered secure active transmissions, milliseconds-long clicks of acoustic energy, like splitting the difference between passive listening and an active search.

"It could work," he said. "Especially if the *San Juan* isn't expecting it."

"With its old equipment, it probably doesn't have the processing power to distinguish a secure active transmission from natural sounds. I urge you to use it."

"Okay, Antoine. You have a point. Go ahead and set it up. Transmit every ten minutes covering a hundred and eighty degrees."

"Thank you, Jake. This could make the difference."

"Well, since your God isn't looking down on us and telling us where the *San Juan* is, this is our best option."

"Maybe He is looking down on us, and maybe He just inspired me to ask you to use the secure active technique."

"We'll never know, Antoine, will we?"

"I will take it on faith."

Five minutes after Remy departed, Jake again risked balancing the combined mass of himself and his chair on its rear legs and his head as he pondered a God looking down upon him.

A thought struck him, like divine inspiration, and he fumbled again to land the chair on its four legs.

"Shit," he said.

He trotted to the control room and darted to the central navigation table, which showed an overhead view of the *Specter's* search pattern. Twenty minutes separated him from the next turn.

"Perfect," he said.

Scanning the room, he noted the absence of Henri and Remy. The fast-learning Taiwanese sailors handled the systems.

"Petty Officer Kang," he said. "Have you seen Remy?"

"He was just here. He told me he was going to line up Subtics for secure active after he ate."

"Fine, let him eat. You can handle this. I want you to line up to transmit a three burst secure active sequence. The frequencies and duration of each transmission are already stored in the system as an alert."

"Really?"

"Yeah, I set them up. That's how the *Ambush* would communicate with us if it needs to. It would be an order to surface and communicate via radio."

"So you want to instead order the *Ambush* to surface by sending it the order?"

"You got it. But I want to do it during a scheduled turn so I can point our active sonar at it without pissing it off."

"That's easy. Give me sixty seconds, faster if you need."

"No hurry."

Fifteen minutes later, Remy and Henri arrived in the control room, rumor spreading like wildfire on submarines.

"What's on your mind, Jake?" Henri asked.

"I need to get a message to Olivia, and I need the *Ambush* to be okay with me coming shallow to do it."

"What message?"

"I'm going to ask for divine intervention."

CHAPTER 22

"Keep turning," Jake said. "Steady course two-seven-zero."

"That's deviating from our prescribed search pattern," Henri said.

"I know. Steady course two-seven-zero."

The deck remained tilted below Jake's feet.

"Transmit secure active pulse sequence," he said.

Remy staring over his shoulder, Kang tapped the screen and sent the chirps of acoustic energy into the water toward the *Ambush*.

"The sequence was transmitted," Kang said.

Remy and Kang burned their eyes on their monitors, seeking discrete frequencies arriving from the direction of the British submarine.

"Nothing," Remy said.

"Henri, all stop. Stop the shaft," Jake said.

"The shaft is stopped."

"Still nothing," Remy said.

"Transmit again," Jake said.

"Still nothing," Remy said. "Still no sign of the *Ambush*, but it must be driving into our baffles. You're running out of time until it's outside the arc of our ability to transmit."

"Quadruple the power and transmit again," Jake said.

Kang sent out the pulses, and ten seconds later, the Subtics system whined with an automated alert.

"Active transmission sequence received from the *Ambush*," Remy said. "It's ordering us to come shallow."

"Okay, then," Jake said. "Bring us shallow, Henri, and raise the radio mast. Line me up with satellite communications to Pierre's phone, and keep watch to see if the *Ambush* tries to contact us directly."

Surface swells imparted a gentle rock on the *Specter*. Jake balanced one hand against the metal railing while holding a phone handset to his check with the other. He heard Renard's voice.

"Yes, my friend?" the Frenchman asked. "What news?"

"No news. Sorry to excite you. But I need to talk to Olivia. I also need the *Ambush* to know what I'm doing, however Olivia wants to communicate with it. The commanding officer doesn't seem to want to talk via high-frequency voice transmission."

"I don't blame him. High-frequency voice propagates along wave tops and is much less secure than satellite links. Excuse me while I find Olivia."

Jake returned the phone to its cradle and pressed a key that routed incoming audio to a loudspeaker. He then turned to a console.

"Let's take a look around, just for fun."

He tapped a screen, ordering the *Specter's* periscope to rise snap a panoramic full-circle picture. Spread across two monitors, the image showed blue sky and white crests of water. Concentrating on the bearing of the *Ambush*, he noticed a tall swell blocking his view.

"Let's try it again."

A new panoramic image replaced the old on Jake's adjacent screens, and he saw a dark line jutting from the water's surface.

"I see the *Ambush's* radio mast. It's listening. Just not in the mood to talk, I guess."

Olivia's voice filled the compartment.

"Hello, Jake?" she said.

He snapped the phone from its cradle for a semi-private chat.

"Can you get a satellite with thermal imaging to search the waters around the Falklands? The *San Juan* is going to have to snorkel eventually, and I want you to catch it when it does."

"I imagine there's already a satellite looking for it. Satellites search for ships all the time. But there's a lot of ocean to cover. This doesn't sound like much of an epiphany."

"But if you calibrate the sensors to detect the heat signature of a snorkeling submarine, you can reduce your margin of sensitivity and widen the search area for a faster and more effective search."

"It could work," Renard said.

"Didn't know you were part of the conversation," Jake said.

"You didn't ask," Renard said. "I suppose you intend to use the *Specter* to calibrate the satellite sensors."

"Yeah," Jake said. "One calibration now under daylight. One in the middle of the night when it's cooler."

"The *Specter's* heat dissipation design is more advanced than that of the *San Juan*," Renard said. "A satellite finely tuned to recognize your snorkeling heat signature would easily see that of the *San Juan*. This could make a satellite search quite fruitful."

"That's what I'm thinking," Jake said.

Olivia challenged the efficacy.

"Say it does work? How long will the *San Juan* remain snorkeling, and how will I contact you if it's found?"

Jake appreciated that she had paid attention to operational constraints during her time spent with him aboard a submarine years ago.

"It's about four hours, if it's doing full battery charge," Jake said. "As for contacting me, you can't. But you can contact the *Ambush,* and it can order me shallow to receive coordinates."

"He must mean extremely low-frequency transmission," Renard said. "It's a strategic communication system designed to contact ballistic missile submarines."

"I bet every British submarine has a wire to receive that frequency," Jake said. "And not just the ballistic missile subs."

"Correct," Renard said. "Of course, we'll need Olivia to convince the United States Navy to lend the use of its transmission stations."

"American policy is to not interfere with this," she said.

"It's impossible to get caught," Jake said. "Nobody can prove that you were looking with a satellite, and nobody can prove that you rousted the *Ambush* to come shallow with a few cryptic characters from a strategic communications system."

"I suppose you're right," she said. "It's just my ass riding on this."

"Your ass is riding on me finding a needle in this forsaken haystack. You have little choice."

"Fine, I'll do it," she said.

"Do you know if the commander of the *Ambush* is willing to talk to me, or is he just taking satellite downloads?"

"If you've got a message for him, you'd better tell me," she said.

"Okay, tell him that I'm going run my diesels as soon as I hear from you that the satellite is watching me and is ready to calibrate its search routine."

"Stay shallow until I can call you back about that."

"Of course. Also tell him that I'm going to use secure active pulses to look for the *San Juan,* just in case it helps."

"Give me fifteen minutes," she said. "You may as well line up to snorkel."

"You must admire a woman who understands submarine operations," Renard said. "I don't believe that a woman ever told me how to run my submarine when I commanded them."

"You're just jealous because I thought of this satellite idea, and you didn't."

Fifteen minutes later, Olivia reported that a CIA satellite pointed at the *Specter* and awaited the heat signature of his diesel exhaust as it dissipated in the shallowest layers of water.

The Royal Navy had agreed to the plan, and the *Ambush's* commanding officer had acknowledged receipt of his new orders to support it.

Jake ordered the *Specter's* diesels to run, and ten minutes later, Olivia told him the calibration was complete. He went deep and continued searching for the *San Juan*, using secure active pulses and hoping that a satellite would augment his efforts.

With no sign of the *San Juan* by day's end, Jake drifted to sleep frustrated. His alarm tore him from a deep sleep in the wee hours, and he crept to the control room to come shallow at the appointed time.

During the phone call, Renard sounded half awake, as did Olivia. But the effort paid off after he snorkeled for ten minutes and established a new sensitivity calculation for discerning diesel exhaust heat from the cooler evening waters.

He trudged back to his stateroom and leapt into his rack. When he awoke the next morning, a depression clouded his thoughts since his first thought involved the recognition that time worked against him.

As he ate breakfast in the wardroom with Remy and LaFontaine, a Taiwanese sailor banged on the door and opened it without waiting for permission.

"Petty Officer Kang reports that the *Ambush* has ordered us shallow," he said.

Henri had the *Specter* on an upward trajectory before Jake arrived in the control room. With his submarine bobbing in the shallows, he ordered the radio mast up.

The news from Olivia disappointed him.

A shipping freighter in the channel to Port Stanley fought for its life after a violent explosion had cracked its keel. Opinions differed on the source of the explosion with some experts calling it a torpedo and others calling it a mine.

"What do you want me to do?" he asked.

"Nothing," she said. "Nothing until we can sort this out. It could be the *San Juan* using a torpedo, but it could as easily be mines laid long ago."

"How will you know the difference? If I assume this was a torpedo and sprint down there, it could end up being just bait to distract me from my hunt or it could even expose me to a shot from the *San Juan* if I run by it fast enough."

"I know. Divers are searching the surrounding waters for mines to see if it's a field or not. That's the best we can do for now."

"How long will that take?"

"Four hours. Maybe six."

"Then I need to decide now if I believe that the *San Juan* is near Port Stanley and shooting torpedoes. If it is, it'll be gone in four hours, and I miss my chance."

"The Royal Navy wants you to ignore it."

"So do I. The commander of the *San Juan* is too smart to risk himself for a freighter. It's a good show of power to remind the world that there is an Argentine naval force, but he wouldn't risk himself like this. Not for a freighter."

"Agreed. Get back to your hunting. You've used up half your allotted days. You don't have much time left."

"You didn't need to remind me."

"Good luck, Jake."

The third day of hunting dragged into the evening, and Jake struggled to choke down his dinner. After the sunset draped the waters above him in darkness, he retired to the solitude of his stateroom. Hope waned until Kang came to him.

"The *Ambush* has ordered us shallow again."

When Jake arrived in the control room two steps behind Kang, he saw a Taiwanese sailor at the ship's control station moving with hesitancy compared to Henri.

"Faster," he said. "Pump water off faster. Use the fairwater planes and our speed to compensate if you make us too light."

By the time he slowed himself against the angled deck to reach the elevated conning platform, his French experts had arrived. Henri took his place at the control station.

"Raise the radio mast," Jake said.

"Radio mast is raised," Henri said.

"Remind me," Jake said. "What's the call sign for the *Ambush,* in case I need to hail it over high-frequency voice?"

"Romeo."

"And we're Juliette, right?"

"That's what happens when you anger a lion. They get to pick the names."

Seeing himself as the lion, Jake choked down his pride.

"Let's see what the news is first. At least that's encrypted, and I don't have to call myself Little Red Riding Hood."

"Establishing the link now," Henri said.

Jake ripped the phone set from its cradle and listened.

"Jake? It's Olivia."

"Yeah?"

"The satellite picked up a telltale heat signature three minutes ago. Put me on loudspeaker. I've got coordinates for you."

Everyone holding a pencil in the *Specter's* control room jotted down the coordinates as Olivia recited them. Jake darted to the central navigation plot and shouted them back to her so that she could hear him over the room's open microphone.

"Correct," she said.

"Hold on, Olivia. Let me start driving towards it. Henri, left full rudder, steady course zero-six-seven."

The deck angled away from the turn.

"Olivia?"

"Yes?"

"I'm eighty-six miles from the *San Juan*."

"What's that mean?"

"It means I can't get there in four hours. Even with my MESMA power source, I can only make twenty knots for two hours. Then I need to surface and run my diesels. That limits me to thirteen knots. I can get there in five and half hours, but not four."

"Maybe that's good enough," she said. "You'll have a good starting point for search for it."

"Do you want to risk your career and many lives on giving that thing a ninety-minute head start?"

"No. But what else can you do?"

"The *Ambush* can sprint ahead and chase it toward me."

"I don't think the Royal Navy will agree to that."

"There's no other way."

"How's it going to chase the *San Juan* toward you?"

"With a torpedo."

"Isn't it dangerous for the *Ambush* to sprint near the *San Juan*?"

"Yeah, but it won't have to. It can sustain thirty-three knots forever. It has time to drive a wide enough arc behind the *San Juan* and then shoot a torpedo at it. It can even get far enough behind it that its torpedo can run out of fuel before hitting, just in case the *Ambush* loses wire control. The point is to drive it toward me so I can use the limpet weapon."

Jake rethought the geometry.

"Scratch that. I have an even better idea," he said. "Make it two torpedoes. One to the right and one to the left. It will drive the *San Juan* down the middle to me."

"Where will you be?"

"Right now, I'm eighty-two miles from the coordinates you just gave me for the *San Juan*. Bearing two-four-seven. Got it?"

"Got it."

Draw a line between me and the *San Juan*. Four hours after you say go, I'll be sixty-six nautical miles closer to the *San Juan* along that line. I'm basically making a beeline there as fast as I can."

"Okay. "I'll talk to the Royal Navy's admiralty about it."

"Hurry."

Five minutes later, Olivia's voice filled the room.

"Jake?"

"Go ahead."

"They apparently already thought this scenario through. They verified that Argentina isn't flying any anti-submarine air patrols near you, and they agreed. But I had to stick my neck out for you. My career is on the line if you run or try anything stupid."

"I won't."

"I know you won't, but I had to remind you. It's settled already. The commander of the *Ambush* agrees, and he wishes you happy hunting."

CHAPTER 23

Three hours and fifty minutes later, the *Specter* rocked in the swells as its diesel engines charged its battery and pushed its electronic propulsion motor to its limits.

Several of the Taiwanese youngsters discovered the misery of seasickness and had retreated to their racks, but enough men remained coherent, and Jake had them alter the weapons load out.

The pivotal limpet torpedo filled tube one. As the second half of the one-two punch, an Exocet missile rested in tube two. Jake ordered a drone into tube three, and heavyweight torpedoes were staged in tubes four and five. The last tube contained a super-cavitating torpedo for no other reason than Jake's desire to have a two-hundred-knot weapon available.

He stood on the conning platform, grasping its encircling railing for equilibrium.

"At least being on the surface allows us to keep the phone line open," he said. "Where's the *San Juan* now, Olivia?"

"The heat signature is drifting almost parallel to you," she said. "It's coming slightly toward you."

"Still no news from the *Ambush*?"

"No."

"No surprise," Jake said. "It's probably too busy sprinting."

"You'll have to trust the *Ambush*," she said.

"This is all about trust and a little luck at this point," Jake said. "There's always slop and a little luck required in submarining."

"I know," she said. "You need to submerge soon."

Her tone sounded sentimental, like an ex-girlfriend bracing to lose him a second time. If he wanted to say goodbye to anyone, it would be his wife, but he preferred to think he would return home.

"I will," he said.

"Hold on!" she said. "The heat signature is going away. The *San Juan* is finishing snorkeling."

"Got to run! Thanks for your help, Olivia."

He shut down the communications to the outside world.

"Henri, lower the radio mast. Open the main ballast tank vents and submerge the ship."

Jake glanced at a screen showing his battery at fifty-five percent charge, which he considered adequate for most contingencies. But he needed to conserve that energy by selecting a slower speed.

"Henri, all ahead two-thirds, make turns for eight knots."

He then walked to the central navigation table and reviewed the geometry.

The *Specter's* sprint and the *San Juan's* drifting had reduced the gap between the submarines to seventeen nautical miles, but the distance proved insurmountable for Remy's ears and for those of his young apprentice.

Jake looked to his sonar operators for hope, but Kang and Remy shook their heads. He muttered to himself, uncaring who heard.

"Patience," he said. "The *Ambush* will come through."

"Should we transmit secure active?" Remy asked.

"I don't want to risk revealing ourselves when we're so close. Ask me again in ten minutes if you don't hear the *San Juan* by then."

For lack of any other option to occupy his mind, Jake glared at the navigation chart. Assuming the unheard *San Juan* remained on its course, he had closed to within sixteen miles of it.

He resisted the urge to stare down his sonar team, but he allowed himself periodic glances. His heart leapt as he saw Remy curling forward in thought.

Then his young apprentice stole the Frenchman's thunder.

"Active countermeasures!" Kang said. "They're on the bearing of the *San Juan!*"

"Agreed," Remy said. "The *Ambush* must have attacked."

"Spin up tube one," Jake said. "Get the limpet torpedo's system running. Enter the Subtics solution for the *San Juan* into it. We will maintain our present course and speed. Keep listening for the *San Juan* to update the solution."

"Flow noise!" Kang said. "It's the *San Juan.*"

"I hear it, too," Remy said. "Assuming a speed of twenty knots and updating the solution."

The chart showed Jake's target fifteen miles away.

"We need to get closer," he said. "All ahead standard."

"They may hear us, Jake," Henri said.

"They're not listening for us. We're quiet enough."

"I've lost the *San Juan* due to our own flow noise," Kang said. "I can't hear through our own flow."

"You will when we get closer," Jake said.

A minute passed. Then another.

"I still don't hear it," Kang said.

"Line up the sonar system to transmit secure active with the narrowest beam possible at one-quarter power aimed at the system-generated bearing of the *San Juan*," Jake said. "After every transmission, line it up again, narrow beam, aimed at the system's latest bearing to the *San Juan* until I tell you otherwise. Got it?"

"Yes, Jake," Kang said. "The system is lined up."

"Transmit secure active."

"Transmitting," Kang said. "Active return! Range, fourteen miles."

"It's not running straight at us," Remy said. "But close enough. It's a steep angle."

"But it will slow down when its commander realizes he's outrun the *Ambush's* torpedoes," Jake said.

"You're probably right," Remy said.

"I am right. We're losing time, and the *Ambush* isn't able to help us anymore. It's now or never. Henri, all ahead full."

The *Specter* trembled with the strain.

Two more minutes passed.

"Transmit secure active," Jake said.

"Transmitting," Kang said. "Active return! Range, thirteen miles."

"Thirteen miles," Jake said. "Since we sped up, it must have slowed down. Damn it."

"I must note that you are within range of a torpedo shot," Henri said. "You can shoot now if you wish."

"I want a better shot."

"I understand."

"Per my calculations in this sound environment," Remy said, "you risk counter detection by the *San Juan* at this speed within eleven miles. Counter detection could be sooner than that if its sonar operators are attentive."

"I'm taking that risk," Jake said.

Another two minutes.

"Transmit secure active," Jake said.

"Transmitting," Kang said. "Active return! Range, twelve miles."

"Jake," Henri said. "The *San Juan* is maintaining its course. You can slow down and control this situation. I appreciate your courage, but use your wisdom!"

Jake glared at the Frenchman. Unlike the confrontation in the wardroom, Henri's features were soft.

"For all our sakes," Henri said. "Be patient."

Running his hand through his hair, Jake played the odds in his mind. He agreed with his colleague.

"All ahead two-thirds, make turns for eight knots."

The trembling subsided.

"Open the outer door to tube one," Jake said.

"The outer door is open," Henri said.

"Can you guys hear anything?" Jake asked.

Remy and his apprentice shook their heads.

"The *San Juan's* commander is cool," Remy said. "He appears to have slowed to his quiet crawling speed. He knows that whoever shot at him still has a large area of ocean to cover to find him again."

"But we know where he is."

"The upside for us is that he cannot move rapidly away from us," Remy said. "We are surely closing in on him."

When he thought nobody was watching him, Jake braved a rare trip to the ship's control station and tapped Henri on the shoulder. The Frenchman glanced up from his seat.

"Thank you," Jake said.

"Of course."

Jake returned behind his sonar team.

"At eight knots," Remy said, "we hold an acoustic advantage over the *San Juan*, no matter what speed it's moving."

"As long as my sonar operators are superior to his," Jake said.

"That's the least of your concerns," Remy said, "as long as you stop bothering them with needless chitchat."

The clock ticked away minutes as Jake maintained his patience. When the solution showed seven miles of distance, Remy curled forward.

"I've got blade rate correlating to five knots," he said. "This tracks with the system's solution."

"Does your apprentice concur?" Jake asked.

"I didn't think to listen for it," Kang said. "But now that you mention it, I do."

"Henri, left ten-degrees rudder, steady course zero-two-zero," Jake said. "I'm putting us on a lag line of sight for the shot."

Jake exercised more patience, and the solution showed six miles of distance.

"Shoot tube one," he said.

After his ears popped, Jake heard the normal announcements of a flawless launch.

"Henri, left ten-degrees rudder, steady course three-five-zero. Time to open distance."

Two minutes passed, and Kang announced the limpet weapon's status.

"Our weapon is in active search mode," he said. "It has acquired the *San Juan*! It's two miles away and accelerating to closing speed!"

"Excellent shot, Jake," Henri said.

"Thanks, but everyone stay focused. Listen for what's going on out there."

"The *San Juan* is accelerating," Remy said. "Heavy flow noise, cavitating screws, too many propulsion plant machinery noises to count."

The report seemed expected, but it lacked elements that irked Jake. He ran down his mental checklist seeking omissions.

"Any countermeasures from the *San Juan*?" he asked.

"None," Remy said. "But it may have expended them all against the *Ambush*."

"Is it turning? Rudder noises? Down-Doppler?"

"It's too loud to tell rudder noises," Remy said. "It sounds just like flow noise. Petty Officer Kang was tracking the electric plant at fifty hertz."

Jake looked to the youngster, who appeared perplexed.

"I'm sure I'm right," he said. "But it can't be."

"Spit it out, Kang," Jake said. "No secrets."

"Up-Doppler on the fifty hertz."

"Impossible," Remy said. "Let me listen."

The Frenchman clasped his hands over his toad ears and closed his eyes.

"He's right, Jake. The *San Juan* accelerated toward our torpedo."

Jake pondered the news as he walked to his chair on the conning platform.

"Holy shit," he said. "That ballsy bastard figured it out. He realized that he just evaded a British submarine only to get punched in the face by me. But he's banking that my weapon is a limpet."

"I would call that stupid," Henri said. "We must be wrong. We must be missing something."

"Our weapon is range gating," Kang said.

"Very well, Kang. How long until detonation?"

"Fifteen seconds."

"Well, Henri. In fifteen seconds, he's going to believe that he's a genius."

"Should we evade his possible counterattack?" Henri asked.

"No way," Jake said. "We're on the best geometry and driving away. The only thing we could consider is to speed up, but I don't want to announce our location. Right now, he can only guess within about a hundred and twenty degrees of arc."

"You could speed up slightly."

"I would, except that he has his sonar team listening for just that. Our best bet is to stick with eight knots, until he fires back, if he even does."

Jake glanced to his monitor and saw the limpet weapon converge on the *San Juan*.

"Detonation has taken place," Remy said. "Limpets deploying."

"Count how many attach to its hull."

"Limpets are attaching and going active," Remy said. "Most of them have attached."

"At least we have the *San Juan* tagged," Jake said.

"Launch transients!" Remy said. "Torpedo in the water! Now another. Then another. It's a ripple launch. I'm sure it's a spread."

Jake sprang from his chair and pounced on his sonar operators.

"Stay calm," he said. "Identify the ones with high bearing rate from the ones that are a concern."

"We'll sort them out," Remy said. "I know what to do."

"I'm waiting until you've identified them all before I speed up. I don't want to drive us into one by accident."

"Good idea. Give me thirty seconds," Remy said.

Jake watched Remy and Kang communicate in shorthanded English, gestures, and nods that revealed the fruits of an outstanding teacher-apprentice relationship. With astounding speed, the duo made sense of chaos.

"The *San Juan* has six torpedo tubes," Remy said. "I assume it launched one torpedo at the *Ambush* and had five available for us."

"How many did it fire at us?"

"Five."

"And?"

"Four of them are drifting behind us. The fifth is a concern, though. You need to evade."

"Henri, all ahead flank, as fast as you can! Cavitate!"

The *Specter* shook.

"Can you still hear the incoming torpedo?" Jake asked.

"No," Remy said. "We won't until it enters active search mode while we're at flank speed."

"Henri, deploy two active countermeasures!"

Deep popping sounds resonated around Jake as bubble makers shot from the *Specter's* hull.

"I hear those," Remy said. "Our countermeasures are active."

Jake turned and leaned over the navigation plot.

"Assume a search speed of sixty-five knots for the torpedo, and give me your best estimate of its path."

As the *San Juan's* threatening weapon appeared on the chart, Jake tapped the screen and commanded a calculation that showed three and a half minutes until impact.

His heart sank as he realized his desperation. He looked to Henri and gestured him to approach and join him. The Frenchman's face revealed the same mortal fear that he felt. Jake kept his voice low.

"Shit, Henri. I don't know what else to do."

"Neither do I. We must trust the countermeasures."

"How did that guy get off such a lucky shot?"

"Fate? Karma? I have no answer."

Jake's desperation became anger.

"Well fuck him. Get tube five warmed up to send him to hell. Have it home passively on the limpets."

Thirty seconds later, tube five thrust Jake's vengeance into the ocean.

"Incoming weapon has entered active search mode," Remy said. "Bearing one-six-two."

Right in our fucking baffles, Jake thought. *Perfect shot. Lucky Shot. If you're there, God, why are you doing this? I tried to end this peacefully.*

"Solution is tracking," Remy said. "Two minutes to impact."

"Deploy two more active countermeasures," Jake said.

The Taiwanese sailor who had replaced Henri at the ship's control station tapped his screen, popping two more aerating distractions into the water.

"Deploy one noise-making decoy," Jake said.

"All countermeasures are active," Remy said.

"Any effect on the incoming weapon?"

"Yes!" Remy said. "The incoming weapon has acquired the noisemaker."

Jake breathed.

"Circling our noisemaker," Remy said. "Now passing through and coming at us again."

"At least that bought us thirty seconds," Jake said.

Henri leaned into Jake.

"We cannot outrun this weapon," he said. "Even if every noisemaker we have gives us thirty seconds of delay, the weapon has the range to catch us."

"One of them may fool it completely," Jake said.

"I wouldn't bank my life on it. Consider surfacing the ship and letting men jump for their lives."

"Maybe," Jake said.

He looked to the sailor at the ship's control station.

"Deploy one noise-making decoy."

The decoy bought another thirty seconds. With two and a half minutes separating him from his demise, he whispered to Henri.

"We're dead," he said.

"Surface the ship, then. Live to fight another day! I'll drag you off myself so that you don't suffer any romantic notions of going down with your ship. Plus, you remember that I can't swim and will need you to carry me."

"Fine. I'll give the order."

Jake made eye contact with the sailor seated at the control panel and drew a breath to bark out his order, but Remy interrupted him.

"Jake!"

"What!"

"The *Ambush*. I just heard it."

"So what? How is that relevant?"

"I think the *Ambush* is maneuvering itself between us and the torpedo."

"Let me see!" Jake said. "Enter the *Ambush* in to the system at thirty-three knots."

Jake watched lines of bearing fan out towards the flow noise that Remy heard from the British submarine.

"Holy shit," Jake said. "Does a British commander have a death wish?"

"Don't question it," Henri said. "Embrace your savior."

"Impossible," Jake said. "This can't be happening."

"The *Ambush* is passing through our baffles," Remy said. "The incoming torpedo is drifting left. It's following the *Ambush*!"

"The *Ambush* is fast, but it can't outrun the torpedo," Jake said.

"Maybe it can," Henri said. "With its extra speed and fresh load of countermeasures, it's possible."

"The *Ambush* has launched a noisemaker," Remy said. "The weapon is circling it and... wait... the weapon is now returning to chase the *Ambush*."

"I need to do something," Jake said. "I can't watch a British submarine take a bullet for us."

'What can you do?" Henri asked. "Shoot the torpedo with our torpedo?"

"It's theoretically possible, especially when there's such a high bearing rate on the target torpedo, but our torpedoes are no faster than... wait."

"No, Jake. I know what you're thinking. It's too risky."

"No, it's perfect. The arc of fire is limited. If I maneuver to the edge of the weapon's usable arc, I can target the torpedo without risking hitting the *Ambush*."

"Command detonate? The *San Juan's* weapon is unlikely to be large enough to allow a proper triggering of the warhead."

"Right. I'll have to guess at depth, but anything close enough should help."

Jake turned to the sailor at the ship's control panel.

"Left full rudder, steady course two-two-zero."

The deck rolled, and as he grabbed the navigation table for support, Jake looked to Kang.

"Already on it, Jake. I've got the best estimate of the torpedo's course, speed, location, and depth in the system, and the super-cavitating torpedo is warmed up. I've ordered a command detonation based upon the system solution, independent of any final triggering."

"Good job."

"The system is recommending no launch until you're pointing within fifteen degrees of the target."

"Fortunately," Jake said. "This little submarine turns on a dime. Let me know when the system clears the shot."

"Now, Jake!"

"Shoot tube six!"

The amazing two-hundred-knot speed of the underwater rocket tested what remained of Jake's patience. It required twenty seconds to accomplish its job.

When it blew up, Jake hoped that it took the *San Juan's* torpedo with it to oblivion while leaving the *Ambush* unscathed. With its blast energy hitting the British submarine at its stern, he expected the vessel's hull to absorb whatever pounding it received.

He felt relieved when Remy reported the *Ambush* maintaining its thirty-three-knot sprint. But his heart sank when he heard that the *San Juan's* torpedo continued chasing it.

"You bought the *Ambush* another thirty seconds Jake," Remy said "You at least temporarily disrupted the torpedo."

"Not good enough!"

"The *Ambush* has launched another noisemaker."

"God, I hope they all survive," Jake said.

"The torpedo has acquired the noisemaker and is circling it."

"Another delay of the inevitable."

"No!" Remy said. "It's continuing to circle."

"Seriously?"

"Our weapon must have damaged it enough to prevent it from correcting its course from a noisemaker."

"Let it circle a few more times before we celebrate."

A minute passed.

"That's three laps around the *Ambush's* noisemaker, Jake. The *Ambush* has a fighting chance now, even if the *San Juan's* weapon recovers."

"Give it another minute."

A minute later, Remy declared the victory.

"The *San Juan's* weapon is stuck in a circle. It's over."

"We did it."

"Our weapon is now range gating against the *San Juan*," Kang said.

Jake had forgotten his vengeance shot.

"Do we still have wire control over that weapon?"

"Yes," Kang said. "Impact in twenty seconds."

I can do nothing and let them die, Jake thought.

"Jake," Remy said. "You need to make a decision. Fifteen seconds to impact."

If there is a God, He needs someone to do his dirty work. May as well be me.

"Ten seconds," Remy said.

If there is no God, then someone needs to render judgment. May as well be me.

Speaking in his ear, Henri offered guidance.

"Our mission is complete," he said. "It's a resounding success. You needn't do this. Think of the aftermath, the peace negotiations."

"Quiet!" Jake said. "Let me think!"

"Five seconds," Remy said.

I feel unworthy to render judgment and deliver death today, Jake thought. *Maybe I've never been worthy.*

"Shut it down!" he said.

Remy tapped his screen and then slumped forward in relief.

"Our torpedo is dormant," he said.

CHAPTER 24

Jake swallowed a bite of his hamburger and leaned back in his chair. The wardroom swayed back and forth as the *Specter* rode the sea's swells.

"We can get back to Mar Del Plata a lot faster than we got here since we can travel on the surface," he said. "We're not hiding from anyone anymore."

"I've already done the math," Henri said. "We can make two hours submerged at twenty knots, followed by four hours surfaced at thirteen knots while recharging the battery. Then repeat that pattern to average slightly more than fifteen knots, or three hundred and seventy miles a day."

"Sounds like someone wants to get back to dry land," Jake said.

"Mar Del Plata is eight hundred miles away," Henri said. "Per my calculations, I'll be drinking my first beer in two days and five hours."

"The lucky bastards from the *Ambush* will be drinking tonight," LaFontaine said.

Jake recalled the latest status report download.

A British swim team had reached the *Dragon* and had placed explosives on its propellers. They had then radioed their readiness to cripple the destroyer to their command, which in turn contacted the prime minister, who then shared the news with Senator Ramirez.

Unknown to President Gomez, Ramirez then contacted the skeletal crew of the *Dragon*. He gave them the choice to surrender the ship back to its rightful owners or to be stranded without propulsion with a dozen well-armed British commandos ready to storm the ship and, if that failed, to blow holes in its side. Given the added news about Gomez's pending fall from power, Ramirez's countrymen agreed to give back the *Dragon*.

Upon news of the *Dragon's* loss, the impotency of the *San Juan* to challenge the British task force, and the British prime minister's preference to deal with Ramirez, President Gomez had resigned his post as his nation's leader. The temporary presidency fell to Senator Ramirez, and he began acting with the decisiveness and ambition of a young and capable man who intended to keep the job.

Ramirez had ordered the *San Juan* to surface and navigate to Port Stanley, where the Royal Navy would assist with the removal of its limpets while keeping its crew as guests in its barracks. Nobody called it an act of surrender, but the *Ambush* escorted the *San Juan*–from below and from behind with torpedoes ready in case the Argentine submarine deviated from the arrangement.

"I agree," Jake said. "There will be drunken *Ambush* sailors before sunset."

The statement left him envious. He wished he could drink away his pain that night, douse an inner anger that seemed to simmer interminably, and quiet the latest ghosts he had created.

After dinner, he had a call to Olivia patched to the privacy of his stateroom. He wanted to learn that his contributions had made a difference.

"I'm sure you read that Ramirez is formally in power now," she said. "The odds are that he'll keep the presidency in the emergency election."

"That sounds good, I suppose. I'm not sure that I care about which politician is in power, but it sounds like you think highly of him."

"I do. He'll do a good job. It's the right thing for the country."

"Now you sound like a politician, all motherhood and apple pie, or whatever they say in Argentina."

"I'm no politician, but I'll be dealing with more of them at the next level. I'm practically assured a promotion to executive when I get back."

"I'm glad your career is working out. Really. I mean it. You've been through some hard shit and you deserve it."

"You just saved my career, Jake. But what the heck, you practically made it anyway. Other than my sex slave ring assignment, every marquis accomplishment I've had has your name stamped on it. I'm running out of ways to say thank you."

Although he expected complete sobriety from the entire crew during the mission, he hadn't declared the *Specter* an alcohol-free ship. He reached into his safe and withdrew a bottle of single malt scotch to quell a few demons.

"Don't worry about it," he said. "You helped me earn my freedom, such as it is, which isn't too bad at the moment. So we'll just call it even."

"Sure. Even it is."

"So you're sticking around Buenos Aires?"

"Yeah. I'm staying close to my source of information until this situation is resolved."

"Sounds like you're enamored with the young playboy president."

"Consenting adults," she said. "It's professional now, but what's wrong with mixing business and pleasure, and who isn't attracted to power?"

"Still direct and honest about yourself, as always."

"What do you expect from a trained psychologist?"

"A wedding invitation if you ever become Mrs. Argentina."

"Deal."

He poured whiskey into a porcelain coffee cup, savored its sweet aroma, and let its fiery taste fill his mouth before swallowing. Semiconsciously, he replenished the glass.

"So what's going on with negotiations?" he asked.

"With the *Dragon* back in British control, the prime minister is holding back the task force while he meets with Ramirez at the bargaining table."

"Really? Why? Did he become lazy all of a sudden?"

"No, it's simple economics. He's got submarines joining the *Ambush* and the *Dragon*. He has control of the sea and the sky, and Ramirez has ordered his troops to restrict themselves to the western main island. The prime minister has no need to spend that kind of money sending an armada seven thousand miles away."

"Make sense. Any idea how this is going to end?"

"If I believe Ramirez," she said, "it will be about sixty-forty in his favor. But he could have embellished his side of the story to impress me. What's important is that the issue of the Falklands ownership, the oil reserves, mineral reserves, fishing havens, and British military presence are all being discussed as one comprehensive agreement."

He started to enjoy alcohol's numbing euphoria.

"Sounds like Renard's plan is working out after all, despite all the screw-ups."

"If you're Machiavellian about it, sure. But I don't think he'll share your optimism, though. He can be tough on himself. You should call him."

"You're probably right."

"I miss you, Jake. It's been so long since we've seen each other."

He doubted if he shared her sentiment, but he owed her an attempt at friendship.

"We have work to do if we're going to become or remain friends. I'm not sure which it is, really. But I would like to stay in touch, at least once in a while. You know, I'd like to hear how you're enjoying taking over the CIA and becoming the queen of Argentina."

"Funny."

"I know. See you later, Olivia."

"Good bye, Jake. For now."

He called his French mentor.

"Great to hear from you, my friend," Renard said. "How goes the journey to Mar del Plata?"

"I'm getting lucky that the seas are relatively calm," he said.

"Excellent. I imagine that you'll have my submarine back in port in just over two days?"

"You got it. Your transport ship is still there, right?"

"Indeed. It will be there to transport the *Specter* anywhere in the world I wish to next take it."

"Riding off into the sunset."

"Yes, and I've been narrowing down the list of candidates for our next opportunity to work together," Renard said. "I've found several of interest, but one in particular entices me."

"Wait, you're already thinking about your next gig? I thought you'd still be beating yourself up."

"I've licked my wounds. At least I hope I have gotten to them all. I may have been terribly wrong about Gomez's loyalty, but my plan still had merit."

"I was just telling Olivia the same thing."

"And I'm hardly ready to retire. The best thing to do is to get back into my routine."

"Fair enough, but I don't want to hear it, Pierre. Not now. I just want to relax."

"As you wish. I have a great opportunity to discuss with you, but we can speak of it later."

Jake tried to imagine which area of the world Renard targeted for his next affair, but he let his mind go blank.

"Can you tell me where you are now?" he asked.

"Far away from Argentina," Renard said. "I have aggravated enough people in that nation that I fear for my hide. I'm sure there are several new people on the long list of hunters who desire my pelt on their mantles."

"When will I see you again?" Jake asked.

"When the time is right, I will find you."

Four days later, news headlines opined that a negotiated enduring peace in the Falkland Islands appeared imminent, and Jake drove home to his wife.

The thought of her companionship struck him as the sole reason he had escaped a life of cursed loneliness. Her presence in the world marked fate's first deviation from its pattern of delivering him constant trials. His relationship with her marked the first since childhood where he felt strengthened and whole by investing emotional energy into it, as opposed to working uphill against something that drained him.

Linda served as his reason to come home alive.

She ran down the driveway before he could stop his Ford Fusion, and she jumped on him as he stepped from the car.

"I missed you so much," she said.

"I missed you too, honey."

"I was so scared that you wouldn't come back."

"I got scared a bit there, too. But nothing to worry about. Just another day changing the course of history."

"Were you involved in all that crap down in Argentina?"

"You know that part of my freedom involves me saying as little as possible about what I do."

"Forget it. I don't care. I'm just so glad you're alive."

"I'm glad you're here to be glad that I'm alive."

As she released him, he realized how much he had missed the touch of her soft skin and her perfume.

"Come in," she said. "I started dinner when you called from the airport."

"What's cooking?"

"Dolma."

"Stuffed grape leaves. My favorite!"

"And my best dish."

In his kitchen, Jake poked at fork at a dark green leaf rolled into a tight cylinder. Steam billowed from it, and he smelled spiced meat and rice.

"It needs to cool off!" she said.

"Kiss me while I'm waiting."

He drew her in and pressed his lips against hers, and then she leaned back in his arms and looked at him.

"I prayed for you every day," she said.

"Thanks. I needed all the help I could get."

"I'm serious. I begged God to bring you home alive. I had bad feelings about this, the worst ever."

"Okay, I get it."

Wearing a hemp shirt, Jake's brother entered the kitchen.

"No you don't," Nick said.

Jake released Linda.

"Huh?"

"You know I can sense when you're in danger," Nick said. "Or maybe I can sense when you think you're in danger. Maybe it's a combination of your reality and your perception, but whatever it is, this was the worst feeling I ever felt for you."

"You're supposed to hide that from Linda."

"He couldn't," Linda said. "He grabbed his chest and doubled over onto the floor while we were watching television. How's he supposed to hide that?"

"I can't help it if he's mister psychic. That's just what he is."

"But you can help it if you run off looking for danger again. You can stop this crap for me. I want my husband to be here with me. I want to grow old with you."

"I'm fine," Jake said. "I haven't died yet."

"By the grace of God," she said. "And I wish you'd stop testing Him."

Jake questioned the existing of his wife's god, but he allowed himself to wonder if some benevolent force beyond his comprehension had spared him from probable or deserved death multiple times.

And he was certain that since some benevolent force had brought her into his life, he should try to stick around to enjoy her.

"Okay, honey," he said. "The next time Pierre calls for me, I'll tell him to go to hell."

THE END

About the Author

After his graduation from the Naval Academy in 1991, John R. Monteith's career in the U.S. Navy included service aboard a nuclear ballistic missile submarine, and a tour as a top-rated instructor of combat tactics at the U.S. Naval Submarine School. Since his transition to civilian life, he has continued to pursue his interest in cutting-edge technology. He currently lives in the Detroit area, where he works in engineering management when he's not busy cranking out high-tech naval action thrillers.

John R. Monteith writes the award-winning Rogue Submarine series:

ROGUE AVENGER (2005)

ROGUE BETRAYER (2007)

ROGUE CRUSADER (2010)

ROGUE DEFENDER (2013)

ROGUE ENFORCER (2014)

ROGUE FORTRESS (2015)

ROGUE GOLIATH (2015)

ROGUE HUNTER (2016)

I hope you enjoyed reading this novel as much as I enjoyed writing it. Whether you loved it or not, I'd appreciate your feedback and I invite you to visit my website at www.subthriller.com.

Thank you,

John Monteith

Made in the USA
Middletown, DE
06 August 2018